THE TALEBEARER

Visit us at www.boldstrokesbooks.com

By the Author

Crimson Vengeance

Burgundy Betrayal

Scarlet Revenge

Vermilion Justice

Twisted Echoes

Twisted Whispers

Twisted Screams

Necromantia

She Wolf

Walking Through Shadows

The Talebearer

THE TALEBEARER

by

Sheri Lewis Wohl

2018

THE TALEBEARER

ISBN 13: 978-1-63555-126-6

This Trade Paperback Original Is Published By
Bold Strokes Books, Inc.
P.O. Box 249
Valley Falls, NY 12185

First Edition: May 2018

Credits
Editor: Shelley Thrasher
Production Design: Susan Ramundo
Cover Design By Melody Pond

Acknowledgments

So many thanks to my editor, my mentor, my friend, Shelley Thrasher. She personifies intelligence, grace, and patience. My life is infinitely richer because she is part of it.

At his best, man is the
noblest of all animals;
separated from law and justice,
he is the worst.

—Aristotle

PROLOGUE

Honest to God, would the woman never die? All the years of listening to her yapping day in and day out was more than any human should be expected to endure. Never measuring up to insane standards. Always coming up short. A person could listen to that bullshit for only so long before the big snap. Well, dearest, that day was today, and the snap was loud enough that the whole county could have heard it.

It should have been easier to put the old girl on the ground, yet she showed surprising resilience when it got right down to the deed. Hitting her in the back of the head with the heavy cast-iron skillet had been an action borne of pure instinct. One bitch too many falling out of her lipstick-enhanced lips and that was it. The frying pan was winging through the air to connect with her head without any conscious memory of even picking it up.

The sound of the iron crashing against her skull had resonated with a most satisfying crunch, and the douche bag had toppled to the floor in a big pink pile. The flowing shirt, always some god-awful shade of pink that she thought was sexy, was spotted with red, and that was at least some consolation. Never having to see that color again was a huge unanticipated bonus.

The moaning that had been going on for at least fifteen minutes was not. It might have been more humane to simply hit her another time or two with the skillet and put her out of her misery, but really, where was the fun in that? After all the years of making life miserable for anyone unfortunate enough to be stuck in her orbit, the opportunity to relax and watch her life slowly flow away held a certain amount of karmic justice.

Besides, there was a fresh pot of coffee, and letting it go to waste seemed wrong. It was better to sit here, enjoy the fresh dark brew, and wait her out. It wouldn't be long before even her feeble efforts at clinging to life would fail. She was on a slow train to hell, and it was enjoyable to sit in a club car and watch the ride.

At first it seemed like all the fun was over once she finally gave it up and died. But the game grew even more exciting after there was a body to dispose of. How to make her disappear was something her dreams were made of.

So many options. Only one body.

Given she was the first, it seemed appropriate that she be given a place of honor. That goal in mind, it wasn't all that difficult to figure out the rest. Everything she needed was in the garage, and the first push of the shovel into the ground proved how perfect the plan was. The ground was soft and yielding, and it didn't take long to prepare her final resting place. Out here where not a soul ever came to sit and enjoy the sunshine and clean air, she would be isolated and alone. No one to be with her and most certainly no one to hear her shrewish voice telling anyone and everyone what to do and how to do it. She would be alone forever. It was a perfect purgatory for a perfectly awful woman.

Rolling her into the deep hole and then shoveling dirt onto her flabby white face until it was completely obliterated was an indescribable ecstasy. It was hard to fathom why it had taken so long to reach this point. The moon was full and showering the area with buttery light. It was a sign declaring the rightness of this action. It was a guiding light showing the way to greatness.

It was the beginning.

CHAPTER ONE

For nineteen years, three hundred and sixty-three days, Liz Boone walked through the front doors of the federal building without incident. Right in the middle of downtown Spokane, Washington, it was a great example of nineteen-sixties architecture enhanced by a courtyard with a water feature and raised beds planted with decorative trees and colorful flowers. Walking through there always made her feel tranquil and happy to begin her day as part of a great organization. That all changed on day three hundred and sixty-four, the day she took a bullet to the chest. On that bright, sunny September morning, when the air held a hint of crispness and a light breeze sent leaves fluttering to the ground, Anthony George Washington brought a rifle to the courtyard of the federal building and opened fire. He left one dead and four wounded. The last thing she could remember about that morning was lying on her back, the concrete cool through the fabric of her blouse, and watching a single leaf flutter to the ground.

Nine months later, Liz now stood looking around her new house, five miles north of the courthouse in distance but about a hundred miles away in character, and feeling more than a little lost. Her palm flat against her chest where beneath her shirt a scar was still angry red, she felt her heart race. Everything was all so different, and that was exactly what she'd been hoping for, even if it was frightening.

For the better part of twenty years her life had been structured and dependable. She understood what she was doing, where she was going, and who she was going to see. It had worked for her, and she'd gone along, as her mother liked to say, fat, dumb, and happy. That was no longer the case. These days she knew precisely jack.

And that was the beauty of it. Her life was finally hers to guide. No longer did she have to worry about those who felt disenfranchised taking out their frustration through the barrel of a rifle. No longer did she answer to a government that sometimes she agreed with and sometimes she didn't. She was free to speak as she wished, protest as she desired, and spread her wings. She was free to be the person she wanted to be, except for one small detail: she was scared shitless.

Even now in this sanctuary she was creating, brand-new to her and without any reminders of the past, panic floated just beneath the surface. Would she ever feel safe again, she wondered for the thousandth time. She constantly worried that she wouldn't. Maybe choosing to stay in the city hadn't been her best idea, and perhaps moving to Seattle might have been better. Except the stubborn streak that had gotten her into trouble more times than she could count wouldn't let her give in to the knee-jerk reaction to flee. Why should she be driven away from the city that had always been her home?

Attila picked that moment to race through the living room. The six-month-old German shepherd slid on the hardwood floor and almost flew into the sofa. Instead, he gently bounced off the front of it and then collided with her legs, tail wagging. It was exactly the diversion she needed. "You're crazy," she told him on a laugh as she reached down and rubbed the top of his head. His fur was soft, his big ears standing up tall.

The collision with the sofa didn't faze him, and he allowed her only a few seconds to pat him before he began to run circles around her. The move to the new house wasn't as traumatic for Attila as it was for Liz. He was adapting extremely well and having a grand time checking out the house and the big fenced yard. The yard, one of the reasons she bought the house, seemed made especially for Attila. He'd marked every corner of it as soon as they arrived and then marched happily back inside. He had Liz, his bed, and his favorite toys, so as far as Attila was concerned, this was home. She loved that about him and wished she could be more like him.

A knock at the door made her jump and her heart start to pound again so hard it was almost painful. She started to run to the bedroom, where she could lock the door and hide. She sure hoped that instinct faded in time, though that seemed unlikely right now. Instead of running for her bedroom, she took a deep breath and turned toward the front door. After checking the peephole, she opened the door to her smiling friend, Meg Zimmer. Meg's smile faded as she looked at Liz. "What's wrong?" Meg didn't even try to hide the concern in her voice. Good friends were like that, no hiding or pretending.

Liz shook her head and gave herself a second before she answered. She wasn't trying to hide or pretend either. She just needed a couple seconds to get her emotions under control. The rapid beating of her heart was slowing, the panic sliding away. No wonder she'd lost so much weight since she'd been shot. Her body probably burned at least two thousand calories every time she went into fight-or-flight mode, and that was just about every day. At this rate she'd be skin and bones before the year was out. "It's okay. I just wasn't expecting anyone." She was proud of how calm she sounded.

Meg's eyes narrowed, and she studied Liz intently before giving her a little nod. Her smile returned as she held out a bottle of sparkling wine and a big dog bone. "I stopped by to celebrate the new digs with you and Attila."

A different type of emotion welled up inside Liz, and this time it was the good kind. It was exactly like her childhood friend to be this thoughtful, and the bone for Attila was beyond nice. She was a truly kind and wonderful person. Meg had been looking out for her since she woke up in the hospital ten days after the shooting. Everyone had been worried, but Meg, a teacher, was particularly concerned. She supposed it was the caretaker part of her personality combined with the fact that they'd known each for a very long time. Even though a part of Liz wished everyone would stop worrying, another part of her appreciated the care. Well, if she was being really honest, a lot of her appreciated the care, especially from Meg. Recovery would have been much slower without her.

Liz smiled. "The bubbly is nice, and you know Attila is going to be your best friend forever now."

"We're already friends forever, aren't we, big boy?' She gave the bone to the tail-wagging Attila, who took it gently from her outstretched fingers and then trotted to his bed. The wine she handed to Liz. "Our little prize is nice and chilled. Come on. Let's blow the cork and christen this place. Oh." A look of concern darkened Meg's face. "You're not still on meds, are you?"

A legit question actually. She'd taken pills, lots and lots of them, in the weeks after the shooting. Some were to dull the pain, some to keep infection away, and some brought her a welcome numbness that she had not been reluctant to embrace. Some days even now she almost regretted giving up the latter. The doc had offered to give her a new prescription, and as tempted as she was, she'd declined, because for the most part she wanted to be clear-headed. Just in case.

She returned Meg's smile and spread her arms wide. "Clean and sober."

"Great. Let's do something about that sober part."

Drinking wine sounded really nice, although she refused to allow herself to take any substance that would dull her senses enough to let her defenses drop. No pills. No drinking to excess. She had to be alert all the time. On the other hand, a glass or two of the sparkling goodness wasn't a bad idea. Relaxing and getting out of control were different. She looked around at the unopened boxes stacked against the walls. Hands on hips, she said, "Just let me figure out which box the glasses are in."

Meg smiled and held out her free hand. "Come on. We'll tackle those kitchen boxes together and polish off this baby while we're doing it. Geez. It'll be just like when we were younger and moving into our first apartments. Mine was that old house up on the south hill and yours…"

This time she laughed. "Mine was that shoebox-sized one-bedroom with the dripping shower. It was such a bitch to make that driveway in the winter. I don't know how many times I got stuck on the hill in the snow trying to make that turn. My dad was so happy the day I decided to move out of there and he didn't have to come rescue me anymore." Sharing memories like this was exactly why having Meg as a friend was a gift.

They were both laughing as they walked to the kitchen and, with what felt like destiny, found the box with the wineglasses immediately. They poured the wine and started in on the boxes. The fizzy goodness was wonderful, and for the first time today, she could almost relax even as she dug into box after box, a tedious task under any circumstance. By the time Meg left, they had not only finished the entire bottle but ordered and devoured Chinese takeout as well. Ever the teacher, Meg even insisted on breaking down the boxes and stacking them in a tidy pile in the garage. It was the most fun Liz had had since before Washington put a bullet through her body.

Once Meg was no longer there, however, silence seemed to hang uneasy over Liz's little house. Attila, with his new bone tucked under one paw, was sleeping soundly on his bed by the fireplace. The month of June around here could be cold and rainy or sunny and warm. This year it was turning out to be one of the nicest she could remember. In short, it was a perfect night for the doors to be open to let in warm summer air. Hers were closed and locked. The beauty of gas heat and central air meant she didn't have to open doors and windows to keep the house warm or cool. Perfect for her wants and, more importantly, needs.

The biggest selling feature that had tipped the house in her favor was the alarm system. Ten seconds after she closed the door behind Meg, it was engaged, and the little light on the panel glowed a solid dark red. It was fully armed, and how she wished it made her feel safe. Perhaps someday it would. Today wasn't that day.

Before Meg could be as much as a block away, the relaxation that the wine, good food, and good company had brought on faded. It was the story of her life these days. She didn't even try to fight the melancholy that draped over her like a cape. Instead, she sighed and decided to give sleep a try. Before she left the hallway, she double-checked the alarm panel. It still showed a steady red for all the door and window connections. Liz walked through the house checking everything again anyway. She stopped at each window and closed the blinds, if they weren't already shut. Like someone who suffered from OCD, she wouldn't be able to even try to rest until she had walked every inch of the house at least once and most days, two or three times. That was her world these days.

It took effort not to repeat the exercise. Maybe she really was becoming OCD, and frankly, on top of everything else, that was about the last thing she needed. As soon as she'd sort of convinced herself all was well, she went to her bedroom. And seconds after that she dropped to the bed. Attila came in and jumped up next to her.

"You have your own bed, you know." He ignored her, as was his custom, made three circles in the middle of the bed, and then lay down. Despite having his own really nice new bed, they both knew she wouldn't kick him off hers. Like double-checking doors, windows, and the alarm panel, his presence made her feel better. Honestly, if she'd known how much comfort a dog provided, she'd have gotten one a long time ago.

She lay back against the pillows and told herself that tonight she'd sleep for more than a couple of hours. Here in this little house in the nice neighborhood surrounded by good and kind neighbors, she was safe. Only her family and closest friends were aware she'd even moved. Attila, her companion and protector, was next to her. The house was buttoned up. She slipped her hand beneath the pillow and touched the cold metal of her handgun. Yes, she was safe. Slowly, as she watched through the open bedroom doorway to where a tiny light glowed softly against the hallway wall, she relaxed, but she didn't close her eyes.

"Ms. Blue?"

Willow Blue turned and smiled at Edie Cahill, her favorite student. Eighty years old and a perfect-attendance student, Edie was a class act. Not only was she dependable, but she was also a ball of pure energy. She put many students in the class who were more than half her age to shame. It wouldn't surprise her to see Edie hit the big one-zero-zero. She was the last one to leave the final class of the night, and the fact that it was now after ten didn't seem to faze her. Most of her class members worked in the nine-to-five world and had to fit their classes in after they completed their work day and attended to their family obligations. But not Edie. She seemed to simply love life no matter what time of day or night. Willow wondered if she ever slept.

"It's Willow, Edie. How many times do I have to tell you that? Call me Willow."

Edie smiled, and she looked at least five years younger. "Just doesn't seem right, you being the teacher and all. In my day, it was only proper to address teachers respectfully."

"You are the most respectful person I've ever met, and you know that we're friends too. So even though I'm your yoga teacher, promise me you'll call me Willow and not Ms. Blue."

Edie nodded and her eyes sparkled. Her white hair hung down her back in a long, thick braid. Would her own hair be that lush and beautiful when she was Edie's age? Somehow she doubted it. "I will do my best. Willow."

"That's good enough for me. Now, Edie, what can I do for you?"

"Well, my grandson, Stan, is coming to town and I thought…" The sparkle in her eyes increased to almost Fourth of July volume. Spunky little grandma.

Hugging Edie, Willow laughed. This woman always made her feel great. "Oh, Edie, you're such a romantic, but I have to tell you a little secret." She released her and stepped back. "Between you and me."

Edie's smile grew as she rubbed her hands together. "I love secrets."

"All right then, I'll share mine. Here's the thing. I don't date men."

Edie's smile faded as she studied her closely. "You don't date men. I don't understand. I know you're not married."

"Think about it, Edie." This lady was sharp, and she had no doubt she'd ultimately get it.

She waited her out in silence. The eighty years she'd been on this earth hadn't dulled her mind one bit. Willow smiled when understanding dawned on her face. "Ohh." Edie drew out the word. "So if my granddaughter was in town…"

"Exactly."

Her smile returned, just as bright as before. She gave Willow a brief hug before she tucked her mat under her arm and started for the door. "Well, you can't blame a grandma for trying."

"No, I can't, and if that granddaughter of yours comes to visit, let me know." She winked.

"That I will," Edie called out cheerfully as she walked through the front door and toward the little orange hybrid she drove to class. No big grandma cruiser for this lady.

She laughed and watched as Edie got into her car and then left. The parking lot was empty now except for her own vehicle, which was sitting right up front beneath a big light. All she had to do was pick up a few things and be on her way. The cleaning crew would come early in the morning, and the studio would be sparkling clean for tomorrow's classes. She loved it here and was still confident she'd made the right decision to move to Spokane from California.

The air was fresh with just a hint of coolness, which with each passing day was fading more and more. The weather was lovely in Spokane, the Eastern Washington city so different from her hometown. Her college friend Meg had also been a guiding force with her promise that, in this place, she'd heal. That she had, and the healing process had brought her more than she'd imagined.

She was just getting ready to turn around when the lights in the parking lot flickered. The disturbance lasted only about ten seconds but struck her as strange. They'd never done that before. She'd have to ask the landlord to check them. She couldn't have Edie or any of her other evening students walking through a dark parking lot. Tomorrow, she'd give him a call.

CHAPTER TWO

Eldon Spicer was worried about Liz. He'd hoped between her retirement and a move to the new house, Liz would return to her old self. Or, at the very least, a bit of her old self. What had happened to her would shake even the toughest, and he'd always considered Liz to be one resilient woman. That she didn't bounce back like a powerful racquet-ball serve shocked him. After nearly a year, she was still suffering, and that wasn't like his Liz.

He wanted to help but couldn't figure out what to do. It hurt him that his friend was in crisis—and there was no other word for it—while he stood around like a lump. The shooting had been tragic, the aftermath a true crisis. When she didn't wake up immediately after surgery, everyone had been terrified she never would. The doctors weren't a whole lot of help either. He'd wanted them to tell him with certainty that she'd recover fine, but they couldn't. It drove him nearly mad.

When she did wake up, everyone rejoiced. At first anyway. It took a few days for the reality to sink in that, while she was back with them, she was different. More than having been a victim of a senseless crime, it went a whole lot deeper. He couldn't put his finger on the exact nature of the change. He only knew it was there. And the fright she lived with day in and day out broke his heart. No one should have to live in constant fear. What could he do? He floated every idea he could come up with, and she shot down everything he suggested while leaving no room to revisit any of it.

That didn't mean he was giving up. Not when it was someone he loved. It simply meant a change in strategy on his part. During the last nine months, Eldon had evolved into a stalker. Not his first choice for the best way to help Liz, but given how stubborn she was, it was the most productive alternative. He intended to keep eyes-on until she was back to the strong, confident Liz. At first it was easy to skulk about and keep her in his sights because she'd been recovering from her physical injuries, and he'd been there to help with no questions asked. As she'd healed, she'd pushed him away, correction, pushed all of her family and friends away. Too many people in her personal space seemed to send her spiraling into a panic attack. Day by day he'd watched in silence as she'd built walls around herself that were difficult, if not impossible, for anyone to break through. It was so unlike her that it made him sad.

Not willing to turn his back on a friend so obviously in crisis, he'd been sneaking around ever since to make sure she was okay. If anyone was watching and didn't know the story, they'd absolutely believe he was a certifiable stalker. In a way he was, but it wasn't the way that required arrest, hospitalization, and a good psychiatrist. All he needed to cure what was afflicting him was for his buddy to find her way back.

Tonight, he'd sat in his car down the block and watched as she'd finished bringing in boxes. It was the last of the move, and for that he was grateful. He'd wanted to help, and she'd let him when it came to the heavy things like furniture and appliances. When it got down to boxes, she'd sent him, and everyone else who'd shown up to make the move as easy as possible for her, on their way. It was just Liz and Attila.

He liked that dog and was thrilled that he was devoted to Liz. It was the one thing that let him leave feeling that she was somewhat protected. He wasn't worried about outside forces harming her but that she would simply give up. Attila wouldn't let her. He was going to have to take that boy a steak one day soon.

He'd been pleased when he saw Liz's friend Meg show up. She was the one person Liz allowed to stay close, and he understood why. The gentle aura that surrounded her drew in everyone who came in close contact. She was a teacher, and probably made a difference in her students' lives. He'd noticed that about her the first time they'd met and had wanted an opportunity to get to know her better.

The timing had never been right, especially not when they'd all been gathered in the hospital waiting room worrying as Liz lay on an operating table. Even then, in that environment so charged with worry and despair, her energy had filled that little room, and he was sure everyone there felt it. It wrapped around him like a warm blanket. Friends and family alike held a vigil until the doctor came out and gave them the good news. She was going to pull through without any serious lasting complications, he'd predicted.

Physical complications, at any rate. What the doc didn't add was that mentally it might be a long time before any of them glimpsed the fun-loving, quick-witted Liz again. God, how he missed her. She was the one person who made life in the office bright. It wasn't that the rest of the staff was bad. Quite the contrary. By and large, they were all great folks. It was an honor to be part of such an important piece of the government. The Third Branch was unique, and it always made him feel special to know he'd been chosen to be part of it.

It was just that Liz was a particularly bright light. She brought life to a place that could often be deadly serious. She took her duties to heart and gave all that she had to her job. At the same time, she never lost her sense of identity. For her that meant joy, and she brought it with her every day she walked into the office. None of them realized how important that was until she was gone. They were getting by and learning to adapt to her absence. It wasn't the same, however, and it never would be again.

That didn't mean she shouldn't find the same joy in her new reality, and that's what had him concerned. That bullet appeared to have pierced more than her flesh, and when they took it out, they took out the light along with it. He was determined to find it again. That was what a person did for a friend.

He just had to figure out how. At her house, the lights in the front room went out. Eldon turned the key in the ignition and drove away. He couldn't do anything more tonight and hoped she would sleep. He wondered if he would.

❖

That last flight had been a piece of shit. Turbulence had made it feel like a roller-coaster ride for at least five hundred miles. Drinks had fallen off trays, people had puked, and not less than ten had sent complaints to the cockpit. What exactly they were supposed to do wasn't clear, but that didn't stop the dumb bastards from sending the flight attendants to the front of the plane. It would be so nice to have a quiet, peaceful, and smooth flight. It rarely happened and sure didn't today.

Home wasn't much better. One hour of peace and quiet. Was that too much to ask for? Apparently the answer to that question was a resounding yes, because it had been a house of chaos since she walked through the front door and hung her jacket in the closet. Field-trip slips needed signing. Soccer shoes had to be found. Homework finished. Clothes readied to be dropped off at the dry cleaners.

She would appreciate as little as five minutes of peace, but it took hours before that became a reality. The whole time that feeling kept building inside her that didn't want to be ignored. It had been this way for months, and soon, nothing would stop it from bursting forth. That was all right because it was time. All she had to do was be patient, play the game a little longer.

When everyone was finally in bed and peace descended, it brought with it a hyper-awareness of what was to be. The computer hummed quietly in the dim light of the office, and the treasured pictures slid slowly across the screen. Weeks' worth of surveillance provided all the necessary information. She uncovered patterns, and plans evolved from there. It wouldn't be easy, but then again, if it were, where would the fun be? Danger held its own allure that fed the hunger inside her. But with each passing day the hunger grew larger, more demanding. Insatiable. With each passing year, the need became greater.

It wasn't a problem really. No one had ever caught on, and no one ever would. Some were special, and it was what made them untouchable. Stealthy and lethal, like a jaguar. Yes, just like a black jaguar. It seemed a fitting moniker, a rare and threatened species with incredible power, compact and well-muscled. A hunter. Worth a check to see how it felt on the tongue.

"I am the Jaguar." Her soft laughter broke the silence in the office. It was perfect.

Now all the Jaguar needed was the certainty that the rest of the household was in deep sleep. Hunting when darkness cloaked the world held its own allure. People tended to be more alert at night, and it made it more fun to snag them when they thought they were being very careful. Most were so stupid. They didn't recognize danger when it came in a familiar package. They trusted what the wrapping told them and didn't bother to look any deeper. No one seemed to recognize her carefully crafted façade. That took the entertainment level quite high, almost intoxicating.

The house was quiet when the Jaguar finally slipped out. Everything she needed was in the expensive designer messenger bag that garnered frequent compliments. Little did anyone realize exactly what she carried beneath the smooth leather flap. The drive wouldn't take long. Wednesday-night traffic was pretty light and, as expected, a fairly empty parking lot once she arrived at her destination. She pulled the car to a stop in a spot where the black paint let it blend into the shadows.

The Jaguar glanced at her Rolex and smiled. It wouldn't be long now. Her intended rarely deviated from her patterns. She was ready when she heard the distinctive click click click of heels against asphalt. She opened the door and stepped out of her car. A little smoke and mirrors, and in the space of a minute, her prey was in the backseat twitching from the charge of the Taser. Loved that little toy.

Now the fun really began.

CHAPTER THREE

*L*iz loved the feel of the sun on her face as she jogged. The
warmth spread across her skin like the kiss of warm honey.
*Attila ran in front of her, happy to fly through the grass without a
lead to slow him down. It was a beautiful, quiet day for a run. So
perfect. Why was no one else out? But it was okay if everyone else
decided to forego the beautiful morning. She liked having this time
to herself.*

*The solitude didn't last long. Not far ahead of her, a young
woman was sitting on a bench, her head bent and her tangled hair
hanging down to hide her face. She wasn't a fellow runner, that
much was clear. Her defeated posture and unkempt clothing told
a different story. It wasn't unusual to see homeless people resting
on the benches that dotted the path. Liz didn't intend to stop, but
something about the lone figure drew her close. It was then she
noticed the debris in the long hair, the torn jeans, and what appeared
to be blood on a shirt clearly not a thrift store buy. For one of the
homeless, that was unusual.*

*"Are you all right? Do you need help?" She had no idea how
she could possibly provide assistance, but the air of helplessness
that surrounded her compelled Liz to ask.*

*The girl brought her face up, and Liz gasped. Her lips barely
moved as she whispered, "I need your help."*

*"Oh my God, what happened?" Any preconceived notions of
homelessness vanished. The serious injuries were impossible to
dismiss. Someone had hurt her, badly.*

"I need your help," she repeated.

"What do you need?" Liz fumbled at her waist where normally she carried her cell phone in a runner's belt. That she didn't have it on today confused her. She always put that thing on. By the looks of this girl, she needed some EMTs right now. Liz needed her phone.

"Find me."

"Okay, I've got you. Where are you hurt?" She was still grabbing at her waist, hoping to touch the phone. She didn't have anything beyond basic first aid, and that wasn't what this girl needed. Where was the damn phone?

"I'm not hurt," she whispered.

Her frantic search for the cell phone stopped. "Sweetheart," she said in a gentle voice. She understood that shock could often trick a person into believing they weren't injured severely. That was most likely what was happening here. "You have blood all over you. Let me do what I can until help can get here for you." She reached toward the injured young woman, knowing that sometimes the warmth of another's touch could be soothing.

She shook her head, her long hair swaying back and forth as dirt and twigs broke free to scatter around her feet like raindrops. "It's too late for that."

"No, it's not too late. I can help you."

This time the girl nodded. "Yes, you can." She took Liz's outstretched hand.

Liz was screaming as she sat twisted in her bed sheets. Sweat popped out on her forehead, and her heart was rat-a-tatting like a machine gun. She sat up and blinked. The room was shrouded in darkness broken only by the tiny light plugged into the hallway outlet. She could make out Attila, who was on all fours in the middle of her bed, the hair at the nape of his neck standing up, a low growl emanating from his throat. His eyes were focused on the open bedroom doorway. The tiny light glowed steady in the hallway.

She pressed the back of her hand against her lips to stifle the screams that still rumbled deep in her throat. When she had that under control, she reached out and patted Attila. "It's okay, big boy."

She could hardly talk and was pretty sure Attila could hear the fear still lingering behind her words.

His growl didn't quite stop, though his body posture relaxed. "It was just a dream," she told him and then managed a little laugh. Despite the terror, the situation was kind of funny. Here she was, an adult woman mostly well-adjusted, explaining herself to a dog. The docs might want to rethink that medication thing.

Her heartbeat calming at last, she swung her legs over the side of the bed and sat with her head in her hands. At the moment, her scars ached, just as they had when she'd been released from the hospital. As the months has passed, so too had much of the pain. They hadn't really bothered her for a while now, so why tonight? Why would a random nightmare cause a physical reaction like that? Dear Lord, she really was finally losing it.

The thing was, she didn't feel crazy. Of course, did anyone who was losing their rational capacities think they were descending into mental illness? She suspected they didn't. Except the dream, if it could be called that, was pretty clear. Especially after the girl had taken her hand. It felt so real, she could swear she'd been running along that path and had touched her. No dream she'd ever had, even when she was filled with drugs, had been so physically real. It was more like altered reality than hallucination.

Oh, she knew who the woman was. Reggie King. Anybody who had watched the news or read the paper over the last two years would recognize Reggie's face. She had been the bright and beautiful local newscaster who went in search of a story and never returned. With her long, curly dark hair, bright-green eyes, and cheerful demeanor, she had clearly had a bright future in front of her.

Until she disappeared. Law enforcement searched for months, and nothing ever turned up. Not a single lead that would help find her. With no leads and no suspects, her case went cold.

Liz wrapped her arms around herself and breathed deeply. What she'd seen shook her deeply, and she blinked hard against the tears that suddenly threatened to spill. She hadn't known this young woman personally, though she had seen her a time or two in the courthouse. Still, knowing what she did now, her heart ached.

What she'd seen left her with a firm conviction as to the fate of the beautiful newscaster.

Reggie King didn't get lucky as Liz had when someone tried to take her life. Reggie King was dead, and Liz sensed that what she'd seen held the clue to where she would be found. But how could she tell law enforcement? She couldn't tell them she'd had a dream and Reggie had come to her. Especially after what had happened to her. They'd just pass her explanation off as a result of her own trauma, and she certainly couldn't blame them for that. In their shoes, she'd feel the same way.

Somehow she had to let someone know what she was sure deep in her heart to be true. Reggie's family deserved to have her brought back home. The killer deserved the electric chair.

Attila nuzzled her neck as she sat there with her head in her hands. Why she'd never gotten a dog before was beyond her. He was so much more than her protector; he was her heart. His simple touch was as healing as anything proffered by modern medicine. Actually, she thought, it was more healing.

"Okay, buddy. I'll figure this out." He nuzzled her again as if to tell her she would indeed do just that.

Her chances of going back to sleep were somewhere between not likely to happen and not a chance in hell. This wasn't the first time since her incident that sleep had run away, which was precisely why she didn't even bother to lie back down. Fruitless endeavors weren't her thing. Instead, she stuffed her feet into her slippers, pulled on a sweatshirt, and headed to the kitchen, turning on lights as she went. Might as well enjoy a cup of tea.

She was holding the tea cup between her hands when she had decided it wasn't too early to make a phone call. Meg was, after all, the kind of friend she could wake up, so that's what she did. She had to tell someone, besides Attila, that is, what she'd seen, or she'd go nuts. She was jumpy enough without sitting here stewing about what to do. It was the old "misery loves company" thing. Meg picked up on the third ring.

❖

Willow was drinking her second cup of tea and reading the morning news on her laptop when her phone rang. She was surprised that anyone would call at this early hour and pretty certain good news wasn't forthcoming. When she looked down at the display, she was alarmed. "Meg? What's wrong?" She chatted with her all the time, though typically not before she even had a chance to take a shower.

"Hey, Willow. Really sorry to bug you at this ungodly hour. I figured there was a good chance you were rolling so decided to go for it."

"You know me so well."

"Even when we were partying college freshmen, you were always the first one up and outside going for a run or some other crazy thing. In fact, I'm surprised I caught you inside. I don't think you've changed that much. Have you already run half a marathon and baked a cake?"

Willow laughed. Meg really did know her. "You hit that nail on the head. Still a morning person, and yes, as a matter of fact, I was thinking about going for a run. Not a half marathon, mind you, and I definitely haven't baked a cake this morning or any morning. So what's got you on the phone this early? You, my sweet friend, were just about the last person to get out of bed any day of the week, and I don't think you've changed that much either."

"Trust me, if it wasn't for the day job, I'd still be that person. Unfortunately, real life took away all the fun of those carefree days. But my call isn't about me…"

Willow listened as Meg explained about her friend Liz, her shooting, and the subsequent issues, including a dream last night that Liz seemed convinced was a vision that required action. Her heart ached as she listened. The story brought back memories she'd prefer to have left in the past.

"I hate bringing this all back up for you," Meg was saying. "I just don't know what else to do. She needs somebody to help her, and you're the only person I know who's been through something similar. If anyone has a prayer of understanding what she's experiencing, it's you."

Just the mention of that awful day in LA made a cold chill slide down her spine. After all this time it shouldn't still have power over her, but it did. Meg wasn't wrong in her belief. Willow had most definitely walked a mile in those shoes. She'd experienced what it was like to have a perfectly great life crash and burn without any kind of warning, and as much as she loved her friend and was willing, on most days, to help where she could, she didn't really want to dig those days in her life back up again. One thing she'd learned since then, though, was that life didn't always play by the rules. Just because she wanted to leave it all behind her didn't mean it was going to happen that way.

"It sounds like it was a disturbing dream, yet a dream just the same. It happens after traumatic events." She said the words even though her heart was telling her something quite different. Calling what was happening to Meg's friend simple was about as far from reality as she could get, and that truth was born of first-hand knowledge. Because of it, her urge to end the call right now was strong. She didn't, though her hand gripped the small device so tight her fingers almost ached. It had taken a long time to get her life back, and while she had no desire to revisit the aftermath of her own shooting, she couldn't turn away from someone in need either. With her free hand, she touched the scar that still marred the smooth skin on her neck. Beneath her fingertips it was rough and ragged. If she gazed at it in the mirror, the redness that had paled somewhat over time would still, at least in her eyes, make it as noticeable as a streak of crimson lipstick. It was only one of the scars that daily reminded her of a moment that had forever changed her.

"I know it does, and I told her the same thing."

"She doesn't believe it." It wasn't a question. A vision and a dream were quite different, another lesson the tip of a bullet had driven home. It was hard to explain to anyone who hadn't experienced a vision. She'd stopped trying a long time ago.

"I gave it my best effort to reason with her." Meg sounded distressed. "You know all about sustaining a life-threatening injury, being out of it for days, being traumatized, and, to top it all off, moving to a brand-new house. I mean, think about it. Moving is one of life's biggest stressors, even without all the other stuff. I told Liz how it could add up to really vivid, powerful dreams. It could happen to anybody even if they hadn't been through what she has."

Meg's logic was sound. "Same thing I would tell her." It wasn't a lie. Despite her own experience to the contrary, it was exactly what she'd do. She was all about healing and not following dark paths. It was entirely too easy to get sucked into the darkness and too hard to claw back out.

"I pretty much heard your voice in my head as I said all that. She kept coming back to me with how she could tell the difference between a dream and a vision and insisting that it wasn't a dream. I've never heard her like this before."

It all sounded so familiar. One thing that had come out of her own incident was the distinct change in her psyche. She'd become far more in tune to the world around her and to the people she let into her life. It was like becoming a psychic. Not that she really believed that's what had happened, but sometimes she'd come to discover she just knew things and couldn't explain how. She'd never experienced anything like it before the shooting, only after. "What do you want me to do?" She hadn't told anyone about her enhanced senses and didn't plan to now. Some things were just better kept quiet.

"Could you talk to her? Like this morning? I'm afraid she's going to pick up the phone and call the Spokane police. I don't want people to think she's losing it. If you talk to her, maybe she'll move more slowly. You know, let it sink in a little and make sure she's not overreacting to an episode brought on by stress. She doesn't listen to me or anyone else because she doesn't believe we can possibly understand. She won't be able to say that to you."

Willow didn't particularly want to call a stranger and kick-start a difficult conversation. Not because she was uncomfortable talking to people she'd never met. No, it was more a conversation like that would open old wounds. Didn't mean she wasn't going to do it. "Okay. I'll give her a call. I don't know that I'll be able to help, but I'll chat with her."

She could almost feel Meg's relief, and a whisper of guilt tickled at her for wanting to stay uninvolved.

"Willow, thanks so, so much. You have such a good heart, and you have to understand that I do grasp this is hard for you. I'm asking an awful lot. I also know, deep in my own heart, that you'll be able to help her. Even more, I'm positive you'll like her too."

"*Amicus meus. Amicus tuus.*"

"Seriously? You're throwing Latin at me this time of the morning? I might be a kick-ass teacher, but Latin was never my strong suit. I wasn't good at that crap after three shots of espresso, and you're throwing it out at me before I've even had one."

"Your friend is my friend."

Meg laughed. "Of course that's what you said. You know I love you."

Willow smiled. "Love you too. Now give me Liz's number, and then quit bugging me and go get ready for work. You have young minds to mold."

"And you have bodies to sculpt. I'll text you her number and address. Namaste."

"Namaste."

Willow put down the phone and stared at the text Meg had fired off as promised. She tapped the display as she studied it. She was accustomed to meeting new people. It was part of her business. Every new class cycle brought both the old and the new to her studio. She met them all with ease and good cheer. None of them asked about the scars. She didn't offer to tell them. Her students were like the majority of people once the redness had faded, most likely quite curious, yet their respect for her kept their questions at bay. She appreciated that more than she could ever convey.

She didn't know Meg's friend Liz, but she understood her. Her body was healing. Her spirit and her soul were not. Willow put a hand over her left breast and closed her eyes. Against her palm, the steady beat of her heart was comforting. Things could have easily turned out much differently for her, and that fact was not lost on her. She had been gifted with a second chance at life, and now karma was asking for payment in return. She would never turn her back on karma.

CHAPTER FOUR

Eldon had slept terribly, and now he felt like he was carrying a soggy sack of cement on his shoulders. The shower had helped, just not enough. How he felt didn't matter much, considering he was expecting the next eight hours to be busy at the court, which translated to the impossibility of being at less than one hundred percent. Every judge in the district would be at the courthouse today, and that always made things a little crazy. Big doings, and he had to make sure every bell and whistle was working, or there'd be hell to pay. Normally he enjoyed a good challenge. Right now it felt more like a burden.

Granted, he had help. Stan, Karen, and Caleb would be all-hands-on-deck with him, so the entire systems support team would be there. Still, he was the go-to guy, and the ultimate responsibility for all the IT systems fell in his lap. His father would say something corny like, "With great power comes great responsibility." He didn't know exactly how much power he actually had, but he was the IT manager for the district, and the job sure as hell carried a lot of responsibility.

Occasionally he wished he could chuck it all and walk away just like Liz. Not that he wished a near-fatal injury on himself. More like trot out those front doors and never walk back in. That sounded bad, considering it really was a great job. Most everyone was super. Still it had its political side, and that's what he grew weary of. If he could just do his job and call it good, it would be fantastic. That wasn't the way it shook out on most days. So much more was involved than simply running the infrastructure of a modern court.

Oh, well, it served no purpose to whine about it, even if his whining was confined to his brain. He knew better than to vocalize any of it. He just had to get through the day, make sure the courtroom being used for the ceremony of their most senior judge, retiring at the tender age of 92 was flawlessly functional, and it would all be good. Yes indeed, he was up to the task despite his fatigue. Once he got going, the adrenaline would kick in, and he would be in the zone. It was where he felt most at home: his brain whirling, his fingers flying across keyboards, his eyes taking in every element of the puzzle that was running a courtroom. He loved the work. The ceremony should be done by four, and then he could make like a hockey player and get the puck out of there.

He wasn't in that zone yet, and that meant he was focused elsewhere. He looked down at his smart phone and debated what he should do versus what he wanted to do. The feeling of tipping over into stalker land hit him again, but damn it, the whole reason he couldn't sleep was because of Liz. Something was way off; he felt it clear across town. He'd never thought of himself as psychic until this thing with Liz. Ever since the shooting it was almost like they were twins. He felt calm when all was going well. Not so much when things were going sideways.

"Screw it," he muttered, and touched her name in the contacts list. It rang three times before she picked up.

"Hey, Eldon."

Liz sounded as tired as he felt. "What happened?" He wasn't going to pretend he didn't hear it in her voice or feel it in his soul. They'd known each other too long to play games. All of a sudden guilt added weight to his weariness. He should have gone by her house this morning instead of heading directly into work. This is what happened when he didn't listen to the little inner voice warning him of danger. He could kick himself.

"Nothing."

Right, and he was tall, skinny, and handsome. "Don't bullshit me, Liz."

"I'm not. Really."

"Then what are you? Really?"

The breath she blew out was clearly audible. "I had a dream."

A dream? Sure, and he'd slept like a baby. "What else is going on?"

"A dream."

"I'm calling bullshit again." He was going to get it out of her one way or the other.

She was silent for an unusually long time. He waited her out. "All right. I thought it was a dream at first. It wasn't a normal dream and it wasn't a nightmare. I know the difference."

"So what exactly are you trying to tell me?"

"I had a vision."

Nope. He wasn't buying that either. "A flashback maybe?" That whole shooter thing was bound to tear anybody up, and if a flashback had dragged her out of sleep, it would be natural for her to sound defeated. She might misinterpret either a dream or a flashback as a vision.

"No." Her response was immediate and firm. "It had nothing to do with me. Absolutely not a flashback. Trust me. It was a vision."

A chill slid over him that was far from comfortable. He wanted to argue and didn't. He owed it to her to keep an open mind, especially if he really wanted to help her heal. "Tell me about it."

"Don't you have work to do? You know, judges' needs and all."

He didn't give a good goddamn about anyone, judges included, at the moment. What he needed was to hear what had happened to her. Until he did, he wouldn't be able to concentrate. "They can wait. Besides the whole staff is here. Things won't fall apart without me in the time it takes you to tell me."

This time there was no pregnant pause. Instead she said, "Meg thinks it's post-traumatic stress raising its ugly head."

Meg wasn't entirely wrong, and the same thought had already crossed his mind. It could very well be PTSD, but if that's all it was, he figured the rock in the pit of his stomach wouldn't be there.

❖

The Jaguar flipped from channel to channel, catching every news broadcast in the area. As anticipated, not one reported the discovery of a body. That was good. Not unexpected but good nonetheless. Besides, it had only been a few hours, and not enough time for anyone to be considered missing. Sometimes it took a very long time for the absence of some to be noticed. Sometimes no one ever noticed. Sad commentary on their lives. Great reminder of how skilled the Jaguar was in choosing her victims.

The house was blessedly quiet at the moment, and she appreciated that. Everyone was gone, to school and to work. Quiet didn't happen often around here, and it was more than nice. It was invigorating. It also meant no one was around to question her intense interest in the local news. No questions were the best questions. Besides, it was great to be able to drink a cup of coffee and reflect on last night without constant interruption.

The gold cross that had been around her neck now lay warm and comforting against the Jaguar's skin. It was a beautiful piece of jewelry, and she could see no sense in leaving it in the dirt for who knows how long. Waste not, want not. Besides, a little souvenir from a night's fun and games was always welcome. Each one became a portable reminder of how easy it was to make someone disappear. Of how easy it was to kill without recompense. Each year it got a little more effortless and the thrill of it endlessly enticing. It was something the Jaguar could do every single day and never tire of it.

The only problem was that issue of enticement. It was like developing a drinking problem. One glass of wine was good. Two was better. A whole bottle fantastic. Yes, it was just like that. The first kill had been euphoric. The second thrilling. Each subsequent event held its own special allure that thrilled to the core, and she wanted more. The whole damned vineyard.

In the beginning it was easy enough to space the adventures out. A simple trinket taken with her when she left was all that she needed to recreate the event in vivid recall. Some might need photos to recapture the thrill. Not the Jaguar. She could recall each and every detail with ease. Over time, the span between them began to shorten as she realized the thrill brought on by touching the souvenirs was fading quicker and quicker. Focusing on the day-to-day routine of everyday life was a drudgery that threatened to destroy the Jaguar's very sanity. It was only the intoxication of the next project that made continuing with the pretense worthwhile. She needed more, and she knew how to get it.

Putting on a mask of respectability was fine as long as the promise of her next night out waited. No one figured out that beneath the shiny, well-cut hair and impeccably pressed suit was a predator. No one guessed that behind the crystal-blue eyes that so many found fascinating lived a jaguar, strong, stealthy, and deadly. It was so easy to fool them all and satisfying to deceive the stupid people who hovered around like a swarm of bees. They all believed they were smart. They weren't.

The coffee grew cold, and without any other distractions, the itch began to set in again. As much as she wanted to give in, she had to ignore it. At least for now. Even the Jaguar recognized that the time was not right. It was far too soon, and that's where danger existed. Pity, really. A new prospect had presented herself just this morning as the Jaguar had driven the youngest to school. Perhaps a touch close to home, but that made it all the more interesting. Why not take someone nearby? It wasn't like anyone had a clue or ever would. It was like being a preternatural creature. By day, respectable, responsible, and loving. A face all recognized and found comfortable in its friendliness. By night, morphing into an unrecognizable predator with a face that struck fear into all who gazed upon it. Like a werejaguar. Human in the light. Jaguar when darkness fell upon the city. That thought brought a genuine smile.

The cold coffee dumped down the sink, it was time to move on with the day. Secure in the knowledge that last night's unwilling yet highly entertaining participant still remained beneath piles of dark, black earth, the Jaguar grabbed the just-cleaned suit jacket and slipped it on. It was snug and well-fitted. In the full-length mirror that graced the front hallway, the image that stared back at her was one of authority and trust. Perfect.

She tugged at the jacket to smooth out nonexistent creases and sighed. Turning away from the mirror, she mentally prepared herself for what the rest of the day would bring. She couldn't ignore family obligations. Work pressures waited. Leather case in hand, the Jaguar stepped outside and breathed in the fresh morning air. The sun was warm, the air clear, and the sky blue. It was going to be a good day.

Chapter Five

The sound of the doorbell sent Liz diving behind the sofa. At her side, Attila hunkered for a second before launching himself at the door and barking with all his power. Her heart raced and she told herself to relax. Attila was only picking up on her extreme reaction to something very mundane. It was simply the doorbell. No monsters waited on the other side.

No gunshot disturbed the morning. Not this morning anyway.

She stood up, blew out a quick breath, and shook out her arms. "Get ahold of yourself, girl," she muttered before running a trembling hand over her hair and heading to the door. "Back," she commanded Attila, who did as she asked, though a quiet rumble still emanated from his throat.

Through the peephole she saw a woman, and not one she recognized—tall, with long black hair and dark eyes. Liz would definitely remember her if they'd met. For lack of a better description, the woman was hot, even with the restricted vision the peephole provided. As the woman waited, she turned her face to the side, and Liz almost blurted out something quite inappropriate. Thankfully she not only caught herself but was safely on the other side of the thick wooden door, so no one could see the expression on her own face. Rudeness had never been a hallmark of her personality, and she didn't want to make it one now.

Composing herself once more, she pulled the door open. "Hello? Can I help you?"

The woman turned her gaze to the open door, and the fine scars Liz had seen through the peephole a moment ago now turned away from her. "Liz?"

The use of her name threw her. "Yes…I'm sorry. Do I know you?" An awful lot of people had floated in and out during those early days in the hospital. Maybe she'd been one of them. Possibly one of the doctors or nurses. Liz hadn't kept track of who they all were, or cared for that matter. She sort of did now.

The smile that crossed the woman's face banished any trace of disfigurement the scars created. "No, but we have a mutual friend. I'm Willow Blue, and Meg Zimmer asked me to stop by and introduce myself."

"Why would Meg do that?" Sounded kind of weak to her.

Her answer was direct. "She thinks I can help you."

"Sorry she bothered you." She shut the door and reached for her cell phone. So much for not being rude. Sending a stranger to her new house didn't seem like something Meg would do without telling her first, particularly after the night she knew Liz had suffered through. Meg had to realize the last thing Liz would want was the company of someone she'd never even laid eyes on, cute or not. She didn't even want the company of family or friends. The phone rang only once on the other end before Meg picked up. "Don't be pissed. You need to talk to Willow. Trust me on this, Liz."

"Why would you send a stranger to my door?"

"Please just talk to her. She can help, I swear."

So many emotions rolled through her: anger, fear, and disappointment. Why did everyone keep trying to fix her? She wasn't broken. "I don't need help."

"Talk to her, Liz, and if you're still mad afterward, you can kick my butt. Please."

She considered just saying no and then thought about her friend. Meg was the last person in the world who would ever try to harm her. "Okay."

"Great. Call me later." Liz pushed End and stuffed the phone back into her pocket. Meg better be right.

Slowly pulling the door open again, she was only slightly surprised to see Willow still standing right where she was when she'd slammed the door, hands in her pockets and with a serene expression. A light wind blew, making her hair fly about her face. "Okay…"

A tentative smile brightened Willow. "I understand this is kind of unusual, and if I was in your shoes I'd tell me to take a hike. Before you do that, hear me out, and then if you want me to go, I will."

She started to say "Hell no" and close the door again. But her second, much stronger, inclination was to pull the door open and invite Willow Blue into her house. She gave in to inclination number two, stepped back, widened the open door, and waved her in. "Ten minutes."

Willow smiled warmly and nodded. "All right then. Ten minutes it shall be."

In the living room, Willow picked one of the two leather recliners. With a big dog in the house, Liz had opted for leather furniture because it was easier to clean. Liz would have grabbed the other one, but she was too late. As if to prove exactly why leather chairs were better when a dog was around, Attila jumped into the other recliner, sat up tall, and stared at Willow. At least he was no longer growling deep in his throat. In fact he seemed delighted to have company, his body relaxed, and what was that on his face? A doggy smile? Was Attila failing at the one job she got him for: protection? Or did he sense this woman was good, and thus, he liked her. Once again, Liz went with number two. Sure as hell hoped she wasn't wrong…twice.

The second Liz opened the door, Willow felt the draw and got exactly why Meg had asked her this favor. Actually two things struck her at once. First, she and Liz were kindred souls. Case in point: the same broken aura that Willow also carried with her circled Liz like a halo. Only those who had suffered as they had would fully comprehend or be able to sense the aura. She was no psychic by any stretch. It was their shared experience that allowed her to understand. Others might try, but they could never really get there.

Second, an immediate attraction hit her. It wasn't like love at first sight or anything like that. It was more a knowing with unexplainable certainty that they would be good friends, that they had more between them than simply having been victims of violent crimes. It wasn't to say she didn't find Liz alluring, because that would be quite wrong. She was, very simply put, lovely. She wasn't a kid, and life was most definitely written on her face. The tragedy that had changed her world, however, had not erased the essence of what made her beautiful. It had failed to break her, and Willow could sense the incredible strength just below the surface.

Though she could sense how powerful Liz was, she didn't believe the other woman had a grasp of her own inner steel. That she was brittle around the edges was crystal clear from the moment she said hello. It was the thing that had Meg so worried, and it wasn't an inconsequential concern. Post-traumatic stress disorder, PTSD, was a terrible affliction that could shake the foundations of even the strongest. She should know. It had very nearly ripped her feet out from under her. It wasn't, however, a life sentence.

She'd been lucky when a mentor came to her and taught her the skills she needed to take back her life. And that was exactly what Meg was asking her to help Liz do. Her initial reluctance to do this particular favor evaporated entirely. It was time to pay it forward, and gazing into the troubled eyes of the woman across from her, she was up for the job. Six months ago that probably wouldn't have been the case. It was amazing the difference half a year and a world populated with kind souls could make.

"Why are you here?"

Blunt and to the point. She liked that. "I'm here to help you."

"I don't even know you, so how could you possibly help me with anything?" The bitterness in Liz's voice was impossible to miss, and she doubted that Liz had any intention of hiding her feelings on the matter. It was actually a good sign. Pretending didn't help anyone, so if she could stay honest, half the work was already done.

Willow's fingers flew to her face, and she lightly touched the scars. She could have investigated plastic surgery to minimize the damage, but as time went on, she moved further and further away from that idea. These scars were hers, and she owned them. Why did she have to hide from what had been done to her? Truth came in many different packages.

"I think you're wrong about that, Liz. I believe you and I have much in common, and I understand a great deal of what you're going through."

Liz was shaking her head. "I can see you've suffered, and I'm sorry, but I don't need any help. I'm okay. My friend worries way too much, and I don't want to waste your time."

"So what you're saying is that you didn't have a vision last night? Liz wasn't the only one who could be blunt.

Liz stared at Willow, open-mouthed. "How…" Her eyes narrowed. "I swear to God I'm never telling Meg another thing."

"Please, hear me out, and don't be angry with Meg. She called me because she cares about you, and I *know* what you're going through. Let's just say I've walked a mile in those shoes."

Liz rubbed her face as if trying to massage away some kind of pain. "Okay, so just for giggles, let's say you understand and have gone through something similar. What difference does that make? What can you possibly do for me that a licensed professional hasn't already tried?"

"You'd be surprised. I had a friend when the world seemed to be falling from beneath my feet. Three tours in Iraq, and then boom. An IED took his legs. PTSD didn't even begin to describe what Ned had been through. For me, it was different, but a lot like what happened to you. I was simply going about my daily life, and then everything was ripped away. I woke up in a hospital with my face in tatters and my life the same."

Liz stared at her before she said, "I wasn't dreaming."

Willow nodded and returned her stare. "I believe you. Neither was I when it happened to me."

CHAPTER SIX

Eldon tried hard to put it out of his mind. He had entirely too much work to do to get sidetracked trying to solve Liz's issues right this second. Still, it haunted him for hours, and he wasn't able to shake it off like he usually could. That feeling in his stomach refused to give up its grip. Because he didn't really have a choice, he put his head down and worked his butt off for the retiring judge's ceremony, though his mind was miles away throughout the whole thing.

Again and again his thoughts returned to that phone call. What Liz had told him rang familiar, and he really wanted to know why. After hours of going through the motions, he realized he wasn't concentrating on his work at all anymore, and he finally had to take a break and sit down at his computer. With deft fingers he began to type. His hasty web search yielded plenty of information in a matter of minutes, and then it all came back to him. No wonder it sounded familiar. No wonder he had a terrible feeling that wouldn't fade.

Reggie King's picture had been on the news, in the papers, and all over social media. One day she was there, and the next, not a trace. She'd never been found, and as far as they knew, the investigation had been relegated to cold-case status.

The description Liz had given him this morning on the phone was an absolute match, from the eyes and hair right down to the clothes she'd been wearing the night she'd gone out to meet friends and disappeared. Liz had most definitely seen Reggie King in her vision, and yeah, all of a sudden he totally believed it was a vision.

He wasn't the kind of guy who believed in visions or psychics or any kind of woo-woo crap. What was different with Liz was simple. Nobody had a dream like that.

Besides, given the trauma Liz had been through, it wasn't a big stretch to think she could have visions. He'd heard of stranger things happening, and despite his pragmatic view of the world, a little piece of him was beginning to buy in. The problem, at least in his mind, was what to do with what she'd seen. Liz had mentioned going to the police, only he wasn't sure what she could tell them that would either make sense or help to take Reggie's case out of limbo. Nothing about the vision gave them anything concrete other than the location, because it was a running path. Hundreds of trails dotted the city, and she didn't have enough additional detail to help nail down where the path might be or why it was important, and that was a shame. He sensed that somehow it was critical.

By the time the lunch hour rolled around, he was almost frantic with the need to do something, even if it was dumb. He raced out of the building and across the street to the parking garage. He was in his car and on the way across the Maple Street Bridge in less than ten minutes. He made one quick stop to run into a store. Throwing a bag on the passenger's seat, he was back in his car, and five minutes after that, pulling in front of Liz's house. Luckily, her new house was a quick sprint from the courthouse. It was in a beautiful old neighborhood that had withstood the ravages of time. It was a soothing place to call home with its old-stand maples and brick cottages all anchored by a great park and historic Masonic temple. He passed them all as he drove directly to her house. A car he didn't recognize was parked in her driveway, and the sight sent him into panic mode. Who was here? Why? Was she okay? Had someone harmed her? Again.

He threw open his car door and leaped out without hitting his head. A pretty good feat for a guy his size. Liz must have seen him through the front window because she had the door open before he was halfway up the walk. "You okay?" His words came out breathless, as if he'd run all the way up here instead of driving. His heart was pounding.

In jeans and a gray T-shirt, she looked more like the old Liz than he'd seen in a while. She wrinkled her brow as she looked at him, another expression that reminded him of the days before the shooting. "Of course I am."

He inclined his head toward the unfamiliar vehicle blocking her car in the driveway. Her gaze cut to the car, and she shrugged. He wasn't sure if that shrug was good or bad. Was she really okay, or was she pretending because danger was inside the house?

"Can I come in?"

She stepped back. "You know you always can."

No, he didn't know that. Not right at the moment anyway. He stopped just inside when he saw another woman in the doorway between the entry and the living room. She was beautiful, and even the scars evident on one side of her face didn't detract from her looks. Nothing about her screamed danger, yet her presence bothered him. At some basic level, the fact that she was standing here without him knowing about it made him feel like he was failing once again in his quest to protect Liz. He needed to pay closer attention.

"Eldon," Liz said. "This is Willow Blue."

He held out his hand. "Eldon Spicer." No reason he couldn't pretend to be polite. For the moment anyway.

She took his offered hand, and her grip was firm, confident. "Nice to meet you."

"Not to be rude, but what are you doing here?" Liz's question was directed to him. "You have the retirement ceremony today."

It was his turn to shrug. "I decided they would all be just dandy without me for an hour."

"That's not like you at all."

"I have a good staff."

"Lame."

"What's going on?"

She did know him. He wasn't the guy who would bail on his responsibilities. Yet that was the reason he was here too. He had a responsibility to take care of her, and sometimes a person had to prioritize. "I was worried about you."

She spread her arms wide. "I'm fine."

He narrowed his eyes. He knew her a little too well, and a declaration that she was fine was her equally lame attempt to blow him off. He'd heard the edge in her voice earlier, and that let him know a lot was going on beneath her calm exterior. Perhaps she was putting on a show of bravado for this Willow. Even if that was the case, he wasn't going to let her get away with it. "Bull."

Liz looked from him to Willow. "Did Meg put you up to this too?"

Didn't he wish? He didn't know Meg nearly as well as he wanted to. She was hot, smart, and every time he was around her, it was like he was in the seventh grade all over again. He was nervous and stammered and in general came off as an idiot. He would give anything to impress her. So far he was sure he hadn't even come close. Not that he was giving up.

He met her gaze and answered her with honesty. "Haven't talked to her. Besides, why would Meg send me over here?"

Liz nodded toward Willow. "Maybe because she sent her to *help* me."

Willow nodded. "She's not wrong."

Eldon smiled at her. If Meg sent Willow, she had to have had a very important reason, and any doubts about her evaporated. "Good."

The plane touched down and not one minute too soon. The Jaguar was about to explode. Emotions had built up so tightly inside that it would be impossible to hold on any longer. It might not be a good idea, but she had to move the next one up. Not doing so would be unbearable.

The airport was loud, and people were pushy. Walking through the crowds was pure torture that made her skin tingle. The air was filled with the overwhelming and nauseating scents of many different colognes and perfumes. The Jaguar hated the morons with the rolling bags, screaming kids, and old people who had no business getting on a plane in the first place. The pretty people with their pocket pets in those stupid carriers were worse than the obnoxious children. As the years went by, it became easier to understand those individuals who finally had enough and began to shoot up public places.

Not that the Jaguar would ever resort to something so vulgar. That was terrorism. She might be many things, but she was most certainly was not a terrorist. Everything had a reason, and it wasn't about random violence. It was abhorrent the way some people blew themselves up or drove cars into crowds of people to make some ridiculous point. For the Jaguar it was far more personal than something politically or religiously motivated.

What the Jaguar did was deeply intimate and important. After she did her work, she left the world in a better state than before, and that made a difference. Everything she accomplished had a purpose. That it was incredibly enjoyable was a side benefit she'd discovered from the very first. It made all the rest of the daily annoyances and bother bearable.

But no one was at the top of the list at the moment. She simply hadn't had time since the last one to do surveillance on the next candidate. Flexibility, however, was an option, though not an optimal one, for it wasn't the best way to operate. Certainly in the beginning the work contained a flavor of chaos. As time passed, more and more order entered into the process, and with that order flowed an oh-so-rewarding sense of calm.

Not right now. Order and logic went out the window when she was in this kind of mood. Despite the short flight day, the familiar anxiety was growing by the second. Getting through the airport took enormous amounts of concentration and energy in order to stay outwardly calm. Once she was in the car, the tremors started, and only one thing could make them stop.

While breathing in and out, in and out, and sitting on the second floor of the garage, she began to form a plan. To say no one had risen to the top of the list wasn't exactly correct. She did have someone to take the top spot. Actually, she probably should have been on the list a long time ago, and now that she seriously considered it, she wondered why she hadn't penciled this one in before now. Maybe it was the universe's way of keeping a ripe prospect in reserve for days like this. A spare, so to speak and, the more she thought about it, a pretty good plan.

As she considered it, the whole plan became clearer in her mind and, without a doubt, more perfect. Of course, when wasn't a plan she devised perfect? Some people just had a way of making something beautiful out of crap. In this instance, it was a case of killing two birds with one stone, which was a fantastic idea; this was getting better and better.

Calm descended as the plan came together with crystal clarity. As if to further punctuate the brilliance of the idea, her flight had landed early thanks to some impressive tailwinds. The end result of that early arrival was that it provided unanticipated time to kill, literally. That brought a smile, a real one, unlike the ubiquitous fake ones that were a necessary part of passing as normal in the day-to-day world. It felt quite good too.

At this time of day she expected the traffic to be light. But that wasn't the case, and it created a longer-than-usual drive. After she finally made it to the street of large, beautiful homes, she passed the house of the intended and got exactly the expected intel. She was there and preparing to head to the golf course, expensive golf clubs being loaded into the back of the shiny Mercedes convertible. Her clothes were trendy and impeccable, as well as coordinated to present the precise image she wanted. Big surprise there. She certainly couldn't hit the links without looking like a million bucks. What would people think? That she was a run-of-the-mill lady golfer? God forbid anyone think she was ordinary. Her obsession with appearance extended even down to the hydration. The water bottle in her hand was the latest must-have model, and she sipped from it now, a smile flirting. If that trendy bottle held only water, she'd be shocked.

With a second long pull from the bottle, she closed it and slipped it into a pocket on the golf bag. She didn't even look around to see if anyone was watching. The arrogance that oozed from her pores was galling, though not for long. The Jaguar had a solution for people like her, and today was the day. The most thrilling thing of all: she'd never see it coming.

CHAPTER SEVEN

Liz sat at the table for a really long time after Willow and Eldon left, tapping the closed cover of the sketch pad that Eldon had produced from a big paper bag. That same bag held two packs of high-grade charcoal pencils, just the kind she used to work with back when she sketched a lot. She had a box on a shelf somewhere out in the garage full of them. Eldon had seen her in the office break room any number of times through the years drawing her heart out, but it had been a really long time since she'd had any desire to create anything. She used to love to draw the glory she witnessed in her everyday world. But these days, she didn't see beauty, and it took too much effort to try to find it. Nope, most of her energy went into trying really hard to stay sane. It was a full-time job.

Though she wouldn't admit it out loud, his idea wasn't half bad. The vision haunted her. She couldn't get the young woman out of her head. Eldon's suggestion that she draw what she saw scared her, as did Willow's encouragement. She saw Reggie's face every time she closed her eyes and heard her voice whenever silence fell. She could almost smell the wet grass and hear the leaves rattle as a gentle wind blew. Yeah, scary.

Willow, on the other hand, was not. Scary, that is. She was as fascinating as she was attractive. The scars on her face might frighten some. Not Liz. They made her even more alluring. That she too was a survivor made them soul sisters of sorts, although it was hard to equate what Liz was feeling with the carefree attitude Willow exuded. The two didn't seem to jibe. Clearly her scars demonstrated the truth of her claim that she had likewise been through a bloody, painful trauma; and frankly, she did believe her. It was just difficult to reconcile her calm and soothing demeanor with the despair that washed over Liz all the time.

The two of them were relative strangers who met on common ground, and that common ground seemed to be random violence. Meg had recognized their shared experience and endeavored to bring them together today. Noble sentiments, though far from the best way to start a relationship. She grimaced when she thought of that word. Actually, she wondered why that word had popped into her head at all. They were acquaintances now and nothing more. Precisely why she ultimately sent her on her way.

So here she sat all alone, except, of course, for Attila, staring at a brand-new sketch pad, big and white and waiting for the touch of the pencil. Part of her wanted to open the cover, and part of her wanted to burn the damn thing. If she had to tell someone why she was conflicted, she'd have to admit she was afraid of what might grow at the point of one of those shiny new pencils. She really was a good artist, and that was the problem.

She was equally afraid of not opening the pad. Somehow she had to get Reggie out of her head, and at least the tip of that bullet hadn't stripped away her ability to draw. Inside her had to be at least a flicker of courage, and she tugged on that now. With a sigh, she flipped the cover of the pad open and pulled a sharpened pencil from the pack. She had drawn a mere fraction of a line when her phone rang.

During the first three rings, Liz stared at the pencil she still held and thought seriously about not answering. As much as she liked the idea of cutting everyone off, even she realized it wasn't a good idea. She was already hanging on by her fingertips, and if she was to have any chance at making it through this nightmare, she couldn't turn into a hermit…tempting as that idea might be.

"Hello." She pressed the phone to her ear.

"Hey, babe. I'm heading your way."

"Eloise, what's going on?" Frankly, she wasn't up to her drama right now. She had enough of her own to last a couple of lifetimes without Eloise's liquor-fueled version. They'd been friends for a lifetime, and she was Eldon's sister, but still, she could be hard to take in anything beyond small doses. Eloise was gorgeous and rich, just as Eldon was. But Eloise hadn't made the transition to adulthood as easily as her brother had. She'd brought all her childhood baggage along with her, and rather than becoming a contributing member of society, like Eldon, she chose to embrace dysfunction. It could get really frustrating, even if she did love the woman.

"I'm heading your way, baby sister. You up for nine holes at Downriver? It's a little late in the day to go for eighteen, but we're good for at least nine. Come on out and play with me. You know how I hate it when they pair me up with some hack. Save me."

Liz was well aware that Eloise was referring to the routine practice of golf courses to pair up singles with other golfers in order to send each group off the first tee as a foursome. "I don't have my clubs unpacked." It wasn't a lie. They were still in bubble wrap and stuffed in the corner of the garage.

"I've got a spare set in the trunk."

Of course she did. Liz didn't know exactly how many sets of clubs Eloise owned, but it was certainly more than two. Every time something new and improved came on the market, she was the first one in the pro shop to buy a set. "Appreciate the offer, but I really have to pass this time around. I'm still settling in, and I'll be honest with you. I'm exhausted."

"Ah, come on, Lizzy. Don't make me go play with strangers. You how that stresses me out." True to form, Eloise was thinking only about herself. It hadn't even occurred to her that Liz hadn't swung a club for more than a year. She might never unpack those clubs.

"They won't be strangers when you finish." Unfortunately the truth behind that statement was disturbing. More than once, Eloise had ended a round of golf with her new *friends*, men or women, by spending a couple hours in a hotel room. Of course by the time she finished a round, whether it was nine holes or eighteen, she routinely polished off the ever-present pint of brandy she carried in her bag. How she could put away as much liquor as she did and still remain standing was beyond her. Her liver had to be a royal mess.

Despite her disparaging thoughts, she valued their friendship in more ways than not. Eloise wasn't a bad soul. Just an addicted one, who displayed absolutely no remorse or desire to change. Bottom line, Eloise really did love her family and friends, her booze, and a rocking good time, wherever she could find it, and not necessarily in that order.

Eloise laughed a little too heartily. Liz glanced up at the wall clock and shook her head as she wondered how much she'd had to drink already. "True enough. You're sure you don't want to play a round? It's been a long time, you know. I miss you."

Right at the moment, if she ever touched a golf club or spent the afternoon with an inebriated Eloise again, it would be too soon. Those clubs could stay in the bubble wrap, and Eloise could go booze it up with some other loser. "I'm sure. Rain check?"

She heard a delicate slurp, and Liz closed her eyes, seeing a water bottle filled with something besides water clutched in one hand. "Fine. Next week."

"Give me a call and I'll see." She'd come up with another excuse then.

"You have simply got to get out of that house, little girl."

The last thing she needed or wanted was a lecture from Eloise. "Call me. I've got to go."

She clicked off the phone before Eloise could say another word. In fact, she did more than just end the call. She powered down the phone. She didn't want to talk to anyone, Eloise in particular, and there was a better than average chance she would try to call Liz again. Eloise wasn't one to take no without a fight.

She should probably call Eldon and let him know that Eloise was driving around while feeling no pain. A good friend would do that. A good person would do that to protect others on the road. God forgive her, but she wasn't a good anything right now, and the darkened phone lay quietly on the table. Today the universe would just have to take care of itself.

Without hesitating, she picked up the charcoal pencil again and began to work. Eldon was right. It was soothing, as if all the tension of her body flowed right down her arm, out her fingers, and onto the paper. The picture began to form without her having a conscious thought, and it felt damned good. She wished she'd thought of this sooner. Or actually thought of it herself.

By the time she finished, her hand was cramping and the sun was beginning its descent over the westward hills. If she were standing on the summit of Snoqualmie Pass, the sunlight would be warm on her face as it slowly sank. As it was, the sun was fading behind the Sunset Hill to the west, and if she could see the freeway from her windows, it would look like ribbons of white and red as the lights of the cars either going up the hill or coming down created what looked like festive holiday lights.

Around her on the table was a sea of paper. Six pages had been torn from the pad, though she didn't remember freeing them from their silver coil. Yet there they were, lined up like soldiers across the top of the shiny walnut tabletop. She remembered putting her head down and touching the pencil to that first empty page, and that was it. As she gazed at the six completed drawings, chills raced up her arms.

Willow didn't go back to the studio. It wouldn't have been a good idea, as her students would immediately pick up on her troubled aura. Wendy, her backup instructor, was more than capable of handling classes for the rest of the day, so she gave her a quick call and told her without a lengthy explanation that she couldn't make it in and needed her to pick up the classes. The expected "no problem" answer was exactly what she needed to hear.

As soon as she ended the call with Wendy, she turned her thoughts immediately to Liz. She was beautiful and troubled, a combination that drew her in like a bee to a flower. What was it about her attraction to wounded spirits?

Actually it wasn't that big a mystery. It was easier for her to relate to those who'd suffered.

She got the walls that Liz had been erecting around herself since waking up in the hospital. Standard operating procedure for the walking wounded. Time and love could break them down, and she was happy to help, especially when it came at the request of someone so generous of spirit like Meg. Only a complete tool would say no. She might be a lot of things, but tool wasn't one of them.

A long time ago, someone had helped her, and she would always be grateful. She firmly believed that what goes around, comes around, and this was her moment to make good on it. She just had to figure out how to give her what she needed. Liz's friend Eldon actually had a great idea when he showed up with a sketch pad and pencils. It was hard to tell what exactly Liz was seeing in the dreams that haunted her sleep, and if she could make it more concrete, great. Even though she was clear on the identity of the woman who spoke to her in the vision, something else of importance seemed to be eluding her. Sketching what was in her mind's eye might help exorcise the demons, so to speak.

She touched the now-faint scars. Once they had been red and angry and painful. Even after the pain was long gone, every time she'd looked in the mirror, anguish had washed over her. Her pure despair had threatened to cripple the rest of her life. As she began to embrace the help offered to her, or as she thought of it now, the gift given to her by another, the emotional scars began to heal at an amazing rate. And more than the inner scars healed. At the same time, the swelling in her face went down, and the redness of the wounds began to fade. Before long, the physical scars became a whisper instead of a scream, and the pain dwindled to a tickle. She had healed more completely than she ever believed possible.

A steady knock on her door interrupted her introspective trip to the past. Just as well. She'd spent enough time in memories of those long-ago days. It wasn't a place she liked to go as a general rule. It was over and done with, and that's the way she'd like to keep it. All that was important lay in the here and now. She refused to live in the past or pin hopes on an unknown future. Here. Now.

A peek out the window revealed a visitor who wasn't a surprise.

"Why did I know it was you?" she said as she swung the door open to Meg. She had to have come straight from school over here.

"Did you get a chance to talk to her?"

Her didn't need a name. "Yes, and come on in." She wasn't much surprised that Meg got right to the point. She was like that when she was worried.

"Oh, thank God. I'd be in a twist if you hadn't. I was afraid she'd tell you to get lost. She's got to pull it together before she implodes, and I'm worried that's not far away." She stepped inside and headed right for the kitchen.

Willow followed her. "I don't think she's as far gone as you believe."

"Really?" The note of hope in Meg's voice made Willow doubly glad she'd talked with Liz. She plopped down into a kitchen chair and propped her chin in her hands.

Well, maybe that wasn't the right way to approach this situation. Willow tried again. "Don't get me wrong. She's far from okay."

Meg began running her fingers through her hair in a blatantly nervous way. "Crap."

Willow put a hand on her head. "Let me finish, sweetie." Meg stopped messing with her hair and tipped her head up to meet Willow's eyes. "Look. Liz is suffering. That's as clear as can be. She's not lost, though, and I know I can help her. If nothing else, I understand her and a lot of what she's feeling. It gives us common ground, and that's an important place to start."

"She's going to get back to her old self, right?"

This was always hard to explain to people. They wanted the fix to just magically happen, and it didn't, even for the most resilient. There was never a way of going back to the way it was before. Things like this changed a person forever. It wasn't something she could explain, so she didn't try. "It won't be overnight."

Meg sighed and nodded. "In my heart, I know that. I just want to hope it'll be soon. Okay, so she'll get back to her old self in her time, but what about the vision she's going on about? That worries me."

Willow met Meg's intense gaze and said with heartfelt honesty, "She'll be fine. Trauma like she's been through does something to a person, and it can bring on the sort of visions, for lack of a better word, that Liz is experiencing. It should pass."

"Should?"

"It's not an exact science." Again, it was too difficult for those who hadn't had to walk through the fire to understand.

Meg dropped her head into her hands again. "No. I suppose not." She looked up once more. "Did it happen to you? I'm kind of guessing it did, by the tone of your voice."

"Something very similar did, yes."

"And you came out of it okay?" The thread of hope in Meg's voice pulled at her heart.

Willow smiled warmly. "I like to think so."

Meg laughed, and the light returned to her eyes. "Ha. Somehow that didn't come out quite right."

Willow kissed the top of her head. "No worries, my pretty friend. I knew what you meant."

"You always do."

CHAPTER EIGHT

Eldon rode up the hill near the stables toward the parking lot on the west side of the Bowl and Pitcher. It was a popular area of Riverside State Park, and he thought maybe he'd picked the wrong place to be right now, considering he'd really like to be by himself. Still, this was one of his favorite biking routes, and riding the lightweight road bike always lifted his mood.

At the parking lot, he unclipped from his pedals and got off the bike. Only two cars were pulled into the spaces marked by the bright yellow lines, and he'd encountered only one other biker in the seven miles he'd covered so far. Maybe his choice for a quiet ride wasn't so bad after all. He loved it up here, and it was easy to think as he stared down at the rock formations so well-known to Spokanites. The river flowed clear and strong around the rocks, and an eagle soared above his head. It wasn't unusual to see eagles here, but the sight still filled him with awe. It always did.

His thoughts turned to Liz, as they did so much of the time lately. He couldn't help it. Some might think he was in the throes of unrequited love. Without question, he loved her, but just not in *that* way, even if she'd been attracted to men, which she never had. He loved her for the wonderful person she was, plain and simple. She was an honest and true friend that he could always count on. She was smart and funny and incredibly talented. She had a piece of his heart and always would, so he just wanted to help her heal. He wanted her to come back.

That Willow who had been at Liz's house when he got there had that same kind of light about her. He didn't know her from Jack, yet something about her instilled trust in him. He didn't often find himself that drawn to strangers. He was to her, and he could see the way she was drawn to Liz. He doubly liked that.

It sure didn't hurt to have another person helping in this journey. That thought made him feel better, and he slipped his helmet back on his head, straddled his bike, and had one shoe clipped back in when his phone rang. It was Liz.

"You busy?"

He smiled, because those two words sounded just like the old Liz. Hope began to bloom in his heart. "Out riding."

"You're at Bowl and Pitcher, aren't you?"

"How did you know?" A dumb question considering she knew him probably as well as anyone, except maybe his sister.

"You always go there when you're worried."

"I'm not worried." He didn't usually lie very well, though at the moment it felt like the right thing to do.

"Sure, you're not worried, and I'm ready to go back to work." She always had a way with sarcasm, her second language.

"Okay, busted."

"Damn right you are. Now pedal your ass over here. You're not that far away, and I've got something to show you."

His heart began to pound, and his initial glee at her sounding like her old self faded away. "What's wrong?"

"Nothing. Just get over here." The edge of exasperation in her voice worried him, and he didn't want to upset her.

He opened his mouth to try to keep things calm, except she ended the call before he could say anything else. Well, so much for trying to be the calming influence. She always did like to get her way, and really, that wasn't a bad thing because it signaled a baby step forward. He clipped into his other pedal and took off, picking up speed by the second. He'd be at her place in nothing flat.

Before he got more than a quarter mile, his phone rang again, and once more he stopped to pull it out of his pocket. Had to be Liz. It wasn't. As much as he felt like he was becoming Liz's stalker, he had the same feeling about June Abrams. Only in this case, he was the one being stalked. She'd moved in across the street from Eloise ten years ago, and from the first introduction, she'd been like a bad rash that wouldn't go away. For whatever reason, June had latched onto him and wouldn't let go no matter what he did, and that included changing phone numbers. Nothing worked.

"Hey, Eldon." Her sugary voice made his back stiffen.

"What can I do for you, June?" He wasn't into pleasant small talk with her. It only served to encourage her, and that he didn't need.

"Well, here's the deal. I just got home from the airport, and I noticed that Eloise's car is gone."

"And that would concern me why?"

Her sigh was overly dramatic. "Well, you and I both know what that means."

"No, we don't. You need to let this go and stop calling me whenever she drives away."

June laughed. "I'd be hurt if I thought you meant that."

"I do mean it." God, was he ever going to get that through her thick skull?

She laughed again. "Of course you don't."

No sense arguing. She wasn't going to listen. "Eloise is okay. I've got to go."

"I'll call you when she gets home."

"Please don't."

"Talk to you soon."

Eldon stuffed the phone back into his pocket and began riding again. He pedaled hard to shove away the irritation that roiled through him every time June called. He'd tried everything he could think of to get through to her that he wasn't attracted to her. It wasn't just that she was a nutcase, but she was married. If she wasn't unstable, if she wasn't married, then maybe, just maybe, she'd be interesting. She was beautiful and successful, but neither of those qualities made a difference considering June was crazy as a loon. He felt sorry for her husband.

❖

The Jaguar was patient. Had to be. Both in the façade that passed for her life and in her real world where all was as she wanted it to be. It was a good trait to possess, for it ensured the capture of all things truly important. Like now. Let the people see what they expected from her and boom—the universe was hers for the taking.

Her intended had come out of the clubhouse, as expected, a few hours later, swaying on her feet. The water bottle she'd brought from home was undoubtedly empty, and the fact she wasn't putting it to her lips every few seconds testified to that truth. It was hard to tell how many drinks she'd indulged in over the distance of the nine-hole round, and then, of course, there were the mandatory cocktails while finishing up the score card. How she could add the score or, for that matter, still stand on two feet was an absolute mystery. Then again, practice made perfect, and anyone who'd been around her very long would realize she'd had plenty of that.

Still, it was crazy to think someone could pour that much alcohol into a body that couldn't weigh more than a hundred and ten pounds and continue to look good. It wasn't fair, considering the abuse she imposed upon her physical being, yet she had a beauty that even booze couldn't take it away. Everyone else had to work at it. Not her. Nothing seemed to dampen that natural allure. The Jaguar knew the one thing that could, and it made her smile.

"Hey," she said as her head came up and she noticed the Jaguar leaning against her car. "Glad to see you. Help a girl get her clubs in the car? I'm toast after that round. I don't think I have the energy to lift that bag." She laughed high and loud as she ran her hand through the tangled curls that had the look of an expensive salon visit.

"I'll put them in the back for you, but let me drive you home." The Jaguar picked up the bag and tossed it carelessly into the backseat. The clubs rattled when they landed, and bits of dirt and grass flew into the air.

"Oh." She waved her hands in the air like she was shooing away flies. The Jaguar wasn't sure if she was batting away the dust or waving at her. "That's nice of you to offer, but really, I'm fine."

"That might be, but it would probably be a good idea to let me take you home anyway. Better safe than sorry." God, that sounded just like her old bitch of a mother, and the mere thought made the Jaguar shudder.

She frowned and stumbled over her own feet, digging for her cars keys in the purse just big enough for a tuck-away flask. "Whoops. Stepped on a rock and almost lost it there for a sec."

Sure she did. There wasn't a single rock anywhere near them on the clean asphalt parking lot. "Come on. I'll give you a lift. You're really not in any condition to drive yourself."

"My car…" Her hand fluttered toward the lovely red convertible.

"It'll be fine here, and you can get it later after you've rested up." Well, somebody could pick it up later, though it would definitely not be the drunk weaving on her feet.

"All right." She laughed again. "Maybe you have a good idea. Besides, we haven't seen each other in forever, and a little ride will give us a chance to talk. Where in the fuck have you been anyway? Let's stop for a drink at the Flying Goat and catch up."

That would be a big fat no. Being seen together was about the absolute last thing that was going to happen. "I'd love to, but not today. I have to get home." What was amusing was the fact that she didn't wonder how they so coincidently ran into each other at a golf course. Only one of them played.

She put her hands on her hips, swayed, and pouted. "Oh, come on. We need to reconnect. You're always too busy to spend time with me." The pout was undoubtedly meant to be cute. It wasn't.

"Another day, I promise." The lies were so easy.

"Okie dokie. Come on. On the drive, you can at least tell me how the world's been treating you. You sure you don't want one tiny little drink? I'll buy."

One hundred percent sure. She had something in mind with a far bigger high than alcohol. "Not today."

With an arm around her shoulders, they began to walk together the half block to where the Jaguar had parked her car. It was tucked beneath a tree and out of the line of sight of anyone coming out of the clubhouse. The plan was a good one. No one paid any attention to them, which wasn't a big shocker. She might be well-to-do and beautiful, but she was a drunk, plain and simple. How many people went out of their way to avoid the club drunk? Pretty much everyone. Worked perfectly for what was to come. No one looked their way because no one wanted to. Everyone was secretly delighted she'd picked someone else to favor with her booze-fueled pleadings.

"God, could you have parked farther away?" she whined.

"You just played a round of golf. This short walk should be easy."

"I had a cart." She snorted. "I didn't *walk* nine holes. Who the hell walks a golf course anyway? Only those who are too cheap or too poor, and we all know that's not me."

Well, wasn't that a surprise. She probably had her cart stocked with a mini-bar. "It's not that far."

"If you say so."

"I do."

When they reached the car, she almost fell into the passenger's seat. Apparently the short walk had worn her out. The interior light that came on when the Jaguar opened the driver's side door made the spots on her expensive shirt show up clearly. No need to wonder what caused them. The odor of alcohol filled the car. Pathetic excuse for a woman. They hadn't driven six blocks from the golf course before she was snoring. Perfect. The noise was annoying, but the no-talking part was delightful because it meant no more inebriated conversation and no more pretending to be pals. That part of their relationship was over. Had been over for a very long time. Soon it would be dead and gone…literally.

CHAPTER NINE

So? What do you think?" Liz had spread the drawings out on her dining-room table and was staring down at them. It was a little like scrutinizing movie storyboards. Once she'd started, she hadn't been able to stop and had worked like a madwoman. At least that's what she thought happened because she still had no recollection of actually doing the work beyond a cramping hand. With each sketch she studied, the tension she'd been feeling washed away a little more. She was as relaxed as she'd been for days. Thank God for Eldon's stroke of genius. Drawing sure beat the hell out of drugs.

Eldon, dressed in the Spandex bike shorts that always seemed so out of character, a loose-fitting, dry-fit shirt, and ankle socks, stood looking down and shaking his head. "Wow." She wasn't sure what he meant, and it was a little hard to take him seriously dressed in Spandex, not that she'd tell him that.

"What does that mean? Wow, good? Or wow, you're more messed up than I thought?"

He tipped his head and stared at her. She was drawn in by his eyes that were such a gorgeous blue. Some woman was going to fall hard for those eyes and the guy that was behind them. It was a wonder no one had yet. "You don't know, do you?"

She threw up her hands. She didn't have the first clue what he was talking about. "Know what?"

"It's easier to show you than try to explain. Where's your laptop?"

"Eldon, what the hell? Spit it out. I can follow. I'm not an idiot."

"Never said you were. Now, just bring your laptop."

She loved the guy, but sometimes he was so damn frustrating. Why wouldn't he simply tell her instead of the "get me your laptop" crap? Nonetheless, she didn't try to argue and instead went into her bedroom and returned with her computer. "Here." She shoved it into his hands.

Without a word, he dropped to one of the chairs and put the laptop on the table. His fingers moved like lightning over the keys as soon as he had it powered up. Not too surprising, considering what he did for a living. When she was working, they used to refer to him as the IT god, because no matter what the problem was, Eldon could solve it. Watching him work now, she had no doubt he'd mine the net until he discovered what he searched for. She was right. After no more than a minute, he turned the machine so she could see the screen.

Her knees felt weak as she stared at it. Slowly, she then sank into the chair next to him. "Fuck me," she whispered. The words trembled as they passed her lips, and a cool wind seemed to waft through her kitchen even though all the doors and windows were securely closed.

"Yeah." He drew out the single word.

The image she studied burned into her retinas, and she blinked to ease the pain. Then, she turned her gaze on him. "What do you think it means? I mean, this is some kind of crazy, right?"

"I wish I had a clue. If I had to guess, it has something to do with Reggie's disappearance. I mean, she comes to you in a dream, and then you draw this. It's like she's giving you a detailed map."

His train of thought was traveling the same path as hers. "I thought the same thing. This isn't any place I'm used to going, so why would it pop up in my unconscious? Sure, I've been by it. Hasn't everyone who lives in the city? The real question is, how did my fucked-up head come up with this?" She wasn't being sarcastic. She knew what it meant to have post-traumatic stress, and it had ruled her life since she'd opened her eyes nine months ago. Still, she'd never heard of anyone else doing something like this. Seeing dead people and drawing pictures that might or might not show where they were. "It's like being a pirate and possessing a treasure map, only in a really creepy, dead way."

"This is no treasure." Eldon's words were low.

Her whole body buzzed as she looked from the picture on the screen to the charcoal drawings on her table. Nobody would doubt that the face was anyone except Reggie, and anyone who'd lived in the city for more than year would recognize the landscape. It was like those really difficult pieces of a puzzle coming together. So what did she do with this?

"Let's call that Willow woman." Eldon tapped the pictures with his index finger.

"What?" That suggestion came right out of left field. Willow was really interesting, and she liked her, which was kind of surprising considering she wasn't into meeting anyone these days. The difference was probably that she got what Liz was going through, but this? How would she be able to help?

"I don't know," he said. "It's just that this is kind of freaky, and even from the brief time I was with her, it seemed to me that she had a clue about what happens to people when they go through trauma as you did. Maybe she'll have some insight. It's worth a shot."

Liz wasn't so sure and preferred not to have her life exposed to any more people than necessary. Eldon and Meg were one thing, but a near stranger something else altogether. She'd allowed Willow in a little. How much farther did she want to take it? "I'm not so sure…"

"Come on. What have you got to lose? Besides, you gotta admit, she's kinda hot." He smiled at her and winked. Damn him. He knew her way too well.

"I didn't notice."

His laughter was light but heartfelt. "You're a horrible liar and always were. That twinkle in your eye is a dead giveaway."

Now she laughed, and it felt good. Maybe calling Willow wasn't the worst idea in the world. "Okay. What the hell, and my eyes don't twinkle."

❖

When Willow's phone rang and she saw whose number it was, she was both shocked and pleased. She'd hoped to hear from the pretty Liz again but really thought it would be days, if not weeks, before that happened. In her own case, despite the generous offer of help she'd received, it had taken her a good two weeks before she'd been ready to open up. She'd expected much the same from Liz.

"Liz." She raised an eyebrow as she looked over at Meg, who sat at the table sipping a cup of tea. A slight smile teased the corners of her mouth, and Willow had a pretty good idea why. A closed book Willow was not, which was another side effect of what'd happened to her. Having one's life flash before their eyes changes everything, including being worried about what anyone thinks. These days, she didn't hold back anything, and she was more than okay with that gift. She'd spent too many years worrying about what people thought and what she said. Not any longer, and it was more freeing than anything she could have imagined.

"I'm sorry to bug you so soon after you left, and I'm sure you have other things to do…"

Well, that was an interesting start to a conversation. Intriguing, as well. "It's fine. You're not interrupting anything major. Meg and I were just having a cup of tea." She wasn't simply being polite either. It really was fine that Liz had called. More than fine, actually. She smiled as warmth rolled through her.

"So, you know how Eldon brought me a sketch pad?"

"I do. It's a good process for you to express yourself with drawing. He had a really great idea." Excellent therapy, and she was going to have to remember that one in case she was in a position to help someone again. She hoped not, because it broke her heart when people had to endure what she and Liz had to. Unfortunately, the world probably wouldn't cooperate, so it was better to be prepared and tuck away every little tidbit of helpful information.

"Yeah, well, I kind of did already."

"That's wonderful. How do you feel? Did it ease any of the tension?"

The pause before she spoke again was telling. "That's what I'm calling about. Any chance I could talk you into swinging by again?

Eldon and I think you might be able to help us make heads or tails out of what I did this afternoon."

Willow's heart began to race. This was even better than just hearing from her. Not only was she offering her a chance to get together again, but she was also intensely curious to see what Liz had created. "I'd be happy to come by. When?"

Again there was that pause. "Ah, would now work for you?"

Surprising. Not unpleasant, yet surprising nonetheless. "Now works great. See you soon." Her pulse began to race. Now was in fact excellent. She ended the call and looked at Meg. "Well, I wasn't expecting that."

"I got that Liz wants you to come by. Why? You said it would probably take her a while before she'd open up to you."

"That's what I was expecting, that's for sure."

"So why ask you to come over so soon?"

"She didn't say, other than she'd been drawing all afternoon."

Meg smiled and her eyes lit up. "I choose to believe it's a good sign. Maybe she's more ready to heal than I'd hoped. I was positive you'd be a great influence, and I was right."

Willow raised an eyebrow. "I know what you're thinking, and trust me, sister, you're off base." Judging by Meg's smug expression, she was patting herself on the back for her mad matchmaking skills. Honestly, the moment she saw Liz she had no question as to exactly what was on Meg's mind. Not that she was discounting the very real concern she had for her friend and her belief that Willow would be able to help. In fact, she was certain that was her foremost concern.

"Really? She calls you back just a couple hours after you meet, and you don't find that interesting?"

"It's not about me." From the gist of their brief conversation, it wasn't about her at all. She wasn't going to discount the possibility it was perhaps a side benefit. It just wasn't the main show.

A smile played at the corners of Meg's mouth. "Of course it's not."

This time Willow rolled her eyes. "Oh, for pity's sake, quit worrying about my love life and focus on seeing what we can do for Liz. She needs help, not a girlfriend."

Meg wasn't about to give up. "The two aren't mutually exclusive, you know."

Willow shook her head. "Come on. Drink your tea and get in the car. I'll drive."

Meg didn't move from her spot at the table or finish her tea. She didn't appear to be in the mood to move. "I don't think she's expecting me. Just you."

"Too bad." Willow took her own tea cup and put it in the sink. Suddenly, she wasn't thirsty anymore. "You're coming along, and that's that."

Meg finally let loose with the laughter she'd clearly been holding back. "Whatever you say. Besides, I am curious."

"Curious about what Liz has drawn?"

"Yeah. That too." Meg set her cup in the sink and quickly disappeared into the garage.

CHAPTER TEN

Eldon was still freaked out by Liz's drawings, and he'd been staring at them for over an hour. When Liz had agreed to call Willow to come back over, he had to admit, at least silently, he was relieved. For some reason he couldn't name, he wanted to know what she thought about them. Maybe it was because he sensed she would be able to impart great insight about what they were and, more importantly, why Liz drew them. Freaky didn't even begin to describe the very detailed, very realistic drawings. Scary was another adjective, but he didn't want to go there.

He was staring out the front window when a car pulled into the driveway and was surprised to see two doors open. Willow got out of one and Meg the other. God, when would his stomach ever stop dropping every time he saw Meg? *Never* was the word bouncing around inside his skull. As he watched her walk from the driveway to the front door, his heart thudded. He was going to pine for her until they put him into the ground. Unrequited love truly sucked, and he was frankly too old for this shit.

Instead of continuing to stand here looking like a love-sick puppy, and he sure as hell didn't want anyone seeing that, he went to the door and pulled it open. He was pretty sure he pulled off a very neutral expression that betrayed nothing of what he was feeling. "I'm really glad you could come," he said as he stretched out a hand to Willow.

"I have to tell you, I'm curious," she said with candor as she stepped into the house. "I'm glad Liz called me. I want to see what she's come up with."

"Curious is good, and I hope you can make sense of this. It's quite frankly creeping me out."

"Make sense of what?" Meg stopped in front of him. She smelled like summer in a field of flowers.

"Hey, Meg." Was that his voice that sounded like it was stretched piano wire? Very macho.

She met his eyes and smiled. Did he see genuine pleasure there or was he imagining it? Odds were on imagination. "Hey, Eldon."

He was stunned when she pushed up on her toes and put her arms around him. Instinctively, he stiffened. "I'm glad you're with our girl," she whispered into his ear. Her breath felt warm and exciting on his skin. His shoulders relaxed, and he wrapped his arms around her in return. The press of her body against his made him want to stand here forever. If he ever doubted the existence of a higher power, it vanished in this second because this moment was the work of the divine. Had to be.

"She needs us," he whispered back into her ear.

Meg broke the embrace, and he reluctantly let her go. "Is she okay? I mean really okay?" Tension seemed to bring her shoulders up and darken her beautiful features.

Nothing too loaded about that question. On one hand, he did believe Liz was doing better. The drawings seemed to pull her out of herself, and he hadn't seen that kind of brightness in her since before the shooting. It was encouraging.

On the other hand, what she had drawn scared the ever-loving shit out of him. It was like seeing one of those TV crime shows laid out in picture format. He wasn't a big fan of those series.

"She's getting there." It was the best and most honest answer he could come up with. Actually he was quite impressed he could talk at all. If he could get over his schoolboy infatuation with Meg, things would be a whole lot easier. Who was he kidding? It was a lot more than that. He wasn't a boy, and what he felt for her went way beyond infatuation. He was also certain it was one-sided and could never come to anything. She had always been kind and sweet and friendly. At the same time, she'd never shown the slightest interest in him beyond that.

Meg's shoulders relaxed a touch. "Good. I hoped Willow would be able to help, and you bringing Liz the pencils and pads was a stroke of genius. Brilliant, really. Why didn't any of those so-called counselors come up with anything like that? I mean, all that time and money, and they didn't even come close to helping her. You did it in minutes."

He had the answer to the unhelpful professional help because he knew Liz almost as well as he knew himself. "She didn't go."

Meg, who was stepping through the doorway, stopped and once more stared up at him. "Say what?"

"She didn't go."

"But her doctors had her set up with on-going counseling. She told me every time I called that she was either on her way or had been to a great session."

Easy answer to that one too. "She lied."

"She wouldn't lie to me." Meg sounded defensive, and a frown turned down the corners of her mouth. "We've been friends forever."

That statement was true about pretty much anything else. She was straight up with her friends, Meg included. This was different. When it came to the issue of counseling, Liz had, in fact, lied big time to not just Meg but everyone. "I'm sorry, Meg, but she did."

"Liz told you that?"

Shit. How was he going to answer that one? He stared at her and then blew out a breath. Might as well come clean, at least with Meg. Sooner or later he was bound to be caught anyway. "Not exactly."

"How does she not exactly tell you?"

"She didn't tell me because, well, I followed her."

"You followed her?" The frown disappeared, replaced by a look of surprise.

"I was worried." It sounded pathetic when it came out of his mouth, even if it was the bold truth. He shoved his hands into his pockets and waited. He didn't look away. He wasn't that big a coward.

Instead of seeing revulsion in her face, he detected relief. "Good."

"Good?" Did he hear her right?

"Definitely good. I like that you had her back."

He'd thought he couldn't fall for her more. He was wrong. Now he should be feeling encouraged and uplifted, and he wasn't. As much as he appreciated her words, he couldn't shake his own uneasy feeling. "In some ways, I feel terrible, like I've become a perverted stalker. I don't want to be one of those creepy guys you read about in the papers."

She put a hand on his arm, her touch warm, soothing. "You're nowhere close to being a creepy guy. You're one who cares, and there's a big difference."

"I do care, although I suspect that's what those guys say all the way to their jail cell."

She shook her head. "No. You're not like that at all. Honestly, if I'd thought of it, I'd have done the same thing. I'm just glad you not only came up with the idea but carried through on it. She's safe as long as you're watching her. Now, come on. We better go in before they start looking for us, but later," she moved her hand to lay her palm flat on his chest, "you and I need to talk."

She had no idea how down he was with that proposal.

It was amazing how long a drunk could sleep. It worked out great because now it afforded her plenty of time to find the right spot. A new area to work in was a treat and one not to be wasted. Usually she had all the groundwork done ahead of time, and that was wonderful in terms of efficiency and time. This was far more of an adventure and not unpleasant in any way.

An easy route from the golf course to the location she had in mind was to hop on Highway 291 and head north. At the turn to the Seven Mile Road, additional inspiration struck, and it was pure perfection. Lots of hiking areas flowing into the interior of the wilderness park and far away from the view of the masses would be the ticket. Plenty of ground to do the work and hide the end result. It was always nice to be able to go back and visit, and this place would provide that opportunity without a great deal of challenge. It was precisely what the Jaguar enjoyed the most, a passion-filled personal secret.

It was still light out when the final location came into focus. She pulled the car into a spot off the beaten track that tucked it into the trees so that only those who were really looking would be able to see it. The people who frequented this part of the massive state property known as Riverside State Park rarely paid attention to other vehicles. They were simply looking for a spot to park in order to hike through the thousands of acres that made up the heavily forested recreational area. The only thing that could cause scrutiny of her car was not having the mandatory park pass on display. She had handled that as she hung the requisite placard from the rearview mirror. As long as a passing park ranger could see the pass, she was golden. Everything was ready. She was ready.

Nonetheless, it was too early to get down to the fun part, and she stayed put, tapping lightly on the steering wheel. It would be a bit of a waiting game, and that was fine except for the continued snoring in the passenger's seat. The Jaguar was surprised her family hadn't knocked her off, if this was her normal operating procedure. It was disgusting on many levels, and good God, that snoring was getting on her nerves.

About the time she thought she couldn't take it a second longer, the sun began to lose some of its shine. Game time was about to begin. She wasn't quiet when she got out of the car, but her guest didn't wake up. From the trunk, the Jaguar retrieved a bag and then walked around to open the passenger's side door. Like a heavy bag of flour, she fell out. Her head thumped onto the ground, and she groaned.

"What the fuck?" Dried pine needles and crushed leaves stuck to her hair when she managed to get herself into a sitting position. Mud smeared her shirt, joining the alcohol stains she'd noticed earlier. "What the hell did you do that for?"

With the leather bag slung over one shoulder, the Jaguar stared down at her. "I didn't do anything. You did. If you hadn't been snoring like an old sow, you wouldn't have face-planted in the dirt and mud."

"You could have given me some kind of warning that you were about to open the door. I mean, really, letting me drop to the ground like garbage? Sometimes you can be a real bitch, you know that?"

Oh yes, indeed, she did know that and was quite proud of it. "More fun this way."

"You're an asshole."

"I've been called worse."

She wiped the back of her hand across her face, smearing mud like blush. "I just bet you have, and you probably had it coming. No more than you deserve for dropping me to the dirt."

"Didn't hurt you, though your hair and makeup could use some work. That shirt probably won't recover either."

"When did you get so mean?"

Oh, what a loaded question. It would take far more time to answer than they had. Well, rather than what she had left, anyway, though she didn't know it. There was work to be done, and now was the time to do it. "I've always been mean. You probably didn't notice. Few do."

She laughed so hard, she began to choke and cough. Spittle ran down her chin. Very unattractive.

The Jaguar looked down at her and scowled. What the hell was she laughing about? The way she was carrying on, if the stupid cow didn't rein it in, she was going to start puking. That would never do. DNA and all that. One reason the projects all stayed a perfect secret was the attention to detail that included not leaving any traces behind. When she stopped laughing, she looked up from where she still sat on the ground, pine needles still in her hair. "Bull. You've always been one of the nicest people I know. Everybody loves you. Well, everybody except my dog."

The Jaguar raised a single eyebrow and told the truth. "Let's just say I'm a good actor." That damn dog was the only one to see behind her mask.

"Not that good. At least until today. I know what an ass you are now." She got up from the ground and brushed the dust off her butt. That wasn't really necessary, considering soon enough it would once more be covered in dirt. Her pretty little crazy expensive outfit was going to be compost. "You're being a real shit right now. Why don't you just take me back to my car, and I'll drive myself home?"

The Jaguar inclined her head to the left. "No, I don't think so. Why don't we take a little walk over here? The fresh air will sober you up." She hoped it would, because it would be a lot more fun if she was completely aware of what was happening to her.

"No, home. Take me home. Unless you've got a big old drink in that bag, I'm not going anywhere with you." She put a hand on the passenger-side door, her back straight and her chin held high. This was the posture of a woman accustomed to getting her way. "Home. Now."

Some pretty big words from someone who, despite her show of bravado, was still weaving and who would be easy enough to drag away from the car like a child in the throes of a temper tantrum. It was clear that, even after her little nap, she was still too drunk to put up much resistance. She didn't have a chance in hell against the Jaguar. "Shut up." The Jaguar slowly pulled on a pair of gloves.

She tossed her head, and twigs went flying. "Fuck you." Cheers to holding onto bravado. She was still spunky. She just didn't realize it wouldn't last long.

The first blow to her face was hard, and it felt glorious. It caused blood to flow dark and red from her nose, a crimson river against her pearly white skin. The punch hadn't broken her nose, as she'd restrained her force. The blow did, however, have the intended result: she shut up, at least for a few minutes, and that was enough. It gave her a second to appreciate the sweet air and sprinkling of stars that were just beginning to shine overhead. A beautiful night for a game.

Her eyes went round and terrified as she covered her bleeding nose with her hand. "What is wrong with you?"

"I'm crazy." It was an honest answer. At this point there was no reason not to admit it. She could do anything she wanted to her, admit anything, and it wouldn't make a difference.

"Why?" she asked through tears. "What did I ever do to you?"

"Your very existence annoys me. The way you waste space on this planet annoys me. I hate everything about you. Now run!"

"What?" It was clear that between the booze and the pain she wasn't connecting the dots.

"I said run, you stupid cow. Run, or I'll kill you where you stand."

The command and the threat behind it finally sank in. Despite stumbling numerous times, she managed to stay on her feet long enough to make it from the car to the tree cover. Good, out here in the open wasn't optimal, but once they were in the trees…

The second blow knocked her to the ground, where she lay unmoving though still groaning. The groaning stopped after the first kick to her head.

Chapter Eleven

L iz was nervous, and not the kind of nervous brought on by stress. No, this was something entirely different and easily identifiable. It all had to do with Willow. She'd noticed it earlier when Willow first came and introduced herself. She had an energy around her that flowed over Liz as well. She'd never experienced anything like it, and well, it was pretty sweet.

Now, as Willow stood at the table and stared down at the drawings she'd worked on all afternoon, the silence was almost unbearable. She still felt that great energy she'd noticed earlier, but something else was there now. Already a little unnerved by Eldon's reaction to them, she desperately wanted to hear another point of view. She should never have been able to draw what she did and in the way she did. This wasn't artistic talent. It was something beyond.

"What's wrong?" Willow's concerned voice cut into her troubled thoughts.

She shook her head. "Nothing."

"You might be able to lie to them," she nodded to the living room where Eldon and Meg talked together softly, "but not to me."

"I'm not lying." She wasn't, not really. Omission wasn't lying.

"You are to yourself as much as you're trying to lie to me."

"I'm—"

Willow put a hand on her arm. "Just tell me. Whatever it is, I'll understand."

Liz looked up into Willow's eyes and felt a little like she was coming home, which considering she was actually in her home was kind of silly. "I'm scared of what you're going to think of me." She couldn't believe she'd actually said that out loud. What was it about this woman that made her share those things she'd been keeping locked up for almost a year?

"Because of these?" Willow waved her hand over the drawings.

"Yes." If she told her how they'd really come about, she'd most likely suggest a one-way ride to the hospital. It felt an awful lot like how she viewed the well-meaning counselors the doctors tried to set her up with. She never believed they'd understand and still had reservations about how far to open up to Willow.

"These are amazing."

That told her absolutely nothing, because she knew she had skills. Not enough to make a living as an artist but better than the average hack. No, it wasn't her drawings that made her nervous, and she was embarrassed to admit to Willow what the real issue was. "Thank you."

"Not really trying to flatter you. Well, maybe a little." Willow smiled.

"It helps." Hearing praise from her did make her warm all over.

Willow's smile disappeared. "Enough with the small talk. Just spit it out. You can trust me, I promise." Her eyes were serious.

"You make me nervous."

In an instant, the stern expression vanished, and her laugh was hearty. "Me? A yoga teacher makes you nervous? That's a hoot and would be a terrible thing for my business, if you know what I mean. You also realize I'm about as unthreatening as they come."

Liz was shaking her head. "You don't threaten me. Not physically anyway."

Her laughter trailed off and she looked at Liz with genuine confusion written on her face. "Then what? I'm not following you, so would you please explain it to me."

She took a deep breath and spit it out. "It's pretty simple. I don't want you to think I'm crazy."

Willow studied her face for a second before she sank into one of the chairs at the table and tapped the drawing that clearly showed a woman's sad face. "If that's what's making you nervous, let it go. Really. Here's the deal, I know you're not crazy. Not one little bit. This woman is missing, and that's very real."

"These kind of make me appear unbalanced." She was looking at the rest of the drawings. She was good, and these were beyond good, given the level of detail she'd been able to create. The more she stared at them, the more she knew they were probably the best she'd ever done. Reggie's face could have been pulled up from memory, given how much air time she'd had when she first went missing. Maybe. But the realism was so deep, it was if she'd sat at this same table while Liz drew her portrait. The rest…well, it was just plain scary. It sent chills up her back and knotted her stomach.

Willow was shaking her head. "No, no, and no. I beg to differ with you. These don't show that you're unbalanced. You may not be ready to hear this yet, and I'm going to say it anyway. They show that you've been blessed."

"How in the hell can you call this blessed?" She couldn't help the way her voice rose or how anger surged through her. Blessed was about the last thing she thought any of this was. Fucked up was way more accurate, and it pissed her off that this was happening to her. Hadn't she suffered enough already?

Willow put a warm, comforting hand on her arm. Her closeness, the smell of her, and the sweet touch helped to turn away the anger. "Easy. You have been given a gift for a reason, and we just have to figure out why. Once we do that, we figure out how to use it."

"Use it?" Get rid of it was more what she was thinking. If this was blessed, she didn't want any part of it. She'd stick with damned.

"Absolutely. It seems to me you're being shown something, or you wouldn't be able to do this. The one thing that's quite clear to me is that we have a mission."

"Seriously, a mission?" Oh, like getting shot and recovering from PTSD wasn't work enough.

"As serious as a heart attack."

Actually, she hadn't thought about it like that. She'd just wanted to get the vision or dream or whatever it was out of her head and onto the paper. A form of catharsis. What to do with it after that had never even entered her thoughts, except for those brief moments this morning when she'd wanted to call the police and blurt out what she'd seen. She'd gotten beyond that urge and figured it was a done deal after the drawings came to her and she laid those beautiful pencils down. "What can we do with these?" She really wanted to believe they were just drawings out of the head of a woman who wasn't exactly playing with a full deck these days. That would make things a whole lot easier.

Willow tapped another of the drawings. It was a pretty good depiction of the area known as Boulder Beach. Out of all of them, that drawing perplexed her the most. When she was a teen growing up out in the valley, she'd played in the river there, just like every other teenager in the West Valley area. It had been years and years since she'd been there. Once in a while she would take Upriver Drive out east. She couldn't remember the last time.

"So, here's what I'm thinking. We take a road trip with my friend Circe Latham and her dog Zelda."

"Your friend and her dog?" Just when she thought it couldn't get weirder. She was now completely lost. Why on earth would they want to drag in a woman and her dog?

Willow seemed tuned in to her thoughts and countered any argument that she might proffer. "Trust me on this. If I'm right about what's bouncing around inside my head, they'll know in nothing flat."

The thing was, Liz wasn't all that keen about bringing in more people to this nightmare of her life. Three of them were already witnessing her insanity, and that was three too many. "I don't know."

"You can trust her. She's a sister of the heart." Willow wasn't giving up without a fight. Liz had to give her points for persistence.

"Your sister?"

Willow smiled. "Not by blood, only in our hearts, and that's plenty good enough for me. I would trust her with my life, and you can trust her with yours. I swear to you."

Liz blew out a breath. Why fight it? Everything was out of control anyway. The way things were going, the whole city would know she was crazy before long. "Okay, call your friend."

"It'll be good. You'll see. Circe is wonderful and everybody loves Zelda." Willow squeezed her hand and then shouted out to the other room, "Hey, Eldon, Meg, come on. We're taking a little ride."

Willow didn't tell Liz she had a bad feeling about her drawings. Well, more like good and bad. It was good for Liz to do them, and she was convinced it was an absolute necessity for her to express whatever she was seeing. She had to get those visions and emotions out of her body, or they'd become toxic. Drawing seemed to be the perfect medium.

But she was quite sure they were more than just drawings that manifested out of a vision. Something very ethereal about them haunted and disturbed her. An undeniable truth lay beneath the strokes of the charcoal pencil, and they needed to uncover whatever it was, one way or the other.

She didn't suggest bringing in Circe and Zelda lightly. Not just because she didn't want to impose upon friends needlessly but also because of the unique nature of what they did. She hadn't told Liz yet. Part of the county's search-and-rescue team, Circe and Zelda were a very specialized K9 team, a recovery team, meaning that they searched for people presumed dead. The more she'd studied those drawings the more she became convinced that Circe and Zelda would be able to quickly reveal what was behind them.

She recognized the specific location in them, as did Eldon. Boulder Beach might be a popular destination, known to most everyone who'd lived in the area for any length of time, yet why come up so clearly in her work? She had an uneasy sensation there was a dark reason why. Combine one missing woman with one unlikely location, and in her mind, it added up to trouble. Who would do the unthinkable in such a popular place?

One easy way to find out if she was right about what she surmised was to bring in a woman with the uncanny ability to see dead people and one dog trained to detect the odor of human decomposition. The combination should put her fears to rest one way or the other. If she was right, however, she worried about how Liz might be affected. Willow saw strength in Liz, yet what she presented to the outside world didn't necessarily mirror what was going on inside. Willow wanted to bolster the strength and help make the fear disappear. She hadn't been lying when she said that Liz had been given a gift. It was. It was also a curse. She wanted to help her make peace between the two.

She called Circe as she headed out the door to her car. The conversation was quick and pointed. Her friend was, as always, willing to lend aid, which was one reason she was careful what she asked for. She didn't want to impose, especially for something like this. In the end, they agreed to meet at Boulder Beach in an hour.

Traffic was pretty much a bitch until they reached the east side of Division. It always was, but once they hit Upriver Drive, it was smooth and easy. Her heart beat faster as they drove the winding road past the houses and the dam that also bore the name Upriver. Across the river, small planes were taking off and landing at the historic Felts Field. The closer they came to Boulder Beach, the more her body buzzed. Like Liz, she'd developed her own touch of otherworldly talent: premonition. Most of the time nothing happened, and then it would hit her like a bat to the stomach. Until she uncovered its origin, it stuck around like a bad case of the flu. She knew she wasn't wrong now; something waited for them along that beautiful stretch of the river.

Circe was already there and waiting when they pulled into the dirt parking area. Zelda was out of the SUV, her body on alert and her eyes focused. Normally the beautiful German shepherd would rush to Willow to say hello and spin in joy at seeing her friend. Not today. She didn't seem to notice Willow, or anyone for that matter, because she had her attention on something unseen in the distance and undetectable, at least to humans, on the wind. Circe might not have her on command yet, but it didn't matter, as Zelda was already on the job.

She gave Circe a quick hug. "Thanks so much for coming. Circe, this is Liz, Eldon, and Meg."

Circe nodded toward them, though she didn't waste words or extend her hand, in which she held several pieces of small equipment. The look she gave Willow was searching, and she didn't need to ask why. Circe was looking for a clue as to what Willow had told her friends about her and Zelda. Had she revealed that this K9 team possessed something more than the normal search capability? In most human-remains detection teams, or HRD as they were called, only the dog had the ability to locate the dead. Not so for Circe and Zelda. They were a double threat. Zelda could detect the odor of human decomposition, and Circe could see the dead. Not surprisingly, she shared this secret with very few.

Willow answered her unspoken question. "We're hoping *Zelda* can tell us if there's anything to what Liz has seen and created. We know the woman she's drawn is Reggie King. We think the rest of these may show us where she is." She held out the pencil sketches, confident Circe understood she'd shared nothing about her unique abilities.

"You think Reggie is here?" Circe pointed to one of the drawings showing a narrow path through pine trees and tall, wild grass. The other drawings were similar, as if a photographer was taking pictures of the same area, only from different angles. A three-hundred-and-sixty-degree view, and all they had to do was figure out where.

"Unfortunately, yes." She glanced over her shoulder at Liz, who stood there pale and silent. She'd been that way since they left her house. Though she'd agreed to this, Willow wasn't convinced she was buying into its necessity. Or maybe Liz understood it was important to follow what the pictures seemed to be showing but would rather be anywhere but here. Willow gave her props for being here anyway.

Circe nodded as she looked over each drawing, one by one. Then she handed them back to Willow. "Okay. Here's what we're going to do. Zelda and I will take a little walk along the shoreline." She nodded toward the beach lined by the boulders that gave it its name. "Given the detail of the pics, I don't think she's there, but we'll clear it first. Then, we'll cross over to the wilderness side and check that area." She inclined her head toward the other side of the street, where acres of trees and brush were maintained in their natural state. It was lovely and peaceful-looking. She was afraid that soon, ugliness would mar its beauty.

Willow had been around Circe long enough to understand the big picture, where she was going and why. Clear the obvious, and then get to the dark recesses where evil liked to hide. It certainly wasn't Circe and Zelda's first rodeo. "Good plan."

It took Zelda a whooping five minutes to cover hundreds of yards of shoreline, her illuminated red collar showing up boldly in the rapidly declining daylight. She moved like the swiftly flowing river she searched along and, for the entire distance, didn't as much as twitch. Watching Circe, Willow was pretty sure she hadn't seen anything either. As suspected, nothing of importance lay along that stretch of shoreline. Following the K9 team, they all crossed the street together and stepped into the trees that were thick enough to obscure a clear view of the road with the beach on the other side.

Willow studied Liz and then laid a hand on her arm. She could feel a buzz beneath her palm. "Are you all right?"

She shrugged and stared off into the distance. "I'd like to say yes, but I'd be lying. Truth is, I don't know. This kind of freaks me out. I know your friend is trying to help, and I appreciate her willingness to do this for a stranger. Says a lot about the kind of person she is. It's the sick feeling in my stomach that has me wanting to run back home."

Willow nodded. It kind of freaked her out too. She knew what Circe and Zelda were capable of, yet this was the first time she'd seen it up close and personal. Nothing had happened so far, and it was still unnerving. It was like the ominous music building up in a movie designed to let the viewer sense danger lurking around the next corner. "I understand, and if you want to hang back, that's fine. We'll let you know if we find anything." If she could shield Liz from any horror that might—most likely did—lie hidden out there beneath the beauty of the natural landscape, she would.

Liz shook her head, and it made Willow feel good to see the strength in her surge. "No. I need to see this through. It's important to understand what's happening to me…what's happened to her. I can't do that if I run and hide because it's hard. I've been hiding for too long."

Suddenly Circe leaned close to Zelda and whispered something in her ear that had her off and running once more. Circe followed the dog, the rest of them trailing behind her. She'd instructed them before she put Zelda on command that, while they were welcome to follow along, they needed to stay well back from her.

For maybe fifteen minutes they walked, albeit quickly as possible, in order to keep Circe and Zelda in sight, through the natural area. Nothing unusual to see. Lots of trees, bushes, and wild grasses. Then Circe stopped and stared, her eyes on Zelda but her body suddenly stiff. "Oh, shit."

CHAPTER TWELVE

Willow's friend Circe was as beautiful as she was serious. Not that Eldon was attracted to her. Not at all. The only draw he felt, still felt, was to Meg. Damn it anyway. He worked to keep his attention on the K9 team and not on how lovely Meg looked walking through the forested landscape.

Despite his infatuation with Meg, it wasn't all that hard to keep his eyes on the action. Zelda was a gorgeous dog, and it was downright fascinating to see her do what she was trained for. It was the first time he'd seen a working dog while it was actually working. It was flat-out amazing. Willow had clued them all in on the way over here as to the search discipline Zelda was certified in, and it boggled Eldon's mind to think about a dog doing something that incredible. She also explained that Circe and Zelda usually only came out at the direction of the sheriff's department. This favor she was extending to Willow was most definitely off the books.

Until right now.

This was no longer a wild-goose chase, a theory, or a long shot. She didn't have to tell any of them they'd found a body. The expression on her face, the tension in her body, and the actions of the dog about twenty yards away made it clear that the supposition had just become reality.

If any one of them had had lingering doubts, he guessed they all now knew what Liz's drawings were trying to show them. Unless he was wrong, and he was pretty darned certain he wasn't, this little hike in the woods would clear up two mysteries: the fate of the missing woman and the nature of Liz's vision. That bullet had changed her life in more ways than one. All he could think was, amazing…just amazing.

"She's there, isn't she?" He was standing right behind Circe, fixated on the very intense, unmoving dog.

Circe nodded and said in a hushed voice, "We need to stay back and not disturb the area." To her dog she said, equally low, "Good girl. Good. Okay, come." Only then did Zelda move. When Zelda approached Circe with tail wagging, she rubbed her head, repeated "good girl," and then pulled a GPS from her pocket. "Give me a sec to mark this, and then we'll head back to the cars." She was intense and serious with her body still full of tension.

He didn't exactly know what that meant to *mark it*, so he stood right where he was without moving. Though he considered himself a cyclist, an outdoorsman he was not. He used a GPS on his bike only to log miles. The type she used now as she studied a small screen and worked tiny buttons was nothing he'd ever handled.

He jumped when his cell phone buzzed in his pocket. Thank God he at least had thought to turn off the ringer. That would have been embarrassing. He pulled it out of his pocket and looked at the display. He almost groaned out loud. "What, June?" No doubt the irritation he felt came through clearly. He didn't care.

"Hey, buddy. Just wanted you to know she still hasn't come home."

"Not my problem, June. Eloise is a big girl. She can come home whenever she wants."

"You're not worried? I mean she could have wrapped her car around a tree or someone could have taken her out to the woods and murdered her. Really, she is your sister. Maybe you should come over, and we'll see if we can find her together. You know, drive around to some of her favorite spots."

Right, like that was going to happen. June really needed to pay more attention to her life and less to everyone else's. "No need to do that. She's fine. She always is."

"You never know, now do you? We've turned into a big city with big-city problems."

Something in June's voice gave him a chill. "What are you trying to say?"

"Nothing. I just think you should pay more attention."

"I think you should pay less. Look, I'm busy, June, and I've got to go." Before she had a chance to respond, he punched off and then promptly turned his phone off. He wasn't going to take the chance she would call back. Frankly, he was sick of June and her obsession with his sister. More like her obsession with him, and Eloise was simply the tool she used as an excuse to call him every freaking chance she got.

The whole exchange with June took less than a minute, and by the time he had the phone stuffed back into his pocket, Circe was saying, "Let's go. I need to make a call."

"You're going to notify the sheriff, aren't you?" Liz's voice shook. "Please don't do that. The last thing I want is for them to know about my involvement. I can't handle anyone asking me how and why we ended up out here."

Circe walked over and gave Liz a firm hug. "No worries. All the sheriff needs to know is that a group of friends and I were out for a leisurely hike when Zelda made a find. That's it. Everyone clear on that? Leisurely hike with no other agenda."

"Crystal clear," Eldon told her. The more uncomplicated they could keep this, the better. He didn't want anyone asking him questions that would be impossible to answer. Or at least answer in a way that made sense in the rational world. Willow and Meg nodded in agreement.

Circe's words were insistent. She was all business. "We need to head back to the cars and wait for the deputies."

He'd really like to get into his car and haul ass home. A forensics team uncovering someone's remains wasn't something he cared to witness. IT guys didn't hang around dead bodies even on their worst days. He was wound so tight, he jumped when a hand touched his. For a second he had the alarming thought it was the grim reaper. Then he realized it was simply Meg who had reached over and taken his hand. Her fingers trembled as they wrapped around his, which was something he'd dreamed of. Well, sort of. He dreamed of holding Meg's hand as they walked side by side along the river. But he'd never envisioned it would come true as they were leaving the site of a body dump, both of them shaking inside.

❖

The phone call distracted the Jaguar only momentarily. Modern technology had its advantages and its annoyances. It was fun to be able to screw with anybody anytime and anywhere. It also meant that people were able to track her anytime and anywhere. Then again, she was good at saying all the right things and at precisely the right moment. It was a gift she used without any guilt. She tossed the phone onto the front seat and then went around to the back of the car.

The folding shovel always located in the trunk was a darned handy piece of equipment. A present from her one and only, who thought it would be helpful should she become stuck during one of the winters where the snow didn't want to quit. So far, it had never touched snow. But he hadn't been wrong about it being handy. It was a pretty efficient way to dig a shallow grave. Certainly wouldn't want to use it for, say, a more traditional grave six feet or so in depth. However, it was sturdy enough to displace the soil so as to create a final resting place for the latest and most satisfying adventure. The right tool for each job.

To say it was satisfying wasn't an exaggeration. The early flight had turned into a godsend. If they hadn't made it into the Spokane International Airport early, this wouldn't have happened. It turned free time into me time. Instead of being stuck at home with both an annoying spouse and bratty children, the afternoon had become a true delight.

Thinking about the look on her face when it had dawned on her what was really happening had been a thing of her dreams. The Jaguar had fantasized about doing this for a long time. A wash of extreme emotions had flowed through her face: disbelief, terror, and best of all, betrayal. It was amazing that she'd had the fortitude to even feel those things, given the sheer volume of alcohol in her system. She had to have been at least three times the legal limit, yet she'd still shown emotions and pain as the Jaguar had kicked her repeatedly. Maybe not such a great thing for her, but for the Jaguar it was perfection. It was always better when they could appreciate what was happening to them.

Of course, as with the vast majority of the games, it had more to do with the Jaguar's skill than anything else. Each one was more than simply a case of having a good time. If that were true, it would boil this down to garden-variety murder. Rather, each experience provided a powerful lesson on how to be a better, more proficient killer.

How to be an unstoppable serial killer. Take that FBI and their so-called behavioral unit. They didn't really have a clue, now did they? They would never be able to understand someone like her or the motivations behind her actions.

That moniker made the Jaguar smile. Serial killer. To be the best when in the company of so many creative others exhilarated her. The difference between her and the others: she succeeded where they failed. The Jaguar continued to practice the craft while all the big names were either dead or incarcerated. Good was good, no doubt about it. She deserved a distinction all her own.

She had never planned this profession. Really, who goes to their high-school guidance counselor and says, "You know what? I want to be a serial killer"? It became the profession of choice once she did the first deed. Only then did all the pieces fall into place and the what-I-want-to-be-when-I-grow-up manifested. Ever since that day, life had been much more fulfilling and a lot more interesting. It was easier to play the normal game when the special moments waited on the fringes. Those unique and satisfying times would always await her because no one could stop her. Not that she was bragging, but nobody around here was smart enough.

Besides, in this day and age of crime television and tons of tell-all books written by profilers and retired agents, everyone knew about the so-called characteristics of serial killers. Of their troubled childhoods, their abuse of animals, and their total hatred of their mothers. The beauty of it was, the Jaguar didn't fit any of those.

Well, that wasn't quite accurate. There was the mother thing, and to say they hadn't been close was an understatement.

Nonetheless, profiles wouldn't do them any good in this instance. If the experts even picked up on any pattern, which to date they had not, they'd still never put the pieces together. No one would ever suspect such a fine, upstanding member of the community of these heinous deeds. Good people didn't kill, right? She smiled. It was clear sailing. Or, rather, unfettered killing. It was the ambrosia that fed her soul.

As much as she enjoyed cataloging her own wondrous traits, it was time to get back to tonight's dirty duty, so to speak. Despite the temptation to linger, that couldn't happen. She had a life to return to and pretend was fulfilling. The scent of fresh-turned earth wafted up into the air, and she breathed in deeply. The sight, the smell, and the sheer physical exertion of tossing shovels full of dirt into the victim's sightless eyes was a great ending to a fun night. Now that was fulfilling.

Nobody who knew the woman at her feet would argue that she'd been a colossal bitch who made the lives of those around her miserable. In the big picture, she was taking up space on the earth for no good reason. Tonight the Jaguar had remedied that miscarriage, and in the end, others would appreciate the deed. No one would miss a rich, obnoxious drunk. Her husband would find himself a free man and be happier for it. At first, he would be upset and sad. After all, he was a good man who simply found himself trapped in a bad marriage. He was too kind to dump her ass, which he should have done years ago. That was the problem with good guys. They lacked the balls to stand up for themselves. She was the kind of person who had to take charge of things for him. She had the balls, metaphorically speaking, to do what needed to be done. This game tonight was more than enjoyment. It was also the finalization of a long over-due divorce.

Her birth family would undoubtedly be relieved. They'd no longer have to make excuses for her behavior or apologize for her misdeeds. The blight on their name would be wiped out, and they would all have to be pleased about that. Though they wouldn't know who to thank for it, they would indeed be thankful.

The only downside she could foresee was that a rich woman disappearing without a trace would raise alarm. It was a given. If she'd been poor, nobody would blink. In this case, money talked, except everyone would think she just took off, given her history of erratic behavior. Drunks could be like that. They would never guess her true fate, and that was as it should be. Some guys were simply too nice to push publicly for a divorce and, even if their plea was silent, needed a little help from their friends.

Asked and answered. You're welcome.

When the last shovel full of dirt covered her completely, the shovel went back into its designated spot in the car. For now, it was inside a plastic bag. On the way home, a quick stop at the carwash would remove any trace of the visit here. She did so like to keep her tools spotless…and clear of any stray traces of blood that might provide DNA.

Back at the makeshift grave, just a touch of clean-up. All she needed to do was camouflage the disturbed earth with a covering of rocks, leaves, and pine needles. It took only a few minutes more to restore the scene to a nice forest landscape. Unless someone looked really closely, they would never suspect that a body lay just below a thick layer of dirt. Nobody would look, they never did, and that was why it was always so easy to go back and visit. All that was important was a location where the occasional hiker was not an unusual sight.

Glancing up to the sky, the Jaguar sighed. Unfortunately, it was getting late now and past time to put back on the mask of normality. Her family would already ask too many questions about her tardy arrival home. It wouldn't be difficult to explain if she retreated now. Stay any longer and that wouldn't be the case. The spousal unit would whine and ask endless questions. God, he could be such a little bitch, it was a wonder she hadn't taken him for a one-way trip.

It was time to put the façade back into place. Fantasies of a life free from pretense and the anchors of a pretend life had to stay that way: fantasy. For now that was fine. Today's fun and games would provide enough energy for her to make it through at least another week.

Maybe.

CHAPTER THIRTEEN

Though the sun went down and the air cooled, they stayed at Boulder Beach long enough for the criminal investigators to interview them in detail and receive confirmation that Zelda had, most definitely, located a body. Liz and everyone else gave the same account, and it seemed to satisfy the sheriff's deputies. It would be hours before the body was removed and most likely another twenty-four hours before the identity was confirmed. Their presence was no longer needed. Thank goodness.

Liz didn't need or want to wait around for confirmation because she knew who they would zip into a cold, sterile body bag and drive to the medical examiner's office. It was the woman who had come to her in a vision to ask her for help and whose face she'd drawn on a creamy white sheet of sketch paper. They kept those small details to themselves and didn't show a single drawing to anyone from the sheriff's department. There was no need. Given the officers didn't even blink at the explanation offered for how they found the body, nothing else was necessary. It appeared they were all very familiar with Zelda and didn't have a question regarding how or why she located human remains. The dog had a job in life, and she didn't turn it off regardless of what they were doing.

From what Willow told them, it wasn't the first time Circe had called in law enforcement after Zelda had provided the unexpected alert of a deceased individual. The way Willow explained it, the deputies would find it more of a shock if someone discovered a body in an area Zelda had been through and she hadn't detected it.

Yeah, apparently she was that good, and given what Liz had seen tonight, she was a believer. That dog was not only beautiful; she was amazing.

Liz appreciated the unquestioned acceptance of Zelda's abilities and her "coincidental" find tonight. She didn't want to have to talk about either her vision or the drawings. It was enough that what she'd done had helped bring this young woman home. Isn't that what Reggie King had been asking of Liz when she appeared in the vision? Besides, Liz wouldn't know how to begin to explain how any of it came to be. As far as she was concerned, there was no explanation.

Sort of. She'd felt different since the moment she woke up. Not just a little different. A lot different. The feeling had nothing to do with the trauma either. She couldn't deny she was struggling with her emotional recovery, but that wasn't it. This other thing that she felt was much deeper. In a way it wasn't a big shocker to find out that the oh-so-clear vision of the woman turned out to be something quite concrete. Even if she hadn't wanted to admit it, it had felt that way right from the start.

Her brother was a prime example. All her life she'd had a deep connection with Steven. He was a bit of a lost soul who'd gone about his life in his own way. Not a bad way. It wasn't like he was in trouble, but his lifestyle was different than anyone had envisioned for him. Bright, talented, and clever, he'd been able to do anything he wanted and excel. Instead of taking those abilities to great heights, he chose a simple life, living it day to day and letting it happen rather than planning a single thing. It had taken him from Spokane to Virginia to California and ultimately to Iowa, where he drew his last breath when cancer came calling. The thing was, she could always tell when he was in trouble. If he was sick, she knew. If he'd been hurt, she knew. If his heart was broken, she knew. When he left this world, a little piece of her went with him.

Until the gunshot that sent her away for a brief while, her only superpower had been that connection with her brother. The moment she'd opened her eyes in the hospital, she'd felt the change. Not that she'd shared that tidbit with anyone. These days the few people she allowed to be around her already thought she was definitely off with her post-traumatic stress. She didn't need to make it worse by admitting that maybe, just maybe, she'd come back to this world carrying a little extra something with her. Nope. She didn't need that stigma at all. PTSD was plenty.

Willow wrapped an arm around Liz's shoulders, and damn if that didn't feel really good at the moment. If she was being completely honest, it would feel good any time. Something about this woman drew Liz to her, and it made her feel better than anything had for a long time. At least one thing felt good. Or maybe two. She couldn't forget her main man, her only man, Attila. He was a bright light in her world, and once he'd entered her life, it was hard to imagine a world without him in it. She had a completely new and in-depth understanding about the power and importance of therapy and service dogs.

It was also quickly becoming clear that she was growing ever fonder of having Willow in her world. Funny the difference a few hours could make. People who'd known her for years would be shocked, especially her ex-girlfriend. The final straw for their failed romance had been the accusation that Liz didn't allow her to get close. She'd vehemently denied it, of course, but her girlfriend had been correct. She'd always held women at arm's length no matter how much she liked them. It would take years of psychotherapy to get to the root of why, though she had an inkling it had something to do with her brother's death. She was always afraid of loving someone deeply and then losing them. When her brother died, her heart had been broken. How crushing would that broken heart be if it was a woman she was deeply in love with? The solution, warped as it might be, was easy: nothing ventured, nothing lost.

"Are you all right?" Willow asked softly.

She turned and looked into her eyes. They were so gentle and full of concern. It was really weird. The compassion in her eyes was heartwarming despite having only met mere hours ago. Her generous heart was unique and special, and it called to her. She started to deny that she had a single troubling thought in her head and stopped. In a flash she decided to take a tiny risk. First steps and all that. She nodded. "I'm not great, but I'm okay."

"You don't look okay."

She gave a short laugh. "Willow, I haven't been completely all right since the morning I started walking into the federal building nine months ago. Oh hell, probably even before that, if I'm being truthful."

Willow laughed a little too. "Fair enough. But this—" she waved a hand to encompass the police cars and crime-scene tape—"has got to be hard. It could bring up many unpleasant memories. It does for me, even after all this time. It's something that's always with you."

Liz shrugged. It was true enough that the morning she'd been shot, the entire courtyard to the building had become a maze of yellow tape, law enforcement from federal, state, and local agencies, and hordes of media hovering on the fringes. If she'd witnessed any of it, she might be chilled right now. She didn't, though, and recalled what the courtyard looked like that day only because she'd watched the news footage later. She had no memory of any of it beyond blissfully heading toward the front door with her backpack slung over one shoulder and a latte in one hand.

This time she was the one to reach out, and she put a hand on Willow's arm. The contact sent a surge of energy all the way into her shoulder. "I'm sorry it bothers you. For me, it's different. I have no memories to deal with because I didn't see any of it except for news accounts later. At the time, I was in another place."

Willow squeezed her shoulder. "Just the same, hanging out here is stressful for you and me. The deputies say we can jet, and I'm ready to do just that. How about we both get the hell out of Dodge and I take you home?"

She could easily catch a ride with Eldon, who had driven himself and Meg here, and given their longtime friendship, that's what she should probably do. As she watched Eldon and Meg talking with their heads close together, she decided that perhaps it might be a good idea to let them make that ride by themselves. Her new x-ray vision was picking up on something brewing between them. If she had to try to explain what she was sensing, she couldn't. It was somewhat like the feelings she'd gotten with her brother. No way to explain.

And it made her happy. Eldon was a good guy and Meg was a good woman. They would make a great couple, and maybe this was the little nudge they'd been needing to encourage that spark to burst into a fire. Kind of a creepy nudge, but hey. The universe had its own ideas of when the time was right.

Like with the woman who was opening the car door for her. When was the last time a woman did that for her? That would be quite a while, considering how long it had been since she'd been on a date. Embarrassing when she gave it much thought. Was she really that big a pain in the ass? That was an answer she wouldn't search for because she knew it would embarrass her.

"You up for a ride home with me?" Willow stood by the open car door and gave her a small smile.

Liz headed her way. "That would be great."

Willow couldn't deny the vibration of excitement that raced through her each time she touched Liz. Pretty freaking cool. Pretty freaking untimely. It would be a whole lot easier if she'd met her at a local bar, maybe during a Poetry Slam, so that it was all coincidental and cool. She'd buy her a drink, they'd talk about the slammers, and get to know each other a little bit.

A relatively recent victim of a shooting who was not only experiencing PTSD but also some kind of ESP wasn't the most ideal situation to lead to a long and romantic relationship. Except none of that made a damn bit of difference to her body. It was screaming yes, yes, yes, while her mind was countering with no, no, no. Okay, to give her mind credit, the timing sucked. To give her body credit, the heart wanted what the heart wanted, and timing be damned.

Liz was quiet as they drove west on Upriver Drive all the way to Mission. Traffic was light until they turned onto Mission, and then it became the normal stop-and-go that Willow so hated. Reminded her too much of growing up in the LA area. One reason she'd picked Spokane was because it was night-and-day different, at least most of the time. There were just some areas that had a significant amount of traffic, though to be fair, in comparison to LA it was nothing. Still it bugged her. She liked calm, quiet, and as few stop lights as possible. Tonight luck was not with her, and they caught every single red light for miles. Thankfully, once she reached Northwest Boulevard, she was back in her comfort zone of peaceful commuting and even caught a few green lights.

It was easy to see why Liz had picked this area. It was old but beautiful, with brick cottages that had fortunately not fallen victim to time or neglect. Most were still as charming, if not more so, than when they were built. People in the neighborhood obviously felt great pride in their area, and she loved it. It would be easy to call this area home.

At Liz's house, she pulled into the driveway and jumped out. She was almost to the passenger's side door when Liz opened it herself and stepped out. "Thank you," she said with a small smile. "It was nice of you to drive so all I had to do was try to relax. Kind of hard to do after all that." She waved back in the direction they'd just come from.

"Didn't work, did it?" Willow got how that felt. Nothing could stop the emotion washing over her like a tsunami. She'd had that same sensation at least a hundred times in the first year. By year two, she'd started to get her legs back underneath her and was moving with forward momentum. She'd still suffered those tsunami moments, only not nearly as often. It hadn't been easy to get through all that, just as she was sure it wasn't easy for Liz now.

In fact, it might even be harder for her. In an all-too-familiar gesture, her fingers flew to her face, where they lightly touched the scars. For Willow, her ordeal was still on display for the world. People were always curious and always sympathetic. Few questioned the time she needed to recover emotionally once they saw her marred face. People understood, or at least they tried to. The scars didn't bother her all that much, but other people's reaction did. She just wished they'd get past them.

For Liz, it was entirely different. Clothing hid her physical scars, so she appeared to be a healthy, well-adjusted woman who gave off an air of competence and contentment. Only people like Willow, who'd been through a similar experience, realized exactly how thin that veneer was and that right beneath lurked destructive emotion. No one could see the angry red skin under her shirt that would one day grow pale but never completely disappear. No one could feel the roiling emotion that came with every crack of lightning or pop of a firecracker carelessly tossed by a teenager just out to have a little fun. No one understood the despair that crept in during the deepest hours of darkness when no one was around or the struggle it took to resist giving up when that despair was overwhelming.

She did. She knew it intimately, and right now she wanted to gather Liz up in her arms and promise her it would someday pass. The only problem? She wasn't sure it would. All those things she'd gone through had been a roller-coaster ride she never wanted to get on again. She'd even had a kind of vision like Liz, and that allowed her to understand oh so much. Despite the many similarities, she'd never had a vision about a violent murder. She'd also never been able to draw a picture that led to the discovery of a body. Post-traumatic stress? Yeah. She understood what to do with that. Despair? Yup. Been there, done that way too many times.

Seeing murder? Not a goddamn clue.

"No." Liz closed the car door and leaned against it. "The whole way back here, all I could picture was Reggie coming to me, only instead of talking to me, now I'm picturing her beneath the ground, all cold and alone. It almost made me throw up."

Willow put a hand on her shoulder. Intuition told her it was the right thing to do. "You have to realize she *was* cold and alone. Now she's not anymore, and that's because of you."

"But what if…"

Shadows darkened her eyes, and again Willow wanted to pull her into an embrace to chase away those shadows. She didn't. "What if what?"

Liz brought her eyes up to the sky. "What if she's not the only one?"

Willow wanted to assure her that no way would another person be found buried in a shallow grave, except that the cold fear that washed down her spine at Liz's words made her afraid. Very, very afraid.

CHAPTER FOURTEEN

Eldon was pretty weirded out. It wasn't every day one of your best friends led a posse right smack to a dead body. It was a good thing in a lot of ways, but it was pretty creepy in a lot more. Right now, it was fantastic just to get far, far away and try to pretend life was normal. He couldn't help but wonder if after tonight it ever would be again.

"What are you thinking about?" Meg was riding in the passenger's seat, still appearing calm. He couldn't figure out how she stayed so cool. He was so far from anything even resembling that, it wasn't even funny. No wonder she'd never be interested in him. When she could have anyone, why on earth would she go for a damaged guy like him?

He kept his eyes on the road and pondered what to say. Play it down to appear more macho? Or just be himself and be honest. He figured he didn't have anything to lose so might as well be himself. He tapped the steering wheel. "I just can't get over what happened. It's too freaky, and geez, I've hiked in that area before. I mean, when I think about her being there all along and just tromping right over her body…" He shuddered, and ice slid down the back of his neck.

He expected her to say that his crossing over the body was not a likely scenario. She didn't. Instead, she said, "Could be. Until the medical examiner does the autopsy, it's anybody's guess how long she's been out there. Anyone who hiked that trail could have walked over her and not have known it."

He shook his head. "That's fucked up."

"I'm sure not going to argue the point because I think you're right on. What I'm actually very grateful for is that Liz found her, and you're to thank for that. Without you, who knows how long she would have been out there."

He glanced over at her, his previous discomfort fading. "Me?" The ice at the back of his neck was suddenly turning kind of warm.

She laid a hand on his arm and smiled. "Yes. If you hadn't given her a way to work through what she was seeing, she'd still be wound up and believing she was going crazy. Now she knows she's not. You gave her an important gift."

"You don't think having a vision that leads to a dead body doesn't make her feel like she's going crazy?"

"Okay. You have a point. It's a little more than morbid. Still, using her artistic talent to express what she'd seen made her so much calmer than the woman I saw earlier. You know, it's hard to believe you're just an IT guy when you have the makings of such a great psychologist."

He laughed, which made him feel a whole lot better. "Good God, me a psychologist? Not hardly. They'd kick me out of school in the first five minutes. They'd be quick to point out I'm not the right guy for the job. I like my code and computers far more than trying to fix people. Computers and networks don't talk back. Not literally anyway."

"You're selling yourself short." She gave his arm a little squeeze before her hand dropped away. He wanted to snatch it back. Because he was basically a very polite guy, he didn't. He just continued to keep his eyes on the road and drive.

Quietly she gave him directions to her house, and after a short but comfortable silence, he pulled into her driveway. It was a nice place, though a little bigger than he would have expected for a single woman. Did she live here alone? He'd assumed she was single and had never actually asked Liz. He swept his gaze over the front of the house and noticed it was completely dark inside. That gave him hope. Perhaps no one else lived here.

"You hungry?"

Her question took him off guard, as he was still studying the exterior of house searching for signs of what? The presence of a man perhaps? "What?"

"Hungry? Like in dinner?"

Until she said it, he didn't realize he was, in fact, starving. "Very," he admitted honestly. His hope that she was single was beginning to gain traction. Then again, she might just be extending the kind friendly invitation people like her were prone to offer.

She smiled and patted him on the arm. "Come on. I've got a couple of steaks in the fridge, and I don't know about you, but this whole thing has made me as hungry as a teenager. I wouldn't have thought I'd want to eat after something like that, but damned if I'm not. I think it's from being around kids all day long. They're always ravenous, and I don't care what's going on."

She had a point. They'd just experienced a situation most people never would in a lifetime. He should be sick to his stomach, not looking for something to put in it. Under normal circumstances their ordeal would have been, well…an ordeal. The only reason, or more accurately, reasons it wasn't had to do with Meg, Willow, Liz, and the team of Circe and Zelda. Meg was also right. Making sense of Liz's visions through her drawings did leave him feeling somewhat rewarded. Coming up with an idea that had given her the tools to solve a mystery and bring a woman home to her family made him feel great. Sure enough, he was definitely hungry, and it had nothing to do with being around kids all day.

Willow's idea to bring in Circe and Zelda was spot-on. Not just because it was successful, but also because of Circe's calming influence. Zelda, though she was wound tight, as most successful search dogs were, was calming because she simply went about her job as if it were totally natural. He supposed to Zelda it was. All of it combined to create an environment that felt more right than wrong.

Oh, murder was wrong, without a question. Bringing some peace to his friend was right. Bringing home a missing woman to her family was also right. Hopefully helping the police identify the killer by virtue of the discovery, yeah, that was way right.

After opening the front door and flipping on an interior light, Meg motioned him in. She led him to the kitchen situated in the rear of the house. It was a good-sized room with signs of recent updating. He liked it. Kind of made him want to cook. Of course, he always liked to cook. A guy didn't get to his level of healthiness by not eating. Except for him, it wasn't fast food, frozen pizzas, or TV dinners. No, he watched the cooking channel like a man with a definite obsession and then tried different recipes himself. He wasn't too bad, either. Looking around, he wondered if he might have found a like soul in Meg.

"Why don't you pick a bottle of wine from the rack while I go change my clothes. It'll only take me sec, and then we can get down to grilling those steaks."

"Any preference on the wine?" He spied the not-too-small rack right next to the moderate-sized glass-fronted wine fridge. Better and better. The messages coming his way said he was in the company of a fellow foodie. He was attracted to this woman for a very good reason beyond the obvious fact that she was gorgeous.

"No preference, except keep it red."

His thoughts exactly. A little over an hour, a little less than a bottle of Milbrandt merlot, and two steaks later, he felt, as the saying went, like a new man. He wasn't thinking about Liz or Circe and Zelda. He wasn't thinking of anything except how pleasant it was to sit here with Meg and enjoy a simple yet lovely dinner. Who would have thought tragedy could morph into a pleasant evening with wine, good food, and excellent company.

"Thank you," he said.

He liked the way her smile made her eyes crinkle at the corners. "You're most welcome. I thought that after today, it would do us good to relax for a little while."

"You weren't wrong."

Clouds passed over her face, and she frowned. "I'm worried about Lizzy."

Now his thoughts did go back to his friend, their friend. "Me too."

"What you did today helped so much."

"But we're not out of the woods yet."

She shook her head. "I don't think so either."

"I have a terrible premonition it's just the beginning. Like we opened some kind of door, and a massive wind is about to blow through." With those words, those terribly honest words, all his peace and contentment of the last hour faded away, replaced by something dark and troubling.

The Jaguar was whistling while driving toward home. It had been a good day. No, scratch that, it had been a great day. She loved to accomplish everything according to plan and with great purpose. Today was outside the norm, and strangely enough, it felt fantastic. The Jaguar had trod a course through pure opportunity and whimsy, which really wasn't her style. Except was it really whimsy?

Driving through the streets where the streetlights cast golden light on the asphalt completely calmed her. She would have to explain the lateness of her arrival in some vague detail. Expectations for family dinners and all that. The work had become such a pleasure, it had taken longer than planned for, which was usually the case. She just couldn't rush the pleasure factor. Creating an excuse was fine, it was always fine, an explanation at the ready regardless of the situation. No one ever questioned the story. Ever. It was an art form the Jaguar had down to a science. Just another outstanding skill she possessed.

It was easier and faster to use the freeway to get home, only it wasn't as pleasant. She much preferred Upriver Drive for its slower pace and prettier view. Well, that and it brought clear visions of what was hidden on the hillside across from Boulder Beach. Anticipation always trilled along her nerves as she neared the beach, and tonight was no different despite the intoxicating adventure just completed. It was all exciting: past, present, and future.

Except that it was different tonight, and that became clear relatively quickly. The flashing lights of police vehicles cut through the air long before the beach came into view. Odds were it would be a swimming accident. Someone drowned. It was the most common occurrence aside from drug deals or fights. Accidents weren't unusual here either, for people routinely discounted the dangerous undercurrents of the river and dove into the treacherous waters like they were as safe as bathwater. Yes, someone had drowned or driven their car into the river when they miscalculated their speed and the angle of the roadway curves. That was definitely it. No one could have come across her treasure buried beneath the trees. She had taken exquisite care to keep her prize safe, just in case.

The police presence was so heavy, the traffic slowed to a crawl, then a stop. Typical in a situation like this. Every gawker for miles came out to see what the police were up to. Usually something like this would send her into a fury. Tonight the Jaguar felt the need to adopt the gawker persona, like the morons ahead of her and behind her on the winding road. It was getting dark enough that it was hard to see clearly, and that was frustrating. The obnoxious flashing lights didn't help. The only upside was that being stopped made it easier to stare without being obvious. Everyone was doing it. She was just another lookie-loo.

The cell on the car seat rang, and while talking on the phone in the car was technically illegal, what the hell? Not a single cop around was looking her way. She expected the name on the display, even though it brought a wave of intense irritation. "I'm on my way home," she snapped.

"You're late."

"Yes, unfortunately, I'm very late. You know how it goes, and I'm trying to get there, only now I'm stuck behind some kind of accident. Hopefully, I'm out of here soon."

"Are you going to make it in time to tuck the kids in?"

"I'm trying." It took effort to keep her voice calm and level. "If I can't make it through this mess for a while, give them a kiss for me."

The sigh was also not unexpected. A purposeful reminder of the long-suffering partner who had to carry the weight of the family once again. "The kids want to see you, and your dinner is in the oven. Just hurry."

The Jaguar flexed and curled her fingers on the steering wheel. "Of course. Love you."

The lie came so easily after all the years of practice, and it was always a quick and easy way to end a conversation. Worked like a charm now too.

"Love you too. Hurry home."

Instead of tossing the phone onto the seat, she threw it on the floor. No more calls tonight. The whining voice on the other end made nerve ends sizzle, and not in a good way. It was infuriating that kind of call could kill a perfectly good buzz. She hated him for it. The brake lights on the car ahead went off, and it inched forward. It was at least a relief to be able to move, even if it was just a few feet, because she could finally get a better view of what was going on around the police presence.

Half a dozen marked cars were parked along the road, and what appeared to be three unmarked cars. They had the *police* look to them, even though nothing on them identified them as law enforcement. Detectives, no doubt. She couldn't care less about the cops. No big threat there. The vehicle that concerned her was the van from the medical examiner's office.

Still, it didn't mean the secret had been discovered. The theory fell apart when a couple of men rolled a gurney toward the van. On it lay a long, black body bag, and they were coming from a direction that held special significance for her and wasn't anywhere near the water. No one had drowned. "Damn it." Watching the techs load the body into the van confirmed her worst fears. It could simply be a coincidence, and the body sliding into the back of that vehicle might not be the same one buried near the big pine tree. That was all fine and dandy if a person believed in coincidence, but really, who honestly believed in something like that? Only a foolish person went down that path. The Jaguar was never foolish.

The annoyance she'd felt at the bottleneck in the road now morphed into something deeper and darker. Fury made a flush course through her body. They had no right to take what was hers.

The road ahead opened up, and the traffic finally began to move. She didn't have the luxury of time to sit here and ponder the hows and whys of the discovery. It was at least fortuitous that she was here to see what was occurring. Actually, when she thought about it, deciding to come home this way was more than fortuitous. It was divine. Another sign the path was meant to be.

As she eased by the last of the police, she began to think about how to handle this situation. She was still disappointed, though her anger was fading and a strong sense of resolve replacing it. The Jaguar was always careful. Now she had to be even more cautious. This particular situation was out of her control. That didn't have to be the case with the others. No way would anyone steal another of the special ones. They did not belong to local law enforcement. They did not belong to the families. They belonged to the Jaguar, and that's exactly how it would stay.

CHAPTER FIFTEEN

Now that Liz had said it out loud, the desperation she'd been feeling since the moment Zelda confirmed her worst fears wrapped her up so tight she almost couldn't breathe. At least she seemed to have found a confidant and understanding soul in Willow. Or to be more accurate, Meg had recognized that Willow was the one person who would be able to truly get inside her head. Actually, the shrinks could get inside her head. But Willow would actually understand what she found there, and that's what she needed right now.

"She might not be." Liz had been worried the body found tonight might not be the only one, and the four simple words Willow had said so quietly chilled her all the way through. It was one thing to think something like that; it was another to have someone else be on that same page. She felt good and terrified at the same time.

"Did this happen to you too?" It would make her feel better to know she wasn't going crazy and wasn't the only one this had happened to.

"Is it too late for a cup of tea?"

The question took her off guard for a moment because she thought Willow was avoiding an answer, maybe to spare Liz's feelings. Then it delighted her. She hadn't moved from the car yet partly because she didn't want to go into the house alone, even though she could see Attila's intense face staring out the big front window as if to say, get your butt in here. Soon, big boy. Soon.

As she looked over at Willow, the tension in her shoulders eased. "Never too late for tea. Come on in, and I'll put the kettle on. No microwaved tea here."

Willow put a hand to her chest and smiled. "A woman after my own heart."

Inside, Attila sniffed Willow once, wagged his tail, and then trotted to the back door. He needed a break outside and was bound to be hungry. He waited patiently for her to open the door. It would be far more convenient to have a dog door put in. Not a chance in hell it was going to happen. Attila was a big boy and still growing. If he could make it through one of those swinging doors, so could a man. No dog door. Not in her world. Ever. She let him out and then filled his bowl with the high-grade kibble he so loved.

She made no apologies about taking care of Attila before putting a water-filled kettle on the stove. Willow didn't comment either, and it said a lot about her character that she didn't have a problem with Liz tending to her dog first. A few more points in the "I like her" column.

From the cupboard she pulled out a tin of good English tea. As she worked, Willow made small talk. How do you like the neighborhood? How did you find such an interesting house? What kennel did you get Attila from? If she intended for her light chatter to put her at ease, it worked. By the time she set the two mugs on the table, she felt as relaxed as she had since before she started drawing those pictures.

"No," Willow said as she stared down at the mug she was holding between her hands.

"No?" What, she didn't like the tea? Liz thought it was pretty good stuff. Her friend Joanie sent it to her from England. The deep aroma filled the kitchen, and the scent alone was soothing, at least to her.

"No. I didn't have visions like yours."

Okay. Not about the tea. Her heart sank. So it was just her.

"But you had something." There had to be more. The shadows that flowed through Willow's eyes as she talked let Liz know there was a lot more to this story. Or maybe it was just that she wanted to believe so badly that she was seeing things that weren't really there.

Willow looked up and met her gaze, nodding slightly. That little nod almost made her cry. "I did, and like you, it rocked me to the core. You know, you hear that saying all the time, but until something like this happens to a person, nobody can really understand what it means. Life is never the same afterward. You know what I mean?"

She got that. "I do."

Willow was still nodding. "And boy, so do I."

"Please, tell me." She wanted to know her story, and yet just hearing that Willow had experienced much the same made a world of difference. The sense of being completely isolated melted away, and that was a first since she'd opened her eyes in the hospital. Again, it took work to blink back tears.

For a second, Willow closed her eyes. When she opened them again, the shadows were gone. Once more her eyes were beautiful and full of light. "It was quite different for me, both in terms of the shooting and the aftermath. Like you, I was going about my normal routine when it happened. But from there our paths diverge. I was walking to my studio on a Wednesday night, and nothing seemed out of the ordinary. I just remember hearing a vehicle coming fast, and even that wasn't unusual where I lived, so I didn't pay any attention. The next thing I knew, I had paramedics swarming all over me, police everywhere, flashing lights, crime-scene tape, and half my face ripped up by bullets. The pain was incredible, though before long they had me so pumped full of meds, I didn't care anymore. By the time they got me to the hospital I had worried family members surrounding me and staring at me like they'd never seen me before. Talk about disconcerting."

"Been there," she admitted, remembering her family's anxious faces when she finally came to. "Who shot you?" She had a hard time seeing anyone with a grudge against this gentle woman.

She waved a hand in the air. "Oh, just your garden-variety gangbangers. Didn't know any of them."

"Why would they shoot you?"

"Wasn't about me at all. It was a classic case of wrong place, wrong time. You never think it could happen to you, yet it really was that random and that simple. There was absolutely nothing personal about the shooting, at least where I was concerned. They were after a guy who happened to be eating in a neighborhood restaurant. I was walking by it when they opened up. Like I said, wrong place, wrong time."

"Holy crap. That sucks."

"It does, although in retrospect, I was lucky. The guy they were after wasn't. I lived. He didn't."

"Did they catch them?" In her case, the shooter was long gone, thank the good lord. Death wasn't something she wished on anyone, except in Washington's case, she still couldn't summon a shred of sympathy. In fact, she couldn't imagine the thought of him still being out there and wondered if Willow felt the same way about her shooters.

She shook her head, and as she did, chills went through Liz. So did embarrassment. Liz had opted to make herself a prisoner of her fears and to surround herself with as much of a fortress as she could construct, complete with massive guard dog. She didn't venture out into the world much these days, and God knows her sleep had been nothing but troubled since she came out of her coma. All of this obsessive self-protective behavior, even though the one who had hurt her was dead. Didn't say too much about the quality of her character.

On the flip side, here was Willow living a full, rich life, all the while knowing that the one, or possibly even more than one, responsible for the scars she'd never be able to escape was still out there somewhere, gun in hand. How did someone get past that? And if Willow could do it with such grace and an ability to hold onto joy, why couldn't she?

Willow stared down at her cup of tea. For a moment, she said nothing. "Strange things started to happen when I opened my eyes."

Excitement filled her. This is what she'd been waiting to hear. "You saw visions too?"

Willow looked up and furrowed her brows. "No. Not quite like yours anyway. Flashes of fire came to me, and it kept happening, over and over. I felt like there was something familiar in the flashes that I couldn't quite catch. I finally decided I just had to concentrate hard, and I would be able to figure out what it was."

"Did it work?" It sounded a little like how she'd felt as she'd been drawing, bringing it into focus.

She nodded. "Surprisingly, yes. You have to understand, I was still in the hospital and pretty loopy. My family was collectively convinced I was under the influence of the drugs they were giving me and nothing of a precognitive nature was happening. Actually, there might have been a grain of truth in that, at least as far as the powerful drugs were concerned, but it was more, and I was convinced of it. I struggled to get past the ambiguity of the fire flashes so I could see what I was certain the universe was attempting to show me."

"And you did." She could tell by listening to Willow that whatever it was, she had found her answers. It made her heart soar. She wasn't crazy.

"Yes, I did. In the middle of the night it was like someone parted the veil, and I could see clearly. The flames were from a fire at my brother's house. That's the part that had been eluding me, and once I channeled my energy into seeing the whole picture, it came to me. Even though I was still a mess and in the hospital, I managed to get to the phone to call him. But he didn't answer. I called my folks in a panic. At first they thought I was haywire from too much pain medication. It was hard to get through to them, but when I refused to let it go, my dad agreed at last to run over to my brother's house. I'm pretty sure they thought it was a simple way to appease me so I would relax. It actually was too, because I didn't intend to give up until somebody drove over to his house."

"It was on fire?" Again that trill of excitement. Not because her brother's house had been on fire. No. It was because they were two of a kind. She wasn't the only one this had happened to.

"It was, although it hadn't kicked through the entire house far enough to trigger an emergency response. My brother, however, was in his room, and the smoke had already knocked him out cold. He was still alive, barely, and Dad got him out. Another twenty minutes and he wouldn't have made it." The shudder that went through Willow's body was easy to see.

"That's incredible." The story gave her the chills.

"After that, I've never had anything else like it. Maybe tiny twinges of feelings that pushed me in one direction or another, but nothing that big or clear again."

How she wished she shared that feeling. "Not for me. It's like there's a whisper in my head telling me we're not done yet. I don't like it. I want so badly to feel the same way you do...empty."

"Empty..." Willow shook her head. "Not completely empty. It's always there just far away at the moment and thus allowing me peace. I wish you the same peace, but perhaps you're simply not done yet."

Liz held the mug between her hands and let its warmth flow up her arms. It helped. A little. "That's what I'm beginning to believe."

"I've thought a lot about what happened to me and decided the universe wasn't ready for my brother to leave the world quite yet. He's a scientist, you see, and doing some world-class research. I truly believe he's going to change the world in a big way, so in my heart, I'm convinced I was supposed to save him."

"That makes karmic sense to me. You saved a life." Liz looked down at her hands still clutched around the mug and let the scent of her fragrant tea fill her. Usually it made her feel better. Not right now. "I didn't save that woman," she said softly.

Willow's voice was strong, firm. "No, you didn't save her life. You couldn't. It was long out of your control, and you can't beat yourself up for that. Liz, you have to remember the incredible thing you did, which is to bring her home, and it's possible you even might keep someone else from losing their life."

All good words, and they should bring her a measure of comfort. "So why do I still feel so weird?"

"Maybe it's like you said earlier, there are more. Just like it was my job to keep my brother alive, your job might be to bring the missing home."

The look on Liz's face was heartbreaking. Mostly because Willow understood what it felt like to step beyond the here and now to glimpse something no one else could. Because of that, those who could relate were few in number. How well she remembered that time in her life and how desperately she wanted it all to be a fluke.

Who in their right mind would want to see a sibling's life in peril? Willow's first instinct had been to blame it all on the trauma and the resulting hard-core medications. But all her rationalizations didn't amount to much because it hadn't been any of those things. The flashes of fire she'd seen had saved her brother's life, and it still shook her like nothing else had ever done, even the shooting. In the intervening years, she'd made peace with the experience and even embraced it because it had spared her brother. That was worth it all.

Sitting here with Liz, it was all coming back to Willow. That same second sense she'd experienced with her brother now washed over her again. She had been truthful when she'd said it had never completely disappeared. The twinges were always there, and now they seemed to be telling her, telling them both, that Liz wasn't done. Maybe she shouldn't have said anything to her, but then again, wouldn't it have been wrong not to? Nearly losing her life had changed Willow in one fundamental way. She no longer cared if she was politically correct or spoke out of turn. Staring death in the face had a way of doing that to a person. The little things didn't matter anymore. Not the intended, or unintended, slights. Not hurt feelings. Not putting anything off until another day. These days, if she felt it was important, she said exactly what was on her mind. No punches pulled. It wasn't that she was trying to be cruel or insensitive. She simply didn't have time to waste.

Liz put her elbows on the table and absently ran her fingers through her hair. Willow liked the way it fell in shiny waves through her fingers. She could sit here and watch her do that for hours. Years. "I want to say you're wrong," Liz muttered.

She looked away from the mesmerizing movement of Liz's hands and studied her down-turned face. "You can't, though, can you?" If she denied it, Willow would know she was lying, even if she wasn't looking her in the eye. She'd hear it in her voice.

Liz brought her head up and locked her gaze on Willow's. Tears pooled in her eyes, making the truth in them waver like ocean waves. "No, because I don't believe you've got this wrong at all. The second you said it, I could feel the truth of it right here." She tapped her finger against her chest. "Damn it, but I could."

Willow put her palms against her own chest. "I feel it too."

The tears were now flowing down Liz's cheeks, and it was all Willow could do to hold back her own. Empathy was another by-product of her experience. It wasn't that she had been unfeeling before. On the contrary, she'd always felt things deeply. But in the past she'd been the strong one, who would never considering crying in public. Now, she no longer even tried to hide her emotions. The work it required to appear in control was too much and unnecessary.

"So what do I do? I mean, she came to me before. I didn't do anything. It just happened. If I'm supposed to be some big savior, how exactly do I make that happen?"

It was a good question, and as much as she wished she had some great answer, she didn't. Like Liz, when she'd seen the fire, it had simply come to her. No mediation or pleas to the universe, just flames before her eyes. She suspected it was much the same with the young woman Zelda had located for them tonight. That woman's face had simply come to Liz, and she had done what she could with what she had.

If they were right, and she was pretty sure they were, given the feelings that assailed them both, more women out there needed to be brought home. A killer needed to be found. The big unknown was how to call up the voodoo at will. Her experience was one and done.

She sat back in her chair and stared across the table at Liz, who looked at her with hope in her eyes. "I don't know, and God, I wish I did. It was different for me."

"You weren't chasing a killer."

She shook her head. That wasn't what she meant. "Not exactly. Fire is a killer, just not the same kind that left Reggie out there under the ground. Whoever did that was very much a human."

Liz got up from the table and went to the back door, where Attila was waiting patiently for her to open it. After he'd eaten his dinner, he'd promptly requested to be let out again. Until now, he'd been very quiet. He trotted in and wagged his tail, seemingly quite content with Willow's presence in the kitchen with Liz, then went past them both to the living room.

She smiled as she watched him and then turned to look at Liz. "It appears our fearless friend there has decided it's time to call it a night. I should probably do the same." It was getting late, and Liz looked about ready to drop where she stood. She understood that kind of bone-deep weariness. The only solution for it was sleep. Lots and lots of sleep.

Liz was shaking her head, a frown on her face. "Don't go."

Willow studied her closely, wondering what she meant. Her shoulders were rigid, her face tight. Was it fear of being alone? Totally justified, given the events of tonight. Or was it something else a bit more personal? Either way, her decision was easy. "I'll stay as long as you need me to."

The moment the words were out of her mouth, the tension in Liz's body visibly faded. "Thanks. I've been such a basket case since I got out of the hospital. I know it's the PTSD. Knowing it doesn't change much. Tonight I'm less worried about any of that and more concerned about these women. It's making me a little crazier than usual trying to figure out how to get it out of here..." She tapped her head. "I just don't want to be by myself tonight while I'm trying to figure this out, if that makes sense."

Willow thought she understood, and it was neither of the scenarios her mind conjured up first. Not fear of being alone or a possible attraction to a scarred-up yoga teacher. She remembered wondering the same thing when she'd realized that her vision really meant something. She'd wondered if she could do more. That's what was whizzing through Liz's mind now. It wasn't much different for her either. She wanted to see where this went, and she wanted to be at Liz's side when it all happened.

That wasn't the whole reason she was excited. Since the moment she laid eyes on Liz, she'd sensed a very real connection. It had been a very long time since she'd met anyone who made her pulse race. To have it be someone who, like Willow, was damaged in some way felt like karma at work. In fact, she liked it a great deal. It made her feel less alone. That single thought stopped her. Until this second, she hadn't even realized she was alone.

It made perfect sense. She had her studio and taught lots of people, both men and women, every day. She talked, she laughed, she guided them to a better life, and then when she was done for the day, she went home alone. She didn't even have a cat waiting for her. Go to bed, get up the next morning, repeat. Lordy, lordy. She truly needed to get out more. It was a sad commentary that she hadn't even noticed until this instant.

"Come on," Liz said. "Let's sit somewhere more comfortable. Would you like a drink?"

Willow smiled. She didn't need to drink. In fact, she hadn't had one since the shooting. No particular reason. It just didn't work for her anymore. Maybe it had something to do with the proverbial life flashing before her eyes. She wanted to experience everything and feel everything. She didn't want a single thing to dull even a second of whatever life she had left, because the one lesson she'd learned from the whole ordeal was that everything could change in a second. She didn't intend to waste one, even a dull one, or lose one.

"No, thanks. I'm good."

"You're sure?" Liz's expression said she thought Willow was simply being polite. She wasn't.

"I'm absolutely sure, but thanks for asking." Once she knew her better, Liz would understand that Willow was honest. Or, as friends often accused, brutally honest.

Whatever she saw in Willow's face seemed to satisfy Liz, and they headed to the front of the house. There they settled in the living room, Liz in a chair with her feet up on an ottoman, and Willow on the sofa, her legs pulled up in a lotus position. It wasn't her house and she barely knew Liz, yet here in this oddly familiar room with just the two of them, the faint scent of cinnamon on the air, and a dog snoring softly on his bed, she felt comfortable. It wasn't like her, especially in someone else's place.

She was the one to break the comfortable silence. "So, let's think about this."

Liz looked at her quizzically. "About what?"

She wondered if Liz felt the same level of comfort. "About how to trigger more visions."

Chapter Sixteen

Eldon had a few minutes of feeling sick to his stomach. When Meg had mentioned she didn't think it was over for Liz yet, dread had washed over him like sports drink dumped over the head of a winning football coach. Cold, sticky, and decidedly uncomfortable. Everything changed when he decided the polite thing to do was leave. He didn't want to. He could have stayed there all night. But he wasn't that guy. His grandmother, bless her soul, had drilled good manners into him.

Sadness had been with him every step he took closer to his car, but Meg walked him to it. Yeah. Walked. Him. To. It. Awesome.

It got even better. When he was ready to get in behind the wheel, she pushed up on her toes and kissed him on the cheek. God, he could still feel the touch of her lips against the five-o'clock shadow that made his skin rough and scratchy. Somehow he didn't think it bothered her because not only did she kiss him, but she laid her palm against his cheek before she said good night.

As he drove toward his own home, he rolled over and over in his mind those last few minutes as he tried to figure out what they meant. He didn't want to read more into what had happened than was really there. At the same time, he sure as hell didn't want to discount what might be implied. If she had even a flicker of something for him then…

No. He refused to get his hopes up. He had too many other things in the hopper to let himself get derailed by desires that more than likely would never come to fruition. He liked her. She seemed to like him. He could easily fall in love with her. She might only see him as a friend.

So he needed to focus on what was really important at the moment, which was Liz and what was happening to her. It was pretty goddamn freaky, for sure. When he'd brought her the artist pad and charcoal pencils he really thought they would be nothing more than a way to release tension. God knows she was wound so tight he was surprised she didn't implode. Then again, who was he to point fingers? She was entitled. Who the hell wouldn't be after what had happened to her?

On the other side of that, though, she was his friend, one of his best friends, and he wanted to help her get her life back. She was never going to be the same happy-go-lucky woman she'd been before that asshole nearly killed her, and that was okay. He'd take her any way she came because she was one of those special people, and if he could do something to ease her back into a comfortable life, that's what he planned to do. He knew both Meg and Willow were on that same sheet of music.

Of course, none of them had any clue that his brainstorm for helping her would uncover the horror Zelda had confirmed. It was a horror but also a blessing, and that's what they all had to focus on. If Liz hadn't seen what she had, if they hadn't asked Circe and Zelda to come along on their exploratory hike, that poor young woman would still be out there in the woods buried beneath rich, dark earth and dried pine needles. They had been looking for her a long time, and he had no doubt her family suffered because of her unknown fate. No family should have to go through that, and the absolute beauty of what had happened tonight was that one lost woman was brought home.

They all needed to focus on the bright light in an otherwise dark night.

That thought comforted him, and he was feeling pretty good when he pulled into the attached garage at his house on 21st Avenue. He liked it here in the odd little neighborhood between the freeway and the Pullman Highway. It was close to everything yet tucked away from the hustle and bustle of most neighborhoods of the city. He wondered vaguely if Meg would like the area.

He'd just opened his back door and stepped into the kitchen when his cell phone rang. It was late, and he couldn't imagine who would be calling him now. The name on the display made him groan. Jason.

He didn't dislike his brother-in-law. But these days Jason always seemed to want him to handle Eloise. It wasn't his job anymore. It had never really been his job, but since she'd paid no attention whatsoever to their parents growing up, the job of reasoning with his older sister always fell to him. Once Jason and Eloise had married, he'd hoped Jason would relieve him of his babysitting duties, and for a few years, he had. Then when she became too much of a handful for him, the calls started. Good old Eldon, who had a way with his out-of-control big sister.

"What's up, Jason?" He tried, as always, not to let the exasperation sound in his voice. He thought he was pretty successful, at least most of the time.

"Have you heard from Ellie?" Nobody except Jason ever called his sister Ellie. His parents didn't believe in nicknames. Hell, he was surprised they didn't call them by their full names: Eloise Elizabeth and Eldon Elias. Yeah, they had a thing with names that began with an "E," as in Eric, his father, and Erzabeth, his mother. If he ever had kids they would not have a name that began with an "E."

"No. I haven't talked to Eloise since last week. Why?" A week without having to control his sister was a very good week indeed.

"She hasn't come home." A note of fear crept into Jason's words, and Eldon didn't know why.

His sister, his beautiful, genius sister, was a lush. She might have an IQ that blew right off the charts, but she also had a substance-abuse problem that was, likewise, off the charts. Her first stint in rehab was at age seventeen. Her second at twenty-five. He was pretty sure Jason hadn't been aware of either of those hush-hush visits when he walked down the aisle with her when she was twenty-nine. If his family was good at one thing, it was covering up. He'd become a master by the time he was five.

"She's probably still at the golf course. Did you call Downriver?" It was her favorite course, even if it was a public facility. She could play at any one in the city, private or public, but she was more often than not found on the links at the popular north-side golf course with its steep hills and river view. For some reason the place called to her, and she returned over and over again.

"No, she's not. I've already called. They haven't seen her for hours."

"She played there today?" She could get pretty plastered by the time she finished eighteen holes.

"Nine holes."

"Only nine?" Less time to put away the booze unless she started drinking early and golfing late.

"Afternoon round, so only nine."

A touch of worry flickered in his stomach. Even with her penchant for booze-filled rounds of golf, Eloise always came home. She was a hard-core alcoholic, no doubt about that on any front. She was also a homebody. She liked having drinks with friends, lots and lots of friends. She also loved hanging out at her expensive home on the Indian Trail bluff and polishing off a bottle of expensive merlot while sitting on the deck overlooking the custom pool. Thank the good Lord she never decided to swim when the bottle was empty. More often than not, she fell asleep in one of the plush loungers, and Jason carried her to bed.

"Did you call Sundance or maybe the Spokane Country Club?" She would sometimes play Sundance if she couldn't get a tee time at Downriver, and on occasion even play at the old country club course, which a local tribe owned and had infused with new life.

"Not there. Eldon, I called them all. I've got to say, I'm scared. This isn't like Ellie, even if she got herself dead drunk."

The one thing he admired about Jason, even if he did rely on Eldon too often to control his wife, was that he really did see her for what she was. He loved the beautiful genius with the kind heart and the scratch handicap. He appreciated the woman she was, when she wasn't drinking, and loved her, drunk or sober. He still wished he didn't call Eldon quite so often.

"Okay. Let's contact her friends." He was running through his mind which of her friends to call first. They both kept in touch with a number of buddies from their formative years.

"Eldon, she doesn't see any of them these days."

His whirling thoughts stopped dead. That didn't sound like Eloise. "Oh, come on. She has friends."

"She *had* friends." The note in Jason's voice was firm.

"What about June?"

"What about her?"

"She called me earlier and told me she'd seen Eloise. If I recall correctly, she also liked to have a drink now and again."

"She's not home. I already tried her, and besides, she won't know anything. They haven't had drinks in a long time."

Jesus, how out of touch with Eloise was he? Truth? Maybe more than he wanted to admit. "What about Kristy?" She was Eloise's oldest friend. Surely there wasn't a rift between those two. They'd been through too much together over the years, the kind of trials and tribulations that forged friendship bonds in steel.

"Kristy hasn't spoken to Ellie in over two years. None of her old friends have. Not Kristy. Not June. Not anybody."

He sank into a kitchen chair and rested his head in one hand. His heart hurt to think that her friends had finally had no choice but to turn away. It had to be bad before Kristy would abandon Eloise because she was the kind of person who didn't give up. "I didn't know."

Jason sighed and then admitted, "I didn't want to tell you or any of the family. I thought I could get her some help. I really believed I could handle her and it would all get better. She's a good person deep down. You understand that, right?"

"She fought you." He wasn't asking a question because he was well aware of what she could be like when she got stubborn.

"Ellie is still Ellie. I've talked to her until there wasn't a single word left to say and got nowhere. She just wanted to have a good time and didn't think she had a problem. She's never thought she had a problem."

"She's smarter than that." He didn't believe for a second she was that naive. Eloise chose substance abuse. She embraced it and understood exactly what she was doing to her mind and her body.

"Of course she is. She didn't want to change, and nothing I said or did made a difference. Even her friends ditching her didn't change a thing. She had her golfing buddies and her thermos. I even threatened to leave. You know what she did?"

"No." He didn't want to hear.

"She laughed."

His heart sank, and his memories rolled back to those long ago nights when he'd hear his mother doing the same thing to his father. The apple wasn't falling far from the tree. "Why didn't you call me before tonight?"

"What were you going to do, Eldon? You've spent years bailing her out of one thing or another, and I imposed on you enough times when I couldn't handle her. I decided it was time for me and Ellie to get a grip on this ourselves. I wanted to find her the kind of help that would get her back to being the person I fell in love with."

"And now she's gone." He wondered if he could make it to the bathroom before he threw up.

"Now she's gone."

By the time the garage door shut and the overhead light turned off, calm had returned to the Jaguar. Oh, it took a supreme effort, given the loss of that very special secret. However, though that one was lost, another had taken her place. Yes, it would have been nice to have kept them all. Sometimes things didn't go as expected, even when the planning had been the very best. It was all going to work out fine. It always did.

It was late. Much later than she anticipated. At least the screaming brats would be in bed and fast asleep. A thousand questions and nonstop jabbering were the last things the Jaguar wanted right now. Silence would most definitely be golden.

Even though the kids were in bed, the chance of enjoying solitude and peace was still about zero. One step outside the detached garage and a full view of the kitchen window was possible. In that window, a frowning face was backlit by the expensive fixture installed less than a month ago. The fixture was still her favorite. The face staring out the window was not. If only it was as easy to eliminate that one as it had been all the others. As tempting as it was, it was too great a risk, even for one as skilled as the Jaguar. Family was always the number-one suspect in a disappearance, thus living with the irritation was a cross she would have to continue to bear.

No sense in putting off the inevitable. It wouldn't be any less painful in an hour, though it really was tempting to turn around, get back into the car, and drive away into the night. Where didn't matter because anywhere was better than here. The Jaguar didn't turn around and instead put one foot in front of the other. The house it was, and the trek across the custom stone path was like walking the proverbial green mile. One day it would change. It just wouldn't be this day.

"About time you graced us with your presence." The sarcasm was so thick it almost dripped.

Oh, how she could have been predicted that greeting…word for word. It made the hairs stand up on the back of her neck and her fingers clench into a ball. It took incredible willpower not to fly across the expensive hardwood floor and put said fingers around that pale neck. How sweet that would feel.

"I got delayed." She took off her jacket and hung it on the hooks by the back door.

"You always get delayed." Now the voice was more of a whine.

She kept her voice level as the mantra repeated itself in silence. Not today. Not today. "Nature of the beast," she said evenly. No need to articulate exactly what beast. It was a secret best kept close to the vest, so to speak.

"I called the airport." So now it was moving into defiance. Like checking up on her was something new. Been there. Done that. What was that line from the popular song: same old song and dance?

A shoulder shrug was meant to convey her indifference. That attitude usually evoked strong emotions from him, and it did so now. The game was the only solace she could garner from this impossible situation. She was stuck with him, but that didn't mean she couldn't have a little fun.

"Your flight came in hours ago."

"I had meetings."

"No, you didn't."

Well, this was new. The typical third-degree revolved solely around the checking of flight arrivals. She never would have guessed he had it in him to do some actual sleuthing. "And you would come by this information how?"

"I checked with your flight crew."

Well, well, well. Things they were a-changing. Part of her was impressed that he actually showed some balls for a change. Only a small part of her. A stronger emotion took the lead and irritation started to flow up her arms like molten lava. "You what?"

"I'm sick and tired of your lies. You weren't in any damned meetings, so where were you?" He turned from the kitchen window, his fists resting on his hips. Something straight out of a dramatic film.

Calm. Calm. Calm. It would not do to let the anger out. It was too dark and deep to be allowed to burst forth. She had to maintain this situation, regardless of its repugnance. The cover provided her safety. Until she could find a method to eliminate the happy little family that didn't jeopardize her or her fine work, she would have to maintain it. But how she wanted to simply put a knife in his heart and be done with it.

Slowly she put the heavy leather case and cell phone on the kitchen island. The small movement provided a few seconds to get herself under control. "I don't know who you were talking to, but they were wrong. I did have several meetings. One with the local airline scheduler and one with a union rep. The union guy talked way longer than I would have liked, but he has an outreach program he wanted to run by me. I don't have an open schedule, so we have to make these things happen when we can."

"Are you serious? Outreach? Since when does the union do things like that?"

"Since they started trying to see if we could all get along. Things change, even in my industry."

"Bull."

Bluff time. The Jaguar slapped the black cell phone on the counter. "Call him. He'll tell you the same thing." The cell phone lay between them. "Last number on my history. See what he says."

It was a calculated risk that paid off despite a few seconds there when it looked like the bluff was going to be called. "Fine. I believe you, but why don't you use that damn thing to let me know what's going on? I'm imagining all sorts of things, none of them good. I was about to start checking with the police and the hospital emergency rooms."

She purposely softened her tone, though his mention of the police almost made her finally lose control. "If I'd been in an accident, you know as well as I do that the police would have let you know. Look, you just need to trust me. Have I ever lied to you before?"

The pause was a little too long. The little shit was having to think about it. "I don't know."

"Sure you do." The sweetness in those three words was nauseating. God, she was awesome.

"I suppose not." This time it was a little quicker. Good. There had to be some payoff for having to play the part of loving spouse.

"I have never lied to you before, and I'm not now. I had meetings that ran way too long and way too late. Yes, I should have called you, and I'm sorry. I'll try to do better next time." She started to unbutton her blouse.

The lies rolled off the tongue so damned easily. The Jaguar smiled.

Chapter Seventeen

For the first time since the unfortunate incident, as she preferred to think of it, Liz fell asleep like a regular person. Of course, for the first time since she'd been shot, she had someone else in the house. Actually, that wasn't quite true. Her mother had spent the first two weeks with her after she'd been released. That couple of weeks had felt like a year. It had taken a whole lot of talking and reassurances to get her mother to finally go home. She worked hard to make sure everyone else left her alone after that. Too claustrophobic with people in her personal space.

Except for tonight. Willow had fallen asleep on the sofa as they'd relaxed and talked softly. Nothing about her being here created any claustrophobia. For a minute or two Liz sat in her chair and simply watched her sleep. She was beautiful, with fine skin and gorgeous hair. Her legs were long and her fingers delicate. She'd love to see her practicing yoga. No doubt she was a master. That would have to wait for another day. Finally, she got up and covered Willow with a soft burgundy throw, resisting the urge to run her fingers through her hair, and then she and Attila went to bed.

As they walked to the bedroom, it struck her as odd how calm Attila was around Willow. One thing was abundantly clear—he liked her. A lot. Until Willow came into the house, he was a hundred percent her dog, and she never questioned where his loyalties lay. She should be jealous about the way he seemed to adore Willow. Should be and wasn't. In many ways she understood how he felt.

Something about her drew both of them to her like the link between two magnets. Though she wanted to believe they had something special between them, she was fairly confident most people felt that way about Willow. It sure didn't surprise her that Willow's yoga studio was an enduring success. When whatever it was that was happening to her had run its course, she would definitely give a yoga class a go. Might do her some good. Probably would do her some good. She was thinking about yoga as she drifted into sleep.

Suddenly she bolted awake. At first she was disoriented. She glanced over at the clock: three thirty. Considering she'd hit the hay, so to speak, at ten thirty, it was amazing. She hadn't slept in that long a stretch since giving up the hard-core meds the hospital had sent home with her. She'd dumped those in the trash about ten minutes after her mom had vacated the premises. Not sleeping was better than being so drugged up it was hard to function. That out-of-control feeling was not for her.

She should turn over and try to go back to sleep. That's not what she did. She got up because she had to. It wasn't that a vision of a dead woman interrupted her slumber and now had her distressed. No, it was something far more concerning, more like electricity running through her body and shooting out her fingers. She was so wired she didn't have a chance of going to sleep again tonight or possibly even tomorrow night.

The thing was, she was pretty sure she grasped what the buzzing meant. She was also pretty sure she knew how to deal with it.

Quietly, she slid out of bed and pulled on sweats and an old T-shirt. Her hair had to be a tangled mess, and that was about the last thing she cared about right now. She was fixated on only one detail. Attila got up as she did and headed to the back door. She let him out, trying to be as quiet as possible. She really didn't want to disturb Willow. Retrieving her pad and pencils from the dining-room table, Liz took them to the kitchen.

Before she sat down, she made a cup of coffee and carried it to the table. It was hot and bitter on her tongue, but she didn't mind. It smelled great. She'd always loved the smell of freshly brewed, good coffee. Blowing out a breath, she flipped open the drawing pad, picked up a pencil, and started to draw. She focused on the paper and the feel of the pencil between her fingers. Work soothed her, and instead of being tired, she was wide awake.

Liz wasn't sure how long Willow had been standing in the doorway watching in silence before she noticed her. Other than her first initial sip, her coffee was untouched and long cold. Beside her, six pages, torn from the pad, were strewn across the tabletop. She stopped drawing and looked over at Willow. Her hand, now that she'd stopped, felt old and crippled. Would she ever be able to straighten her fingers again? The skin was dented where she'd gripped the pencil. Black smudges marred the outer edge of her hand.

"Hey." She stretched her cramping fingers and grimaced at the pain that shot up her arm.

"I'm really sorry I woke you. I was trying to be quiet."

Willow shook her head. "You didn't wake me up."

"I thought if I worked in here, the light wouldn't bother you, and I'd be quiet."

"No problem." Willow walked to the back door, where Attila was softly scratching to be let in. Once she opened the door, he trotted through and went to stand at his empty bowl. She laughed. "I think someone wants breakfast."

It was way too early for him to be eating, and Liz was going to say as much until she looked at the clock on the oven. It was almost seven. Where in the hell had the last three-plus hours gone? This was insane; she felt like she'd just gotten out of bed. She started to jump up from the table, but Willow put a gentle hand on her shoulder.

"Just tell me where the food is, and I'll take care of Attila."

"You don't have to feed him."

"I know I don't. I want to. Food?"

"The pantry." She pointed to the double doors that opened onto a walk-in pantry.

"Got it. Keep drawing. I didn't mean to interrupt you."

Attila's tail was wagging as Willow grabbed his bowl, filled it, and put it back down for him. The hours outside didn't appear to have traumatized him much, as he wagged his tail and began to eat.

Liz smiled. "You're going to have a friend for life, you know. One sure way to that big boy's heart is through his bowl!"

Willow smiled. "I hope so. He's a great dog." She rubbed the top of his head, and he leaned into her.

"He is, and he's a wonderful friend. I've needed his unconditional and unquestioning love."

"You have so many friends who love you too."

"I do, and trust me, I feel very fortunate. It's not the same as with Attila."

"You needed more than they could give you. Trust me, I get it."

She was sure she did. Willow seemed to understand everything she was feeling. She didn't judge, didn't try to make it better. Her empathy alone was like a salve to an open wound. Meg's instinct to put her and Willow together was more important than she would probably ever know. She'd have to someday try to tell her how much she appreciated what she'd done.

She dropped her gaze to the fruits of her three-hour fugue state. She didn't remember drawing these sketches, even though her hand testified to the reality that she had, indeed, created them. It was chilling and exciting at the same time. "Would you take a look at these and see what you think?" Liz slid the now-seven sheets over to Willow, who sat down across from her. "You want a cup of coffee?" She wasn't a fan of cold coffee and was all for a fresh mug of the stuff. Maybe she'd even drink it this time.

"Sure." She sounded distracted as she spread out the drawings, side by side, and studied them. Liz wasn't sure if she really wanted a cup of coffee or was simply responding without thought. She'd go with the assumption that she did want one.

Liz grabbed her cold cup and dumped the contents into the sink. It took only a couple of minutes to fill two mugs with fresh, hot java. The brewing coffee made the whole kitchen smell great once again. She took the two cups of dark brew to the table and slid one across to Willow. "What do you think?"

A cloud seemed to pass over Willow's face as she looked up and locked gazes. "I think we need to make another call."

"A call?"

She nodded and tapped one of the drawings. "Yes. Circe and Zelda have another search to do."

Willow had come awake, disoriented for a few seconds. Then it all came back to her, and warmth had flowed through her whole body. The way they'd sat together in Liz's comfortable living room and talked had been the most pleasant thing to happen to her in ages. Granted, it had all come about because of something terrible, yet it had been something wonderful.

Her thoughts returned to that day that had changed her life. It wasn't fair that she'd been minding her own business and ended up scarred and wounded. The journey to recovery had been long, painful, and difficult. Once she'd gotten over the typical "why me" whining, she'd found a way to plunge forward with her life. Sure, this existence was different from what she'd planned. What she'd discovered along the way was that it didn't mean it was bad. Right now was a really good example. Had she not been in that place at that particular time, she wouldn't be sitting across from this fascinating woman right now. She firmly believed every single dark cloud had a silver lining. Sometimes it was just hard to see.

The warmth had been with her from her waking moment until she'd walked into the kitchen and saw what Liz had been doing while sitting at the table for hours. Shades of the pictures she'd drawn yesterday lay spread across the table, only this time the drawings reflected a different place and face. That little twinge of apprehension that had been with her after Zelda made the disturbing find now blossomed. Liz's very talented fingers had once more brought into the light images meant to remain secret.

"I recognize this." She pointed to the drawings that were vague and yet distinctive. They showed headstones on a gently sloping, grassy area. Despite having lived in the area a relatively short amount of time, she'd driven by that spot a hundred times. It caught her attention the first time she'd seen it because it seemed so out of place among the rolling fields of wheat and alfalfa. As it was one of her favorite routes to Mt. Spokane, she noticed it each time she made the trip to the mountain to ski or hike.

"It's the old cemetery just south of Mead."

Liz squinted and stared down at her drawings. "I don't know what you're talking about. This isn't ringing a bell with me at all."

"I'll bet you've probably driven by it a dozen times or more and didn't notice it. Most people don't, because for decades it was left to decay. It garnered attention recently because of the north/south freeway project. Thanks to that construction, it's been spruced up and preserved. It's pretty cool piece of history if you ever stop and really look."

"You think this guy buried her there?" Liz pointed to the picture she'd drawn of a young woman with long hair and piercing eyes. She was beautiful yet had a trace of anguish in her eyes. Liz shuddered.

"It's a distinct possibility," she said. Absolutely, not *distinct*, is what she was thinking.

"Kind of a ballsy place to hide a body, if that's what he did."

Willow ran a finger lightly over the woman's face, careful not to smudge the charcoal. "He's got balls, all right, and yes, that's most likely what he did. Actually, if you think about it, it's kind of a brilliant move. A body in a cemetery? Nobody would give it a second thought or even consider looking there. Whoever he is, he's smart. We need to call Circe again."

Liz put a hand on her shoulder, and its warmth went right through her shirt to her skin. It felt great. "Yes. That's exactly what we need to do. This is so messed up. If she is there, I want to bring her home."

Willow looked at her face and noticed the dark circles under her eyes were gone. She might have been up for a while, but she must have managed to grab some rest. That was terrific. There was that silver lining again. "It is most definitely messed up. I still believe in a way it's a pretty good thing. If another dead woman is out there, maybe this will help bring peace to her family."

Liz began to tap the table with her index finger. "This makes me a little twitchy. I mean, yeah, we want to call Circe and Zelda, and I know if she's there, Zelda will tell us."

"I agree, so what's bothering you about giving them a call?"

"There's no way the cops are going to buy another just out-for-a-walk theory, and oops, we stumbled on a second dead body with the cadaver dog we just happened to have with us. Especially not if this place is where you say it is. Not exactly the kind of area people just hike around. They're not going to believe us, and I don't blame them. They'll want answers if we're right about this."

Liz did have a point. That would be stretching believability a bit too much. The cops didn't question Zelda's abilities, and that played to their advantage. But two casual hikes, in two days, uncovering two bodies? Definitely a stretch even for the most gullible, and she had yet to meet a cop that fit that description. She did know someone who could make it work. "We're going to have to bring Circe's wife, Diana, into the mix. She's a cop, and I know she'll help."

"She'll think I'm crazy."

Willow laughed, which amazingly took the tension down a touch. She could see Liz's shoulders relax. "Trust me, neither Diana nor her partner, if she decides to bring him in, will think you're crazy. Those two have seen a lot, and they have very open minds."

"You're sure we can trust this Diana? I'm not up to having someone put me under a microscope."

Willow put a hand on her arm. "I wouldn't lie to you, and if I say Diana is trustworthy, you can take that to the bank."

Silence fell between them, and Willow thought at first that Liz would say no way, and she couldn't blame her if she did. If that was the case, they'd simply figure out another way to follow up on what the drawings seemed to be showing them. She was about to say the same when Liz nodded slightly and said, "Let's give this Diana a call."

CHAPTER EIGHTEEN

Eldon tried really hard to get some sleep. It didn't work at all. He tossed and turned, and finally he grabbed his cell phone from the night stand. Once more he punched redial for Eloise. He'd done that at least a dozen times over the course of the night, and the call history attested to that fact. It also showed that not once had she picked up.

Now he stood at the window and watched dawn roll over the city in a fiery display of color. It was quite impressive, and if he wasn't so worried about everything, or so it seemed, he might actually find it inspiring. He looked down at the cell phone and saw that he was going to have to plug it into the charger soon. Only thirty percent of battery left. What if Eloise was trying to call him? He didn't dare push it too far. One more time he tried his sister's number, and one more time it went straight to voicemail. Even dead drunk, she always picked up when she saw he was calling. She never, ever, blew him off. One thing about their relationship had never changed: blood was thicker than water.

He understood her demons, even if he didn't grasp all her reasons for choosing to deal with them through chemical intervention. Growing up had been hard for both of them. Very hard. Coming from an affluent family didn't make life easier either. In fact, sometimes he believed it was much harder. They were a prominent family and everyone knew their name, so they were held to a higher standard. Perfection was the presumed benchmark.

Behind the gorgeous shrubs, the acres of immaculate lawn, and the massive brick home, things were light years away from perfect.

He'd long ago lost count of the number of times he'd found bottles of vodka hidden in the toilet tanks throughout the house. He threw each of them in the trash, right after he emptied their contents into those same toilets. Every time he checked, a new bottle had taken its place. Still, he got rid of them over and over. As soon as he did, his mother replaced them with brand-new bottles.

Eldon and Eloise closely guarded the truth of their mother's extreme alcoholism. It was their family's dirty little secret. They were Spokane royalty, as their family was largely responsible for building the city in its early days. No one wanted that image tarnished. Thus their father ignored what was happening at home and left it to his children, from the time they were quite young until they left home, to deal with a mean drunk for a mother. Eloise became the stand-in mother while he was the enforcer, at least in the beginning. It was a big order for a couple of kids.

It all changed when Eloise finally broke, and that was the only way he ever thought to describe it. The cuts, both physical and mental, were too deep and the damage too great. His sister couldn't take it anymore. Looking back, he figured she was maybe eleven or twelve when she took her first drink. From then on, Eldon had to maintain what order there was in the house. Each year their father grew more distant, their mother grew more erratic, and Eloise became more delicate. How he ever got out of there with anything even close to being well-adjusted was a gift from God. He didn't take it for granted either. He was acutely aware of how lucky he was to have survived.

Now, shades of his past were coming to visit again. After he'd left for college, his mother had hit one, more likely two, vodka bottles a little too hard. In a historic home with lots of steep stairs, that wasn't a good idea. Booze and stairs don't typically mix well, and for his mother they became a deadly combination. Dad found her at the bottom of the staircase, her neck broken, and a later autopsy revealed a blood-alcohol content so high it was amazing she'd even been walking. At the time of the accident, Eloise was holed up in her room with the music blaring and her own bottle of booze tucked in a gym bag. He'd wondered as they'd been standing at the edge of the grave if the absence of their abusive mother from their lives would free Eloise. It hadn't. Her demons were evidently too ingrained to be released.

After the funeral, he'd stayed for a few weeks and, when he'd left, had felt that his sister could very possibly be recovering somewhat. She had created that illusion to lull those around her, like Eldon, into believing she was going to be fine and could be left on her own. Her skills at maintaining a façade of normality were amazing, and for years she pulled it off. He'd believed she was better. Not that she ever became as bad as their mother. At least he hoped not. After she got married he gave himself a lot of distance and had some freedom from his eyes-on duty with his sister, at least for a while. At first it was like a giant weight had been taken off his shoulders.

The lesson he learned was that distance didn't make a lot of difference. He continued to worry. He loved his sister deeply. For so many years all they'd had was each other against a father who had checked out on the family and a mother so messed up she rarely left the house. The only love they ever felt was from each other and perhaps their cook, Eva. Although now he wasn't convinced Eva really loved them as much as he'd thought. She might have simply felt sorry for them. It really didn't matter because what she'd given was what they needed at the time. A feeling of being loved.

Right now, it scared him at a very base level that Eloise was missing, and that's exactly how he thought of it. Usually where she was concerned he knew what to do. That wasn't the case now. He didn't know what to do, and God forbid, he was afraid of what he might have to do. It was the nightmare that had always lived in the back of his mind and that he'd hoped would never come to pass.

As he stood staring out the window and contemplating his next move, the cell phone he was still holding rang. His hopes soared. It had to be her. He glanced down with hope in his heart. It died as quickly as it had come. He put the phone to his ear. "She's still not home." Jason. His heart sank. In the four words, he recognized the fear in his brother-in-law's voice because it echoed what he was feeling.

"We've got to find her." His mind was racing with every possibility he could imagine.

"I've made all the obvious calls. Every single hospital and minor emergency facility in the city. She's not in any one of them." His voice cracked.

"Well, at least we know she wasn't hurt in an accident, and that's good. She's just got to be passed out in her car somewhere. We need to call the police." He hated the thought. It wouldn't be her first run-in with the cops, and she'd managed to finagle her way out of each encounter. Probably not this time. A jail cell was a very real possibility, and it was still infinitely better than an accident where she might have been hurt or worse. He wasn't ready for that, and neither was Jason.

"The police called me."

The ice that rushed through his veins was glacial. "What did they say?" He didn't want to hear the answer. He'd received one other call from the local police, to tell him about his mother. He was a whole lot older and wiser these days, but that didn't mean squat when it came to a loved one.

"The groundskeeper at Downriver Golf Course reported that her car has been sitting in their parking lot since yesterday. It was there when he left last night, and it was there when he arrived first thing this morning."

He was grasping at straws. "Maybe she started walking home and fell asleep along the way." It wouldn't be the first time she'd done something bizarre. She could be very well snoring under a tree somewhere. *Please, God, let her be asleep somewhere.*

"Her purse was in the car."

Oh, man, he was piling on the bad news. He didn't have to explain to Eldon what that meant. Eloise would never, repeat never, leave her purse behind. It wasn't because of money or credit cards. She never cared about those things, probably because she always had them. Her connection to the purse was far more elemental. She kept a flask inside it.

❖

Breakfast was tense. Not the fault of the family. Oh, no, they were chipper and happy and endlessly annoying. No one was aware of the fact that the news was building a fire inside the Jaguar that threatened to erupt. All her hard work, the planning, and the secrets were now out in the open for the whole world to see. The anger from last night surged once more.

The news broadcasts consistently showed the woods across the road from Boulder Beach exploding with police and news crews. A person would think that by this time they would be done out there. What more could they glean today that they hadn't uncovered last night? Apparently quite a bit, if the news reports were to be believed. The perky news anchor reported that it would be hours yet before law enforcement cleared out.

It wasn't fair and it wasn't right. Good work had been accomplished with her, and she should have stayed hidden there forever. It wasn't fair that they could just come in and undo everything. The newscasters were giving credit to a group of folks who'd been out walking with, coincidently, a cadaver dog. A fucking cadaver dog. What were the odds? Too high to be an accidental hike through the woods.

It was too coincidental. No way did that kind of thing happen out of the blue, so how did they know where to look? She'd never left a clue behind, not one single clue, yet somehow these people had gone straight to her.

Without trying to appear too interested, the Jaguar flipped through the various channels, catching each of the reports on the main network outlets. She might discover something if she listened close enough to what was being reported. Channel Six was pay dirt. They were playing a loop of video captured the night before, and she couldn't believe she hadn't noticed when she'd driven through. There in the background was a familiar face, and the newscaster so very helpfully pointed out that he was one of the "hikers." Eldon Spicer. Well, well, well. How about that? He always was a nosy little bitch. The buzzing in the Jaguar's ears was so loud, everyone had to hear it. No one seemed to notice.

For the next half hour, the Jaguar pretended not to care about the morning news. Once everyone was gone for the day, peace reigned once more, and it was easier to think about what to do. How did Eldon know she was hidden in those woods? There was one good way to find out. A little visit perhaps? Or maybe something a little stealthier. It wouldn't be a good idea to reveal much. Not at this point. Too many exciting projects on the horizon and one very important one completed the night before. He was a smart guy so she'd need to handle him with care. She was good at that kind of thing and would find out how much he actually knew one way or the other.

It was bad, though, because this was hitting too close to home, particularly after last night's game. Taking her down had been a long time in the making, and what had happened was totally justified. There was no way she could have known that on the same night Eldon would stumble upon the carefully hidden grave. In some ways, it shouldn't be a total surprise. He always was a pain in the ass, and it was very clear that some things hadn't changed. Not without a little help anyway.

There was one way to see what he was up to, and obviously he was up to something. He was a techy and had no damn business traipsing around in the woods. He should have had his ass in front of a computer like any other self-respecting nerd. The idea of Eldon hiking through the woods with a damn cadaver dog was too ridiculous to consider except that, from everything she saw on the news, that's exactly what he was doing. Then again, one couldn't always believe what was being reported. Spin was always part of any news story.

She glanced up at the wall clock. A little past eight. If Eldon was going to work, he should be there already. The court had to be an eight-to-five gig. But if last night's trauma weighed too heavy, he might have used leave time to take the day off. Why not? He was a fed, and didn't all feds earn about a week a month in leave? That gave her a great idea.

Most of the day was open to practice surveillance, and the Jaguar was able and ready. Actually, it wasn't all that much practice because it was a skill refined over years of waiting and watching. How else could such fine work go under the radar for so long? It was also aided by years of working varying hours. Sometimes day. Sometimes night. It was a perfect profession for someone with such extraordinary abilities in off hours. No circadian rhythms to throw her off and no pattern for some professional, or these days skilled amateur, detective to discover. Yes, she really was that good. She grabbed her keys and headed out to the garage.

Driving to the Spicer casa provided more time to think things through. Really, she didn't have any reason to worry. Just because one lovely had been uncovered didn't mean a thing. Even if Eldon had some kind of special knowledge it didn't signal that the rest of her work might be exposed. All the others were safe and sound, just where she'd left them. And besides, if following Eldon revealed something dangerous, she could handle that too. Men could disappear just as easily as women. Wasn't normally her thing, but hey, as she'd so recently discovered, sometimes it was fun to change things up.

At the house, it wasn't a huge surprise to see his car still parked in the driveway. In fact, it was exactly what she was hoping for. She pulled to the curb about a hundred yards down the block and settled in for a lengthy wait and watch, except that didn't exactly happen. Less than five minutes later, Eldon came out and got into his car. So much for the long haul. Good. No time to get bored. When he backed out of his driveway and headed down the street, so did the Jaguar. It was actually pretty fun to tail him. Kind of like being a spy.

The house he ultimately stopped at was a lovely little place in the Audubon Park neighborhood. Eldon got out of his car and walked with a determined stride directly to the front door. An attractive woman of medium height with brown hair wrapped her arms around him in a bear hug. Well, now, wasn't that interesting? Was she a new girlfriend? Something about her looked familiar, though she couldn't figure out why. Probably one of the faces she saw on the news about last night. Yes, she was sure that was it.

A smile chased away some of the shadows. She might be Eldon's girlfriend or not. Didn't matter one way or the other because his actions clearly demonstrated that he cared for her, which was more than enough to mark her as the new target. What a good way to get Eldon's attention off what had happened last night. There was some power in the old saying, "When it rains, it pours." For Eldon, the pouring rain was about to turn into a hurricane. She glanced down at her cell phone and decided it was a perfect time to make a call.

CHAPTER NINETEEN

Words couldn't express how glad Liz was to see Eldon. Over the phone, she'd heard the strain in his voice, and initially she'd blamed it on the stress of what they'd witnessed last night. Lord knows, they'd all felt it. She didn't have a clue how Circe and Zelda could do what they did again and again. It had taken a toll even on Zelda because dogs experienced the tragedy too.

Now that she saw Eldon, she was certain that while last night had certainly affected him, much more was going on. He had dark circles under his eyes and stubble on his face that, while it made him look kind of sexy, also hinted that his normal routine had been shot to hell. He never started the day looking like this. As many years as they'd known each other and worked together, she'd seen him rattled before, and he didn't react like the man standing in front of her right now. His phone rang just as she put her arms around him. He pulled it out of a pocket, glanced at the display, and grimaced. Then he shoved it back in the same pocket and returned her hug.

She pulled him inside, shut the door behind him, and stopped him just inside the entry with a hand on the arm. "You can take that call if you need to."

He shook his head. "No. It's just June again, and I really don't want to talk to her."

"June?"

"Long story. Suffice it to say she's a pain in the ass that I don't need right now."

"What's wrong? Has something else happened?" She didn't see the sense in wasting time with trivial greetings or by pretending she didn't notice he was off the norm.

"Eloise is missing." His voice sounded tired and sad.

If it had been anyone else, news like that would be a bombshell. In this instance, she knew his sister far too well. In fact, she'd wondered many times how long it would be before Eloise self-destructed. Could very well be it was right now, though her choice of this moment was awful. One look at his face told her this observation was not what Eldon needed today.

Eloise was so different from Eldon. Liz had always been friends with him and not at all with his sister. Oh, she'd tried way back when. Eloise was hard to get chummy with even when they were children, and even more so as they got older. Being one of the few people who was aware of what went on behind the grand doors of the equally grand house, she believed she understood why. Or at least she deluded herself that she got it. Until the gunshot, she hadn't truly comprehended how trauma could take a perfectly fine person and turn them into a neurotic. Oh, my, did she understand now. All she had to do was look in the mirror to see the proof of the theory.

Even realizing what she did now, she had a hard time wrapping her head around what such a childhood had to have done to two innocent children. Her history was worlds apart from theirs, and it had nothing to do with money. She'd been blessed with a great family and a pretty darned normal upbringing. Despite that solid base to carry her through hard times, she was aware that since she'd awoken in the hospital, she'd been off, or as her oldest brother had not-so-diplomatically pointed out, she'd been, and continued to be, a basket case. The few seconds it took to pull a trigger had created her situation. Eldon and Eloise had endured years of abuse.

Eldon, unlike his sister, had turned the tragedy of his childhood into incredible strength of character. Of all the people in her life, he was one of the smartest and most solid. How he did it was a mystery. But he had clearly decided somewhere along the line to thrive in spite of the hideous hand he'd drawn in the parent department.

Eloise, not so much. What had happened in that house had affected her deeply and irreparably, and Liz had always thought it was such a shame. She was beautiful and equally as smart as her brother. With a great husband who loved her in spite of her flaws, she had what it would take to rise above circumstance. She didn't. Not as a child and not as an adult. As each year passed, she seemed to fall deeper into the same hole that had swallowed their mother.

Now it seemed she had taken the one final tumble. She was probably dead drunk and passed out in her car somewhere. Liz's heart felt heavy. Such promise destroyed. Such a heavy burden for those who cared for her.

Liz kept her hand on his arm as she looked up into his face. "She called me yesterday to try to get me to play a round with her. I just couldn't do it."

"You're not her babysitter." His voice was heavy.

True enough, though would it have changed anything? Probably not. "Have you checked with the police?" In this instance, it seemed like the first and most logical thing to do. Nobody liked to make that call, but sometimes it was the most appropriate thing to do.

"The police contacted Jason. They found her car."

In a weird way that news was actually a relief, because at least she hadn't killed anyone. That Eloise routinely got behind the wheel with a blood-alcohol level way over the limit was not an unknown fact to either her or Eldon. She'd heard that at one point, Jason had tried to take her keys, but she'd managed to get another set made. No matter how Jason or Eldon worked to shut her down, protect her, she circumvented each and every best effort. From the things Eldon had shared over the years, exactly like their mother.

Liz moved her hand from where it still rested on his arm to his shoulder. It felt like a steel rod. "That's good. She's not hurt, and she didn't hurt anybody."

"It's not really good." She could swear he tensed even more, if that was possible.

"If they have her car, she has to be close by. It's just a matter of time before they find her. She's really not into hiking."

"Yeah. You'd think she'd be around, wouldn't you? She loves that car."

And the bottle of vodka that was typically under the front seat, though she didn't mention that bit of knowledge. Dread started to pool in her stomach. Maybe things weren't quite as good as she thought. Maybe she should have forced herself to go yesterday. "She wasn't there? I don't understand. Where would she go?"

He shook his head. "Worse than that, her purse was in the car, and you know as well as I do she wouldn't leave that bag behind."

Her head hurt. "Oh, Eldon, this is bad, and we don't need an Eloise mystery on top of everything else." That remark sounded cold, and in a way it was. It was born of a long history of having to watch Eloise. From the time he'd gotten his driver's license, she'd been with Eldon any number of nights as they tracked her down to bring her home before she got into serious trouble. It was an ongoing battle that Eldon still fought, despite having the assistance of her husband, Jason. What he could do by himself in their younger years now required the combined energy of two adults.

"Jason is trying his best to find her, but I just can't shake the feeling that this time something has gone terribly wrong. I'm pretty sure he's thinking the same thing." He closed his eyes and breathed deeply.

If pushed, she'd have to admit that so was she. This didn't feel like another of Eloise's nights of excess. Every night was one of excess for her, and it was hard to pinpoint one that was more so than the others. On the other hand, given everything that had happened since the first set of drawings had flowed to life under her pencil, it was possible both she and Eldon were overreacting. It was easy to jump to the worst conclusion when it could be as simple as Eloise taking off in a drunken stupor and now sleeping it off under a bench or in someone's yard. No, she'd never done anything like that before. Didn't mean it couldn't happen now.

"Let's wait to hear from Jason. We have to stay positive and believe she's passed out somewhere. She'll wake up and call just like she has a hundred other times." She expected him to argue. He didn't. He simply nodded and headed to the kitchen, where her drawings were waiting.

"You did these last night?" He was standing across from Willow and staring down at the pages torn from the artist's pad on the table between them.

"Early this morning. I did manage to get some sleep, but as soon as I woke up, this is what happened."

"There's something here."

"I agree," Willow said as she stood beside Liz and looked at the drawings as well. "She's on to something."

Liz agreed with them. The drawings sent an eerie sensation sliding all over her. This was far more than art. "We're calling Circe and Zelda again. I need to show them these." Eldon was studying the sheet that depicted a woman's sad face, and his complexion was even paler than when she opened the front door. "You recognize her?"

He nodded. "Yeah. I wish I didn't, but I do. From what I recall, she went missing about a year ago. Could have been longer. Not really sure without looking it up. I do know this is the same woman whose face was all over the local news."

She vaguely recollected it, but like a lot of things since the shooting, the memory had grown hazy. The last few months, details of many things didn't stick with her. Not like they had prior to the shooting anyway. Whether it was a physical thing or a mental one was anybody's guess. Honestly, she hoped it was the latter, because that meant she had a chance to recover a part of what she'd lost. The doctors all had the same mantra: patience. She'd taken it as good advice in the beginning. Over the last several days, it was beginning to get on her nerves.

She looked around at the fortress she'd been busy creating, suddenly a little embarrassed. It hit her in this intimate moment with these two great people that she, quite simply, needed to get over it. Bad things happened to good people all the time. That didn't mean such an incident had to rule life from that point forward. It was time to join humanity again.

As if sensing her distress, Attila leaned into her legs. The reassurance was all she needed. She hadn't asked for the so-called superpower that had been manifesting itself over the last few days, yet there it was nonetheless. She didn't appear to have an ability to turn it off, so she might as well embrace it and start living the life that was now hers. It might be different, but different might be exactly what she needed. The people around her right at this moment were a good example. She had incredible friends and family. She had everything she required to have a good life in spite of what had happened.

As to Eloise, well, they'd figure that out as they could. Who knew what could happen. She might show up while they were dealing with this mystery and be her normal unrepentant self. As irritating as that could be, Liz actually hoped it would be that simple.

"Well then." She squared her shoulders and picked up the stack of drawings from the table. She looked at Willow and then Eldon. "What are we waiting for? Let's go find her."

It wasn't that Willow had been trying to eavesdrop. She hadn't, though she'd still caught most of the conversation between Liz and Eldon. The two friends had a lot of history, and part of it had to do with a sister who had a substantial substance-abuse problem. The scenario wasn't foreign to her. Many of her students had struggled with precisely those issues and came to her after getting clean and sober. One of the most beautiful things about yoga was its way of restoring a damaged soul. She bore witness to that one firsthand, even if substance abuse wasn't her particular cross to bear.

Her monkey on the back ran the same course as Liz's. Post-traumatic stress had kicked her ass for months. People simply did not go through huge ordeals without coming out on the other side bearing scars. They might tell you they were fine. They were not. She certainly used that line over and over, and even believed it was the truth, most of the time. It was a lie. It had been a really long time before she could say she was fine and be telling the truth.

Her heart went out to Eldon. No, she didn't know him well. It didn't matter if they were recent acquaintances, as she recognized a good soul when she met one. His goodness radiated around him like a halo. She also liked the way he looked out for Liz. More people needed friends like him. Hell, she needed a friend like him. She could have used an Eldon when she was recovering.

Without yoga and all it had taught her, she might not have made it through. It was amazing how many people couldn't look past her very visible scars. It had been such a hard time, especially in the beginning when the wounds were still healing. They were raw and red and glowed like a neon sign. She hardly went out at all because she hated all the stares. Nothing felt normal or good.

After a few weeks, it had all changed. She grew weary of hiding. After all, what had she done wrong? Nothing. When that truth hit home, her whole outlook changed. Rather than dwell on her losses, she chose to look at the bright side. That included all the great people she'd ignored in the beginning. For all those who stared in open horror, a lot of people couldn't have cared less about her outward appearance. Those were the family, friends, and acquaintances who focused on her spirit. They saved her. She embraced the good and found a way to release the bad.

In fact, she'd made many more friends after the incident. Maybe before her ordeal she too had focused on the outside of people rather than the inside. It was a sad commentary for someone who had devoted her life to something that required introspection much of the time. She'd thought she'd been a good yoga teacher before the shooting, and all modesty aside, she probably had been. Now she truly understood others' inner beauty, and instead of simply being a good teacher, she was now a great teacher.

Whether she could help with Eldon's sister was a big unknown. She did seem to have a way with those who were lost and trying to find their way back. Usually it was through her yoga classes and the spiritual journey that came with practice.

She turned to study Liz, who was intent on getting the bus rolling. Drawing the new set of pictures had put her in an action mode. Eldon was still not moving from his spot next to the table. He continued to stare down at the top of it, even though Liz had picked up all the drawings. His mind appeared to be somewhere far away.

"Can I help?" She stepped up and put a hand on Eldon's shoulder. *Oh my* was what she didn't voice. Beneath her palm, vibrations let her know that whatever was going on with, she presumed, his sister was scaring him at an elemental level. She didn't know him, yet she sensed that fear made him tremble, and that was an unusual emotion for him. If she could see auras, she bet his would scream terror, and that made her afraid too.

His eyes were haunted as he looked at her. "Thank you, but no," he said in a low voice. "I doubt there's anything anyone can do. We've all tried for years and now…now, I don't know what she's done. I don't know where she is."

"We'll find her." Liz's voice was calm and confident, though Willow had the feeling she was putting on a show for her friend, who up until this moment had been the strength holding her together. Funny how things could change in a second. Didn't she know it? Didn't Liz know it too?

"Your sister, right?"

He nodded. "It's no big secret. Everyone in town knows she has a significant drinking problem." She noticed he couldn't say the word alcoholic. Of course, if it was her sister, she wasn't sure she'd be able to either.

"Something's happened, though, hasn't it?"

"Yes. You have to understand that it's not unusual for her to be late, even hours late. If you wanted to have dinner at seven, you would tell Eloise it was at five. Then she might make it on time. Last night, she didn't come home at all, and even after all her bizarre behavior, that's something she's never done before. She always comes home regardless of how drunk she's gotten or how late. She always comes home…" His last words trailed off softly.

A chill washed over Willow as though an Alaskan wind had just blown through the kitchen. It was the same feeling she'd had when she'd glimpsed the fire at her brother's house. The spirit that had gifted her with that bit of vision seemed to be telling her now that darkness was all around Eldon's sister. She didn't share with him what she was feeling. It wouldn't do any good.

"How can I help?"

Again Eldon shook his head. "I appreciate your offer. Right now, none of us can do anything. Her husband is working with the police. We just have to wait until we hear."

Waiting around under circumstances like this was the kiss of death. The best thing any of them could do was to be active, release some endorphins, and keep their minds busy, not dwell on the *what ifs*. When it was time to help his sister, they would know. In the meantime, they had to keep their forward momentum going.

"We need to roll." Liz was moving toward the door again, this time with Eldon's shirt sleeve in her hand.

"Give me a sec." Liz let go of Eldon and turned toward Willow, who made a quick call before sliding the cell phone into her pocket. "Circe and Zelda are on their way." Then she put a hand on Liz's arm and thought about how much she loved the warmth of her skin. She could hold onto her all day and that would be just fine.

Liz gave her a look that told her she understood. It also showed a clearness to her eyes that hadn't been there before Eldon arrived. Strength was coming back to her in this hour of need. It was a defining moment, and damned if Willow didn't hope she'd be around to see more of those.

Eldon, still waiting by the front door, seemed to shake himself clear of the fog he'd been in since arriving. His mind was most likely still on his missing sister, but he was also beginning to really process what he'd seen in the kitchen.

"Was it another vision that made you draw the pictures?"

Liz shook her head. "No. Not this time. It was weird and more like my fingers drew the pictures without the need of some ghost coming to me. They just sort of magically happened. I don't know how to explain it that will make any sense."

Willow was hoping they'd get rolling without a whole lot of discussion. Action was what they all needed right now, except talking about it didn't shake Liz up all over again, as Willow feared it might. In fact, didn't seem to affect her at all. If anything, it was the opposite. Her voice was confident, her back straighter, and her eyes clear and focused. This was, she suspected, more of the woman who had been around before the bullet pierced her skin. Oh, hell yes, she liked this woman.

"We have to check it out." Eldon's confidence seemed to be returning as well. Good. They were going to need him.

She gave him a single nod. "Yeah, we do, and only this time we've called in reinforcements."

"Isn't that what Circe and Zelda are?"

"Sure, but trust me when I tell you her wife is a cop with a very open mind." She loved Diana and was confident she'd be a huge help.

This time he gave her a quick nod. "Good plan."

"Just like a Girl Scout." Liz winked.

Yes, Willow really liked the woman she was watching right now. A lot.

CHAPTER TWENTY

Even as shook up as he was, Eldon had felt better once he got to Liz's house. Just being around Liz always put him in a better mood. She was simply one of those people. Throw in Willow, who was a very calming influence on all of them, and it was even better. It wasn't just him either. The difference her presence was making for Liz was clear already, and it warmed his heart. Meg had called that one a hundred percent. Another instance of Meg's unconscious demonstration of how special she was.

They were still standing in the kitchen when the doorbell rang. He'd known who it was because he'd sent her a text. He hadn't asked her to come. He'd hoped she would.

Liz brought Meg back to the kitchen, where he and Willow still waited by the back door. Meg stopped right behind him and put her hand on the small of his back. The gesture was soft yet intimate. He didn't want her to ever move her hand. He hated that he might be blowing this out of proportion, yet deep in his heart, he didn't believe he was. After all his hopes and doubts, they were forging a connection, and he prayed it didn't fall apart once this thing with Liz, whatever it was, came to an end.

"When are Circe and Zelda coming?" Liz must have told her they were waiting for the K9 super team.

"They're on the way," Willow answered. "We're going to buzz out to the cemetery as soon as they get here."

Eldon had taken the drawings from Liz and was staring at the one with the rows of old, leaning headstones. It struck him as an odd place for another body to be buried. Well, a body that wasn't supposed to be there. "You really think she's there?" He stared down at another drawing, this one with the likeness of the lovely young woman's face.

Liz blew out a long breath. "She's there," she said with conviction. "I know she is."

"What is wrong with people?" he muttered. What kind of person would kill like this and leave bodies hidden so their families never knew what happened to them? Of course, that was a stupid question, given where he lived. Over the years, more than one serial killer had made the state their home. Ted Bundy, Gary Ridgeway, also known as the Green River Killer, and of course, way too close for comfort, was Robert Yates, who was currently sitting on death row in the Washington State Penitentiary at Walla Walla. Yates was particularly gruesome, considering he was a regular-looking guy who could have been anyone's next-door neighbor and who also buried one of his victims in a flower garden beside the home he shared with his wife and children. The creepy factor of that guy was off the charts.

So, thinking that this kind of evil couldn't find its way back to Spokane again was particularly flawed logic. It bugged him even given the painful way he'd grown up. His mother had been some kind of crazy and had damaged both him and his sister. Deep down he held tight to the belief she was simply a flawed human being and not an evil one. To think otherwise would be more than he could process. Bundy, Ridgeway, and Yates were far more than flawed. Eldon truly believed evil made their souls as black as a cloudless night. Now, he had to wonder if another black soul was sharing their airspace. No, that was stupid and it wasn't a question. Someone out there was spreading their evil and he, or she, needed to be stopped. Must be stopped.

He stared over at Liz, and something flitted through him that he couldn't quite define. It wasn't a bad something either. He'd been so worried about her since the shooting and feared she would be lost to them forever. She was falling down the rabbit hole, as the saying went. Until now, that is. Today for the first time in almost a year he saw something in her that gave him a surge of hope. It was wonderful and creepy all at the same time. She was regaining her confidence and strength, and she was doing it by helping catch a killer.

"Come on," he said to the three women. "Let's wait outside for Circe. Is Attila coming along?" He loved that dog and could easily load him up and take him home. He was pretty sure Liz would come after him like a tornado if he even tried to coax her dog away. Liz and Attila had bonded from the first second they laid eyes on each other, and the love between them was steel strong. Maybe when all this was over, he'd find his own Attila.

Liz smiled and patted Attila on the head. He wagged his tail. "No, he's going to stay here to hold down the fort." Attila wagged his tail harder and ran out of the kitchen to the front room, where he promptly jumped up on the sofa. Apparently, he knew exactly what his job was.

"You sure he's actually holding down the fort?" Eldon stood in the doorway between the two rooms and looked over at the very relaxed Attila. He didn't look on alert to Eldon. He looked far more like a dog about to take a lengthy nap.

"Don't let his relaxed posture fool you. He can turn it on a dime."

"If you say so."

Attila groaned and rolled over on his back with his feet straight up in the air.

Everyone laughed, which helped defuse the tension that kept growing as they waited for Circe, all of them knowing what they would find at the end of their day's quest. Or so they thought.

Well, well, well, wasn't this an interesting twist? Eldon had gone from his house to the lovely little brick house near Audubon Park, which coincidentally was right near Downriver Golf course. Could the universe be trying to send her a message?

No, it had to be nothing more than a fluke. Or perhaps not. As the Jaguar watched, Eldon came back out of the house with three women right behind him. One, a tall woman with brown hair, stood particularly close to him. That was a surprise. She wasn't the same woman he'd been hugging earlier when he first arrived, and something about this one seemed even more special than the other one. He was a guy just full of surprises.

When had Eldon gotten himself a girlfriend, because it seemed pretty darned clear that's what he considered her to be. He'd always been such a loner. He wasn't a bad-looking man, with his thick auburn hair and deep-green eyes. Throw a kilt on him and he'd make a perfect Highlander. Still, through the years, he'd been more of a nerd than a stud, and the women he shared his life with were few and far between. Captain of the football team he most certainly was not.

Things were changing, judging by the picture presented right now. The body language between him and the woman almost screamed of the distinct interest between them. Good little bit of information to tuck away. The woman could play an important part in the game, should the Jaguar need another bargaining chip to shut down the nosy Eldon. He never was very good at knowing when he was out-matched. A curse of the rich and smart. They were too arrogant to know when they were beaten. Or about to be beaten.

The two other women followed Eldon and his girlfriend out the front door. One was the dark-haired woman he'd been hugging earlier. After a better look at her face, she still felt that something about her rang familiar. In all reality it could be something as simple as she had an average face, which she had. The other woman was more striking and more easily remembered. Tall and thin, with jet-black hair, she was a stunner even from this distance. Like Eldon and his little girly, the two women seemed to have a link. Body language was telegraphing loud and clear that they were together or, if not together yet, wanted to be. Strangely, she too looked a little familiar, although she was sure they'd never met.

Then it hit her why. All of them had been together last night in the crush of police vehicles out at Boulder Beach. In all the news clips she'd seen, this was the group standing in the background beside Eldon. This whole crew had been responsible for finding what had been hidden quite well for so long. All that was missing was the damn dog and its handler. The moment the thought hit, the missing piece emerged. An SUV pulled into the driveway, and the handler got out. The dog had to be in the back. God damn it. Fury burned in her like a winter fire.

"You guys ready?" The dog handler stood just outside the SUV with one hand still on the driver's side door.

Eldon held out a stack of papers that he handed to the shorter, dark-haired woman. "Yeah. Let's get this show on the road."

"Where are we going today?" The woman who was now holding the papers stepped over to the handler and showed them to her. What were they? She could hear their conversation from here but couldn't make out any detail about the things they handed back and forth.

The K9 handler nodded, her face grim. "I know this cemetery. I've driven by it tons of times when I've been heading to Mt. Spokane to ski."

The hair rose on the back of the Jaguar's neck. No. No way could they be going there. It was one of the most perfect places ever, and coming up with it had been a stroke of genius. Very little traffic and nearly forgotten except for a quick, sideways glimpse when driving through the miles of plowed fields and around the gently curving road. How would they know? How could they know?

The handler returned the sheets of paper to the woman, who slid them into a pad...an artist's pad. What the fuck had this woman been doing? That anyone would know what was nestled amongst the bones of the long-dead was an impossibility that defied explanation. That someone could actually draw the secrets that hid beneath the shaggy grass and old, dying trees was simply not possible.

Except that as they pulled out and drove out of the neighborhood, the Jaguar staying a discreet distance behind, fear began to creep steadily in, causing a knot to form in the middle of her stomach. The road less traveled was being heavily traveled at the moment by five adults and one dog with the ability to smell the odor of dead bodies. The people should be run off the road and the dog shot.

Shit.

CHAPTER TWENTY-ONE

The farther north they drove, the more Liz's stomach tightened. It was as though she was getting sick and her body was telling her to get ready to puke. Except it wasn't sickness assailing her. It was dread making her feel like she was going to have suffer the black plague. Once they let Zelda loose to do her job, Liz knew exactly what she would do. She would run to a spot on the edge of the cemetery and alert her handler to the presence of human decomposition. Once the sheriff's department was called in to investigate, the face they would uncover in that shallow grave would be a familiar one.

Well, that wasn't exactly true, given that they already had the cops with them. Circe's wife was indeed a gun-toting, badge-carrying law-enforcement officer, and one who didn't seem to think Liz was one iota crazy. Honestly, she was surprised at how good it felt to be taken seriously. Ever since this thing, whatever it was, had been visited upon her, she'd been feeling less like the walking wounded—which was how she'd been feeling since waking up in the hospital—and more like someone who needed a licensed professional. Until now anyway.

Circe and Diana made her not only feel sane, but they also made her feel important. That was an unexpected change. They took what she showed them and studied it with intense concentration, the kind they would give any other piece of solid evidence. That felt great, and more and more she was beginning to shift from damaged-goods status to maybe okay.

It also didn't hurt that she now sat in the back of Eldon's car with Willow holding her hand. For a long time she'd harbored doubts that she would ever be able to get close to anyone again. More than her body had been shattered in the courtyard that day. The shot had demolished her trust of other people. Giving people, all people, the benefit of the doubt had been a hallmark of her personality. But not now.

For months she hadn't been able to trust anyone except a few of her family members and very close friends, like Eldon and Meg. Nothing about either one of her friends had ever changed. Not in the way they treated her or in the way they talked to her. Everyone else in her life had been tiptoeing around her like she was a broken doll. She'd never told anyone, but sometimes she thought of taking an easy way out. Going to sleep and never waking up held a certain appeal that was hard to resist. That her two friends treated her exactly as they did before meant more than she'd ever be able to tell them and helped remind her there was hope.

Except she did have a little secret—she'd known about both Meg and Eldon watching her on the sly. They thought they were being as stealthy as afternoon shadows. They hadn't realized she wasn't so far gone that she hadn't caught them now and again. She'd have called them on it except that it made her feel good to know they were there. With Eldon, Meg, and Attila to help, she'd been able to hang on. Barely.

This morning, she woke up feeling completely different. More like the old Liz, and man oh man, did it feel fantastic. It was crazy considering what was going on. Here she was seeing things, drawing people and locations impossible for her to have any knowledge of, yet she was certain she drew the undeniable truth. Murder most foul. Murder uncovered, and she was the one doing the uncovering. She was regaining some of the power she'd lost as that bullet pierced her skin and changed everything. Her body, her spirit, her soul—they were all returning.

"I'm okay, you know," she said quietly to Willow. She didn't want her to think she was so scared someone had to constantly hold her hand. Earlier dark thoughts and emotions about how this had come about threatened to overwhelm her. Not anymore. Now that they were here, she was anxious, and not out of fear. She was eager to bring a woman home. It was as though she'd been shown her destiny and she was grabbing it with both hands.

The corner of Willow's mouth turned up in a smile. "I know. I've known since the moment I saw you that you were okay. You got this." She squeezed her hand.

"Really?" She should probably pull her hand away. She didn't.

"Really. Even at the first hello, I could read strength in you, and you're getting stronger by the minute. The woman I saw sitting in the kitchen this morning was a world away from the one I first met."

"I feel stronger. I'm not afraid anymore."

Willow leaned into her, and she loved their contact. She loved the way Willow smelled—rich and earthy and intoxicating. "I'm glad. I've thought about what's happening to you and have decided what it means."

"And…" She wanted to know what Willow thought.

"You're a talebearer."

"A what?"

"Talebearer. It's like there's a story out there being written by a killer. You are the one the universe has chosen to tell the tale, and by doing so, you'll balance the scales of justice."

She kind of liked that. One thing bothered her though. "All I'm doing is finding the lost. Nothing I've drawn so far has anything to do with the bastard or bastards who killed them."

"Who knows how this will all play out. It could all be connected, and what you're doing might be all the cops need to find the killer."

Liz shook her head. She'd argue except there was nothing to argue about. She felt the truth of Willow's statement all the way to her toes. For whatever reason, it was important that she follow it through to the end and let it take her where it would. Someone or something was working within her, and it was up to her to convey the truths being shared with her to the outside world. At the same time, even as vague and unsettling as it was, to be useful once again was priceless.

It wasn't simply a sense of fulfilling some sort of purpose, either, that had her heart swelling. The touch of the woman sitting next to her was more than healing; it was thrilling. She'd dated her fair share of women and, until now, not a single one had set her pulse racing by the single act of holding her hand. She'd given up hope that she'd ever discover that special something everyone talked about. For the first time ever, she was beginning to believe she understood. The last twenty-four hours had been filled with new and wondrous things.

"Well, all right then." She leaned back against the car seat and watched out the window as the fields whizzed by. It didn't take very long to get from her house to the old cemetery. By the time they negotiated the narrow gravel driveway and parked in the tiny lot carved out at the top of the hill, her nerve endings were on fire. A part of her would like to believe she was wrong about what had flowed from her fingers onto the paper. She wasn't wrong, and another part of her was grateful for that certainty. Out there somewhere, a lost soul waited for them and had been waiting for them for a long time.

It took only a few minutes for Circe to get her dog ready, and quickly enough, she was off and running. She, as well as everyone else, expected Zelda to traverse the cemetery as they'd seen her do last night in the woods. She'd cast out a long way, her nose down and her eyes focused. Liz was shocked and, judging by Circe's expression, decided she wasn't alone in that feeling, when Zelda wheeled around, crossed the road, and headed toward a field on the other side. The wild grasses that grew in the unworked field had been recently mowed, so it didn't make sense that Zelda would go there. Surely there couldn't be anything else, particularly not a body, given the way the earth had been so recently worked. Something was obviously off with the dog.

Zelda didn't give the mowed field more than a quick sniff. Instead, as she raced along the tall weeds of the stretch of land that separated the field from the highway, she seemed to be intent on her search, as if she was on the scent of something. Indeed, when her head snapped to the left, the weird feeling Liz had been experiencing since they left became strong enough that she doubted whether she'd be able to hold back this time. She really didn't want to throw up in front of everyone.

The truth of what she was seeing in Zelda's behavior flooded her. She stood by the car and glanced over at the old, leaning headstones. There was no body—no unexpected body—in the old cemetery, despite what her drawings had seemed to indicate. She wasn't wrong in believing they were here for a reason because there still was a body. It was simply a matter of letting Zelda do her job.

"She's got something," Circe said as she followed Zelda to a patch of land high with wild grass.

In many ways it didn't make sense, at least not in terms of how accurate her first drawings had turned out to be. The drawings that had flowed from Liz's fingertips clearly showed the rolling hills and headstones of this cemetery. Zelda had zero interest in the cemetery. This was no longer about her artwork and was instead all about Zelda. Liz followed Circe as she too crossed the road. Zelda's body language told anyone with decent vision that the dog was certain. She was totally committed to the trained response she was exhibiting for Circe. The oh-so-skilled canine was picking up the distinct odor of human decomposition.

So maybe she wasn't quite the talebearer Willow thought her to be. Her accuracy was only fifty-fifty at this point. Then Liz turned and studied the area. As she gazed at the land across the road, it all fell into place. From this spot, the view across the street was exactly as she'd drawn it.

More than the trained response that Zelda was giving Circe, the haunted look on Liz's face told Willow everything she needed to know. Once again they'd found a missing woman. They'd all come here expecting to find a victim hidden on the fringes of the cemetery. Rather than in the cemetery, the woman had been buried here on the edge of the field, as if someone wanted to make certain she was hidden for eternity. Here there was no risk of someone stumbling upon her inadvertently.

It made sense in a warped way. She remembered hearing one time that bodies could not-infrequently be found buried along the edge of cemeteries. Particularly in years past when families who couldn't afford plots in cemeteries would sneak in at night and bury their loved ones on the fringes, feeling that they were doing the right thing by still getting them into hallowed ground. When she'd seen Liz's pictures, that's exactly what she'd thought had happened.

From all appearances, it wasn't quite that way. No, this was a case of a killer wanting to hide his or her dirty deed, not some well-intentioned family member. One body in an out-of-the-way wilderness area close to town, and a second in an out-of-the-way acreage, also close to town. Whoever was killing these women was thinking through their disposal pretty carefully. It was even scarier to consider someone with that kind of thought process.

Willow wondered when she'd made up her mind that this was a single killer. Liz was seeing nothing that indicated these two women were connected. Statistically speaking, friends or family had most likely brought about their deaths. That was what the experts always said. Those closest to the victims committed the vast majority of murders, and the numbers bore it out. She didn't have any trouble believing that to be true, yet Willow had a really strong feeling that wasn't the case here. These two women had died by the same hand, and it wasn't that of an angry boyfriend, husband, or lover. She shivered.

What was it about being a victim of violence that opened up the doors to another dimension? Willow's experience had been brief but intense, and it involved someone very close to her. She hadn't experienced anything even near what was happening to Liz, who seemed to be channeling some kind of pipeline directly to evil. Willow could only hope the evil didn't find its way into Liz's soul.

She studied her now as Liz stared into the distance with a somewhat stunned expression. They had all come out here fully expecting this end result. That expectation didn't change how surreal it all felt when it actually came to pass. As she looked at Liz, a light began to glow all around her, as if a spotlight had been trained on her. It was then that Willow embraced a certainty that no matter what kind of evil Liz was tasked with uncovering, she would come out on the other side healthy and, hopefully, happy. She wanted to be there to see it. Darkness was not going to get a chance to wrap its ugly arms around Liz.

"What am I seeing?" Liz asked so only she could hear. She was standing totally still and staring at the hillside cemetery. "I don't get it. Tell me this happened to you too and that I'm not some kind of psychic freak."

Willow took her arm and walked her away from where the rest of them stood talking quietly near the spot Zelda had indicated. Diana stood off to the side with her phone pressed to her ear. Presumably she was calling in for reinforcements. How Diana planned to explain their unique expedition was an unknown. Really, she didn't care. What she did care about was getting all this out of Liz's head and making certain that poor young woman was brought home.

"You're seeing truth." It was as simple as she could think to break it down. The thing inside Liz was seeking only what was honest, and it radiated from her mind and through her talented hands. The universe had a way of pulling out those with a bright light and kind soul. She was so drawn to it. To her.

"That might be, but it sure is a fucked-up truth."

"Only for whoever is doing this."

"Whoever? Makes more sense that it would be multiple *whos*. What makes you think it's one person? Maybe I'm just clueing in on victims, and it doesn't matter who hurt them. My only job is to find them. The cops are going to have to figure out the rest. "

The argument actually held a lot of weight. Willow didn't have a single rational explanation for why she felt like a single individual had killed both women. She only knew that she did. More than a sense of knowing, she was certain she was right. Maybe it was her own brand of superpower kicking back in. It hadn't appeared since they'd pulled her brother out of his burning house. Though she'd assumed it was essentially gone since she'd had no additional strong bouts of sight, that didn't mean it was. She kept coming back around to a single idea, and it was so strong she wondered if it was like seeing the flames.

"I have a theory about what's happening to you, and it's not quite that you're clueing in on only the victims."

Liz looked confused. "It's got to be. Nothing else makes sense."

She shook her head and took Liz by the arm, leading her back across the road and toward the car. "You're definitely picking up on something here, only I think you're channeling a killer. You're seeing the world through the killer's eyes, and that's how you're doing these drawings."

Liz shuddered. "No way. I think you're wrong. What about the first woman who came to me? I mean, it was such a deliberate vision. Why would that happen?"

She shrugged. "Maybe it was like the flames I kept dreaming about, and I think that was because I was in tune with my bro. It puts people like you and me into some kind of psychic space, and the channels cross now and again. For you, it was when the woman came to you. She opened the door for you, and after that, the images that flow from your fingertips come directly from the killer's mind. That's why I believe it's a single person. You're inside a killer's head."

"Another serial killer? No way." Liz shuddered. "It's crazy that our city would have another one. It's more than creepy. It's insane, and I sure as hell do not want to be inside their head."

A chill filled Willow, and she held onto Liz's hand. She didn't want to freak Liz out and felt that it would be a great disservice not to say what she was certain was true. "As much as I hate to say it, yeah. I think you're on the trail of a serial killer."

CHAPTER TWENTY-TWO

This time they didn't wait around for the troops to arrive. They'd had enough of that last night and weren't interested in a repeat performance. No more interviews and definitely no more probing questions. They hightailed it out of there. Eldon drove Meg, Liz, and Willow back to Liz's house. He probably should have stuck around with Liz to make sure she was going to be all right. Today he didn't have the heart. Besides, she had Willow with her, so he was confident she'd be okay. He and Meg got back into his car.

No one had any questions as to who they'd find when the soil was moved aside because they knew. Eldon couldn't concentrate anyway. Initially, it was a good diversion. As soon as Zelda confirmed what they all were expecting, he began to obsess about Eloise again. He couldn't help it. No matter what, she was his sister.

He kept waiting for his phone to ring and for Jason to tell him she'd come home bedraggled, wrinkled, and hung over. That she was fine, or at least would be once she got some sleep. He checked the display on his phone so many times he was surprised the battery hadn't died.

That, or June calling him again. Her tenacity would be admirable if it wasn't so incredibly annoying.

His cell never rang. Not while they were on the way to the cemetery, not while they were there, and not while they were on the way back to town. It was maddeningly silent, which made him want to scream or throw it out the window, at least where it concerned Jason. No calls from June was a good thing.

"We'll find her." Meg put a hand on his arm. He almost flinched and then caught himself. She was the one person in the world he would never shy away from.

He ran a hand through his hair and absently tried to remember when he'd actually combed it last. "This is the longest she's ever been away. She gets totally messed up and has passed out in her car more times than I care to count. But she's never bailed on her life before. She might be dysfunctional, but she's not suicidal."

"I don't believe she's bailed now."

That really was the kicker. He didn't either, and that's what worried the ever-living hell out of him. The longer he went without hearing from her, the more convinced he was that something had happened to her. God damn it, why hadn't Jason called yet?

"I have an idea." Meg turned to face him. The car was parked in the driveway, and Liz and Willow had already disappeared into the house.

"I'm open to anything." If he could do something instead of sit here, it would help a lot. The diversion of the cemetery investigation kept his mind busy for a significant amount of time. Now he was back to obsessing about Eloise.

"Let's have Liz draw her."

His hopes for a great plan fell like a boulder dropped from a cliff. He ran his hands through his hair again, this time rubbing his scalp as if it would help erase the tension that made his entire body stiff. It didn't really work, and the idea of having Liz draw Eloise frankly creeped him out. His grand plan to have art help Liz had worked out in that so far it had brought two dead women home. Not quite what he'd intended. Good end result nonetheless.

He didn't even want to consider asking Liz to draw Eloise. It seemed to him that would invite bad luck. It might help law enforcement clear up a missing person mystery, but his sister wasn't a victim. At least not of a killer. She was a victim of their family secrets and of her own unexorcised demons. That was all.

"No." His voice was quiet but firm. "I can't ask that of her." He looked out the side window before turning to stare into her eyes. "I don't want to ask her."

Meg laid her hand against his cheek. Her small palm felt nice on his cold skin. "I understand why you wouldn't want to try. If you don't want to ask Liz to give it a go, we won't ask her. I promise you, though, we'll find her. I know we will." Then she did something that shocked him. She leaned across and kissed him.

It was the fucking drawings. A good set of binoculars had finally provided an adequate view of what the woman held, and the impossibility of them was hard to accept. For years everything had been simple and a total secret. All it took was a little planning, some knowledge of the area, and skill. The Jaguar had it all, and life had been perfect. Whenever the mood hit, another one was out there waiting for a visit from her. Until yesterday. First one was taken away and now another was being ripped from her. Pissed off wasn't even close to the emotions she was experiencing at this moment.

She'd followed them from the house in the Audubon neighborhood to the cemetery and back, and now to another house in town. It was like being in a bad dream. She wanted to wake up and to make it stop, but she couldn't. It just kept moving forward with disastrous results.

And that damned Eldon was part of it. That would never do. The way the one woman held the drawings and the artist pad showed she was obviously the artist and at least partially responsible for the discovery of the bodies. The real question was how she knew what to draw? There was no evidence, no clues, nothing that would allow anyone to know who and where. She had been beyond careful. Her mama didn't raise a fool.

How Eldon fit into the whole thing was still unclear. Not that the details mattered a great deal. He was going to pay the price for being part of this, and it was his bad luck. He'd always seemed like the good son while his sister had been a giant pain in the ass. Perhaps that assessment had been off. Perhaps Eldon was just as big a pain as his sister. Well, she had a remedy for that.

Holding the steering wheel, the Jaguar's hands began to tremble. Last night's discovery had seemed like a fluke until now. Whatever was going on here was far from chance. This situation was something out of her worst nightmare. It wasn't fair. After all this time, her secrets should be safe and not dug up by a bunch of cops or, even more insulting, uncovered by a stupid dog. Yet, that seemed to be what was happening.

She zeroed in on one woman, the same one who'd been hugging Eldon at the front door of the house. It was her fault, she was certain of it, and something was going to have to be done about her. But first, she'd have to figure out the appropriate disposition for Eldon. He couldn't be around, and he couldn't be hanging with that woman. She had to stop the double threat immediately. It would take some thought, though not too much. In two days two secrets had been revealed, and that was two too many.

The Jaguar pulled back onto the road and drove slowly past the brick house. Eldon was walking inside and didn't pay any attention to the single car passing by. She needed to go back to her tried and true methods, and that meant developing some plans. She just didn't have the luxury of the time she usually did. She had to make these plans immediately. First things first, however. It was time to make the rounds. It had been a while since she'd visited the whole circuit, and right now she wanted to make certain everyone else was still safe and sound. She refused to lose anyone else because of this group of misfits.

The first stop was only a few miles away. She didn't need to get out of the car, as it was easy to view the special spot from the car. All looked peaceful and the ground undisturbed. No one who walked through realized that she rested a few feet below the green grass. Her site was still as perfect as the day she'd been put below the dark earth. Nothing quite like a state park to *park* a body or two, and what an incredible view. Couldn't argue with perfection.

It took almost half an hour to drive to the next spot, which was a particular favorite. Two people were sitting on the boulders with their feet on the wild grass that grew freely. That brought a genuine smile. Little did they know they were sharing their cheese sticks and water bottles with a third party. Wouldn't they be surprised? Like the spot at the base of Mt. Spokane, all was still as it should be.

One more and the circuit would be complete, at least in the immediate area. There were others, but these were the most important. The last one required a bit more finesse to check on. That was the problem with being the first one. Jaguar hadn't fully developed her skill and forethought at that point, and it showed. Well, really only to her, as no one else knew what had happened. The police had made a token investigation attempt before letting it fade to cold-case status in the SPD files. The Jaguar was greatly pleased to be responsible for not just that particular one, but also for a stack of those cold-case files. It just went to show how much a person could learn and put into practice. It was a badge of honor, even if no one else realized it. Too bad the girl scouts didn't have merit badges for murder, or she'd have a sash full. She laughed and drove home as she couldn't check on the last one until darkness fell.

The hours ticked by with agonizing slowness until finally it was time. Everyone was busy in the house when she slipped out the back door. She left so quietly no one noticed she'd gone. It was always this way. Out like a whisper, in like a ghost. She drove away into the night.

The street was dark, and one of the streetlights was out. Years ago, it had been a nice middle-class neighborhood where kids ran around unsupervised until late at night, the only parental instructions being something along the lines of "be in by eleven." Games of hide-n-seek, kick the can, and other improvised entertainments were common when they were younger. As their teenage years approached, more adventurous endeavors like drinking rot-gut beer and smoking joints behind the shaggy hedges replaced the games. That was a long time ago, and this was a different place now.

Things had changed in the intervening years, and peeling paint and cars that no longer ran and were parked on yellowed grass had replaced the once-nice street lined with tidy houses, green lawns, and two cars in the driveways. Another streetlight down on the next corner sputtered as if it was also trying to die. Kind of like this neighborhood. It too was sputtering and on the verge of extinction.

Fitting that number one should still be here. The decay of the neighborhood matched the decay in her soul that had begun long before she took her last breath.

A school at the end of the street had a big parking lot, which would be great during the day. It was empty at this time of night, and her car could catch attention. An apartment complex across the street was a different story. She parked between a pick up and a battered van. Her nice vehicle might stand out if someone was really looking, and that was a chance she had to take. She decided it was dark enough outside that no one would look close enough to notice it didn't really belong.

It was likewise easy to make it back down the street without being seen. After all, years of practice made it a simple matter. People rarely forgot things they learned early, even if the playing field morphed. This path was so familiar, she could traverse it blind.

Five houses down was a one-story rancher with a single attached garage. It had always been one of the smaller and shabbier houses on the block, even before the neighborhood took a path downward. Once upon a time, the front door was red. Now it was almost pink, as it had faded so much, and most of the paint was peeling off. All around the house the windows were boarded up from the inside, and a shiny padlock had been installed on both the front and back doors. No one had lived in the house for a very long time, but that didn't mean it had gone unused, despite what the neighbors would undoubtedly report if asked.

From the overgrown shrubs in the back, it was a simple task to scan the backyard. Weeds were waist high, and not a trace of the scraggly grass that used to be there remained. It had never been one of those pretty yards where the family had dinner on the patio table and watched the sunsets. The patio was cracked, and weeds pushed up through them. This wasn't new. The patio had looked like shit for years. They'd never had a dinner while sitting on it and most certainly never sat here watching a sunset. Despite its shabby nature, one patio section had been added, and it differed from the main section because it had only a few thin cracks. That was good. In fact, it was excellent and exactly what the Jaguar was hoping to see. It meant nothing had been disturbed, which, given the state of the area, was an ever-present concern.

The fortress the house had become was pure perfection. This place had, if nothing else, become a refuge for self-preservation, yet suddenly it became more important. Oh yes, it was still about self-preservation, but in a completely different way. The key slipped easily and silently in the back-door lock, just as it always did. Inside it was pitch black, courtesy of the boards on all the windows. She didn't need to use the penlight because this was a simple courtesy check. The silence of the interior was the only confirmation she needed that everything was as it had been left after the last visit. Not even so much as a mouse moved inside, thanks to the poison stationed around the house. This was not a place to share with anyone, human or otherwise, except by specific invitation.

Once more outside, it took her mere minutes to retrace the path to the car. The parking lot looked exactly as it had when she parked the car between the pickup and the van. The thought that the day had started out badly faded away as the Jaguar backed the car out of the space and drove away from the old hood. She no longer feared discovery. Instead, excitement rolled in like a fast-moving summer storm.

CHAPTER TWENTY-THREE

L iz hadn't gotten much sleep last night and had a hunch tonight wouldn't be a whole lot different. Her body still buzzed, even after going for a run with Attila. It was the only thing she could think of to do when everyone left after their return from the cemetery. It was also a first. Ever since she'd healed enough to be able to run again, she'd been doing it on the treadmill. She'd always hated the things until she'd discovered she could run on them in the safety of her own home. Exercise and safety was exactly the combination she treasured. Today was the first time she'd hit the streets in a year. It was fantastic. Of course she waited until it was dark. If no one could see her, it was hard to be a target. Still, it was a step forward, and she'd take it. Circe had promised to call and update them once the sheriff's department finished. She figured that would take all day, and she didn't see any sense in sitting around waiting for her phone to ring.

After Eldon and Meg had gone, Willow seemed really reluctant to leave her. She liked her hesitation, though she craved some alone time to process all that had happened in the last twenty-four hours. It was wonderful to have someone so understanding hang with her. To ask her to stay would be selfish on her part, and she had enough character flaws to deal with lately without adding selfish to the list.

Besides, Willow had classes to teach, and Liz didn't want to be responsible for taking her away from her job. The people in her classes counted on her, and frankly, Liz had been handling her life, or what passed for her life, by herself for a long time. She was going to be fine. In fact, she felt like she might be more than fine…finally.

The run actually did help a bunch. There was a lot of magic in releasing those endorphins and working muscles, except she remained incredibly worried about Eldon. It was still hard to work up much sympathy for Eloise. She'd been creating her own hell for a long time. That sounded cold, but when someone refused help year after year, after a while it was difficult to find the energy to offer any. Like a counselor had told her during her worst days in rehab, "You can't help someone who doesn't want to help herself." The advice had worked in her case, and she'd pulled her head out, so to speak. Eloise never had.

Eldon was different. She worried about him just like he'd been worrying about her. It was time for the shoe to be on the other foot. He'd been watching her back since the day of the shooting. Now she was watching his. He wouldn't be okay until they found Eloise, and so that's exactly what she intended to do, regardless of how she felt about her. She could figure out only one way to do that.

After showering and changing clothes, Liz sat at the table with the pad in front of her, tapping a pencil on the blank surface. Seemed like the right thing to do except she still didn't know how to make her newfound skill work on demand. The first time, the dream or the vision or whatever in the hell it was triggered it. The second time, it was as if the pictures simply flowed from her unconscious mind and through the tips of her fingers. No real thought to it. It just happened.

Right now she was getting precisely squat. Nothing came into her head, and nothing shot out of her fingers. Big fat lot of help she was turning out to be. Failing those she cared for once again. Willow's voice filled her head, and she had to backtrack. It wasn't exactly true. Her drawings had brought two women home. That wasn't a small feat, and she certainly wasn't failing.

Tapping the pencil against the blank page she couldn't help wonder why she could draw the women but not the one killing them. At first she hadn't wanted to believe, as Willow did, that one man, one person, was killing these women. The more she thought about it, the more she began to believe that it was one man. In her head, if it was one killer, it had to be a man. She'd never heard of a woman doing something heinous like this, especially to other women. Willow was most likely right about the single killer. The thought of her drawings coming directly from a killer's mind, however, creeped her out. She hoped Willow was wrong on that count.

After sitting at the table for half an hour, she got up and paced around the kitchen while shaking out her arms. She tried to relax and allow herself to open up to whatever the universe might send her way. After a few minutes she sat back down and picked up the pencil again. Still nothing. The more she concentrated, the more her head hurt. This was a futile exercise. Finally, she gave up, put the pencil down, and laid her head on her arms. In the hallway, the grandfather clock she'd inherited from her grandparents chimed four times. Where had the day gone? Why was she failing when it was so important? She owed Eldon and had to do this. She closed her eyes and willed herself to relax.

The next thing she knew, someone was pounding on the front door and yelling. "Liz! Liz!" Attila was barking and jumping at the door, his tail wagging. He recognized the voice, and after a second, so did she.

Liz rushed to the door and didn't pay any attention to the papers that floated to the kitchen floor. Hearing Willow's voice was both a surprise and a great pleasure. It had been hard to try to return her life to what might be considered normal. She hadn't wanted it and hadn't wanted anyone to get close. It occurred to her now that she'd done a complete one-eighty in a really short amount of time. She loved having Willow around and here at the house as much as possible. She felt so much better when she was nearby. To hear her now was fantastic. She was so frustrated by her lack of ability to channel at will, it would be great to have someone to vent to.

"Hi." She opened the door and smiled, expecting to see an answering smile. She didn't. Not even close. "What? Has something else happened?" Her first thought was Eldon. More likely Eloise.

Willow took one of her hands, and she noticed immediately that Willow's were shaking. That was a surprise. Willow's words come out in what sounded like panic. "Where have you been? I've been trying to call you for over an hour, and I know I knocked on your door for at least two full minutes. Attila's been going nuts. I thought…"

What? No way. None of that made any sense. She'd been right there at the kitchen table resting her head on her arms while willing something to happen. She'd have heard the phone ring, and Willow couldn't have been knocking more than thirty seconds before she woke up. It was only when she heard the knocking that she even realized she'd dozed off for a second. "I don't know what you're talking about. I was right here. I didn't hear the phone ring, and I came to the door as soon as I heard you."

A concerned yet puzzled expression crossed Willow's face. "Seriously, Liz. I'm not kidding. I tried you six times by phone, and I've been here for a while knocking on your door. Just ask Attila."

Attila was currently doing circles in front of Willow, and she had to admit he did appear a little frantic. Granted, he liked to circle, a trick she'd taught him when he was a pup. Still, it wasn't like him to spin like a top. He was out of his normal stride. "Okay." She drew out the single word as she watched Attila give up on the circling and trot into the kitchen. "I was trying to draw something, maybe channel Eloise, and nothing was happening. I put my head on my arms and thought if I closed my eyes for a minute or two, then perhaps I'd be able to create a drawing that could help." As she said the last word, the clock in the hallway chimed. What chilled her was that it chimed seven times. Her horror must have shown on her face.

Willow squeezed her hands gently. "What time did you close your eyes?" Her voice was just as gentle, and the tension that had been there earlier was gone.

No way. There was just no freaking way. "Four." The single word came out as a mere whisper.

As if to punctuate the truth that three hours had passed, Attila came back from the kitchen with his stainless bowl in his mouth. He promptly dropped it at her feet, where it rattled against the hardwood floor like a dinner bell. Two hours late and counting. The dog had always been able to tell time, at least when it came to dinner time.

She stared from Attila to the clock to Willow. "This doesn't make sense. I was only asleep a few minutes. I know it. I'd only just closed my eyes when you showed up."

Willow held out her arm, where she wore one of those watches that was also a fitness tracker. It read seven-oh-one. "I got here at five minutes to seven and thought I was going to have to break down the door." The fear returned to her eyes and gave serious weight to her words.

At her feet, Attila nudged the bowl, and it clanged once more against the hardwood. As freaked out was she was, some things couldn't be put off. She leaned down and picked it up. "Come on," she said to Willow. "Let's feed his majesty and then figure out what the hell happened to me." Her words were calm. Her heart was pounding.

As Willow studied her, she appeared satisfied that nothing terrible had happened, and her shoulders eased. "Probably exhaustion, and not just in the last few days."

"What do you mean?" It wasn't like she hadn't rested at all. God knows she'd had time on her hands since opting for retirement. She should feel guilty about leaving as early as she did, but she didn't. It had been the right thing to do for more reasons than just having been shot. The politics got pretty old no matter how nice most of the people were. She missed some of them.

"It took me more than a year to find peace. I thought, like you, that I was healing and resting and putting myself back together. In a way, yes, I was. But it was all superficial. I got enough rest to heal, but I wasn't really rested. Does that make sense?"

Too much, actually. Month after month she'd told herself all was well and she was moving forward. If she'd learned anything in the last few days, it was that it was a big lie. She had used an incredible amount of energy simply going through the motions. No wonder her friends were worried. Now she felt alive for the first time in a really long time, and that included before the attack. She understood what she was able to do was important. Creepy but important.

She stepped through the doorway into the kitchen, intending to give Attila his dinner and stopped so suddenly, Willow bumped into her. The scene was surreal, and what she saw made her legs shake. At the same time, everything fell into place. "I think I know what I was doing the last three hours."

Willow was shocked, yet not, both at the same time. The kitchen table was covered with sheets torn from the artist's pad that was far thinner than it had been when Eldon first brought it. Three sheets lay on the floor, one face up and the other two down. She leaned over and picked up all three. As she touched the sheets of fine paper, her fingers trembled, and the sound of them rattling together echoed in the now-quiet room. It was almost as if they were charged with electricity, and in a strange way she supposed they were. Whatever was flowing through Liz was nothing short of an electrical storm, and it went right from her fingers into the pictures. It was incredible.

The first sheet she looked at had a face that was pretty though not beautiful. Short, dark hair curled around a high forehead, and her eyes were just a touch too close together. She supposed that's what kept her from being really attractive. She was pretty sure if they were to search lost persons in the area, this face would pop up.

The second two drawings were landscapes but showed two different areas. It wasn't like the last couple of instances where Liz seemed to be channeling the dead. Those focused on one person, one location. This sketch was already veering in another direction.

"You don't remember doing any of these?" Willow picked up a fourth drawing from the table, and this one reflected a woman's face, a little older than the others she'd drawn. This woman's eyes radiated intense sadness, and deep lines creased her brow. She obviously had internalized sorrow quite deeply.

Liz held Attila's stainless bowl, now full of kibble, in one hand and with her free hand tapped her fingers on the table. "Not a single one. It's crazy to think I did all this and don't remember. This one worries me." She touched the picture of the woman with the sad eyes that Willow still held.

"Why this one specifically?"

She sighed. "It's Eloise." Then she turned away to set Attila's bowl in the raised feeder on the floor at the end of the counter. He began to attack the food with the enthusiasm of the young dog he was, and for a moment neither of them did anything except watch him eat. After a moment Liz turned to stare at Willow, her eyes full of concern.

Eldon's missing sister. Willow's stomach lurched, and she was pretty sure Liz's did the same. The unspoken thing between them was hanging heavy, and neither wanted to give it voice. So far, Liz was two for two in finding dead women. If these two pictures kept to the pattern, it meant Eldon's sister was now among them.

"Oh, Lord." She stuffed her hands into her pockets and rocked back on her heels. Talk about a feeling of the world spinning out of control.

"That's mild compared to what I'm thinking. Tell me I drew her in that fugue state, or whatever in the hell it was, only because she was on my mind. Tell me that's all it was and that she's not like the other two. Please."

Willow couldn't and didn't. Lying wasn't her strong suit. Truth was. Instead of even trying to come up with something to say, she pulled her hands out of her pockets and spread her arms. Liz didn't hesitate. She walked into her embrace and began to cry. "I'm sorry." She kissed the side of her head. It seemed like the right thing to do. The only thing to do.

"This is fucked up."

Definitely an understatement. "Absolutely."

"Why couldn't it just be women I don't know? Eloise has to be okay. She just has to be. She might be a giant pain in the ass, but she can't be dead. She can't, and I can't show this to Eldon. Oh my God, Eldon. This will kill him."

Willow laid her cheek against Liz's hair. "I don't know why this is happening to you, but it is, and it's important. We also can't hide it from Eldon. That wouldn't be fair to him."

"It's awful, and what if it's like the others?"

"So far two who were lost have been brought home. If Eloise is one of the lost, we have to bring her home too. You know that's what Eldon would want."

"I want Eloise to come home alive."

Liz's tears were gone now, and so Willow held her out at arm's length so she could look into her eyes. "We're not certain anything's happened to her."

"Everything I've drawn so far has led us to a grave. I'm sensing a pattern here. You can't say you don't see it too."

The truth was, she did. She wasn't going to admit it. "Two times doesn't mean it's always the same." She said the words, although she didn't much believe them. Liz's superpower seemed to be uncovering a killer's dirty deeds, and what she was staring at now appeared to indicate that her friend Eloise was a victim as well. But wait. Wasn't that jumping ahead quite a stretch? Two similar incidents did not a pattern make, just as she'd said to Liz. Beginning of one maybe. That's all.

Liz's eyes were haunted. "I don't have a good feeling about this."

Willow kissed the top of her head again and wished she had the courage to kiss more than her hair. "I'd be lying if I told you I don't have a bad feeling too. I do, but just the same, I'm trying to stay optimistic. The one thing we have going for us is that we know you'll be able to help, and that's what we have to focus on right now. Agreed?"

She nodded, though Willow detected hesitation in the movement. "Agreed. I like that. My job is driving the pencil. I hope that's all it is."

"You got this. Why don't you let the big boy out." Attila had finished the kibble Liz had given him and was now pacing in front of the back door. "I'll try to put some order to these." She waved at the papers strewn across the table.

Liz gently petted Attila on the top of the head. "Sounds like a good plan. Come on, chow hound," she said as she opened the door. "Let's get you some fresh air and green grass. Go take care of your dog business."

As Liz was letting Attila out, Willow studied the pages Liz had torn from the pad. It showed, as she kept looking, two distinct scenarios. The one with the younger, dark-haired woman appeared to be a drawing of a hill near the Valley. Wasn't that where one of Yates's victims was discovered? Was this person, whoever he was, emulating the area's most infamous killer? It certainly seemed so, if the pictures Liz had drawn indicated anything.

They'd have to turn them over to Diana and let her sort it out. She wasn't up to another trek with Circe and Zelda. After today, she'd seen enough to last her a lifetime. She didn't know how Circe did it over and over again. Of course, she'd asked her about it once, and she'd said it bothered her more to know a body was out there somewhere in the dark and the cold and not be able to bring it home. Finding a body meant that the person would no longer be lost and alone, and her family could embrace some measure of peace. Willow sort of got that but still couldn't do what Circe and Zelda did with such professionalism. She'd be a basket case in no time.

The second set of drawings, the one related to the woman Liz identified as Eloise, depicted an area she didn't recognize at all. Unlike the others, it wasn't wilderness or an urban area with undeveloped property. It was a house in what appeared to be a lower-middle-class neighborhood. The house was sad, with boarded-up windows and a lawn that had been let go for many years. The edges of the neighboring houses didn't look much better. As she laid the drawings out, side by side, the portrait of a dying neighborhood seemed to develop in greater detail. There was distinct sadness in the work, but it was more than that. Something at the edges made her uneasy, as if behind the sadness suggested a presence that reeked of evil.

With Attila happily running the perimeter of the backyard, Liz came to stand beside her. Surprisingly, she took hold of Willow's hand and their fingers entwined. It was a shock, a good one, and happily, she didn't jump like a scared cat. Instead, she let her fingers tighten a bit just to let her know she was here for her. "Do you recognize this?" Willow tapped the center picture of the house.

Liz shook her head. "Not at all. I wish I could remember drawing them. What was in my head? Why was it in my head? And why would it link to Eloise?"

"Could this be her childhood home?"

Liz gave a snort. "Not even close. Eldon and Eloise came from a prominent Spokane family. They lived on the hill, and their house would swallow this little thing. Let's just say money never was an issue. Still isn't. Eldon works, but he doesn't have to. He's just the kind of guy who makes his own way in the world."

"I got good vibes from him right at the start."

"It's because he is a good guy."

"Did your family have money too? I mean, you've known him since you were kids, right?" It made sense, if Liz, Eldon, and Eloise had grown up together.

Again Liz snorted. "Money? My family? Not even close. I met Eldon and Eloise because we all went to the same private school. For their parents it was no big deal. Everyone in their family went there. For mine, it was a huge financial commitment. They had strong feelings about sending me and my brothers to the best school they could, even if it meant sacrifice. It was a great experience, and I made incredible friends like Eldon and Eloise. Well, mostly Eldon. Trust me, though. Our neighborhood was nowhere close to theirs."

"Well, that doesn't help us much then, does it?"

"Not at all. You know, Eloise wasn't really a snob. Don't get me wrong. She liked her expensive cars and nice clothes. She just didn't have a stick up her butt like a lot of the other rich girls I knew from school." As she said the words she realized how true they were. It was so easy to get caught up in the years and years of her booze-fueled behavior that Liz forgot that sometimes Eloise could still show her gentle, kind side. "On the other hand, I can't see her ever being in a house like this or even having a friend who came from one. She kept to herself pretty much, and the few friends she had mostly lived on the hill." Every family of prominence in the city had lived on the South Hill for over a hundred years and nowhere near the northside neighborhood where her family had lived, still lived. Growing up, they all made jokes about the "South Hill snobs."

"So what exactly is this trying to tell us?"

Liz shook her head. "I don't have a fucking clue."

Willow decided a little diversion might help them clear their heads. Maybe then they could approach these drawings with fresh eyes. "Dinner?"

"What?"

"We'll think better if we have something to eat. I'm going to run over to the Flying Goat, grab a pizza, and then I'll be back. Once we chow down, our minds will be firing on all cylinders, and we'll figure this out."

At first Liz shook her head but then stopped. She put a hand to her stomach and smiled. "You know what? I am kind of hungry. You grab the pizza, and I'll open a bottle of wine."

Willow bumped fists with her and headed out the door. "Be back in a few."

CHAPTER TWENTY-FOUR

Meg's hands cupped his face, and she stared into his eyes as she leaned through the open car window. He'd followed her from Liz's house to hers and now sat in her driveway bone weary and frantic. Even on his worst days, he couldn't remember feeling like this.

"You go home, go directly inside your house, and sleep for at least an hour," she said. "You hear me? I don't want any argument."

"I don't think I can." Eldon was so wired he wondered if he'd be able to sleep anytime in the next week. Or month. Or year.

"If you want me to show up there with food, you will do as I say." Her voice softened. "Please."

With those eyes and her intoxicating scent, how could he argue? "I'll try." Big words he didn't think would help. Until they could find Eloise, he doubted he'd be able to close his eyes. In terms of finding out where Eloise was, the afternoon had proved to be as uneventful as the morning. It was as if she had simply vanished, and that wasn't like her at all. She was a little like a tornado, leaving a path of destruction behind her, only right now they couldn't find so much as a breadcrumb to tell them where she'd gone. He closed his eyes and sighed.

Meg kissed him. Not like a pal either. No, her kiss was firm and meaningful, and he could hardly believe this was happening. After all his pining for her, what he desired most was coming true. He wished he could enjoy it more.

If his lack of enthusiasm bothered her, she didn't let on. "I'll be there in an hour, give or take, and we'll eat. Maybe by then Jason will have heard from Eloise, and she'll be safe and sound at home."

"I hope so." He said the words. He didn't believe them. The little voice in the back of his head was telling him it was too late, but he tried hard to ignore it.

"Sleep," she reminded him as she pressed her lips once more against his. Then she spun and headed toward her house without looking back at him. Fortunately he didn't live that far away because he was used up. All he wanted to do was get home and hope he woke up to find this all a bad dream. At the house, he pulled into the garage and went in through the back door, thinking about both Meg's kiss and her command.

Sleep, sure. Eldon plopped down into a soft chair and leaned his head back. Thoughts whirled. Even with the chaos that had defined his early years, the last twenty-four hours were the worst of his life. So many times he'd wished Eloise would vanish so he didn't have to put up with her dysfunction. So he could have a normal life like everybody else. Now that she had, he would take back every single one of those wishes. He wanted his sister back, broken as she was.

To appease Meg, he attempted to close his eyes and sleep. Sure, his eyes would close. His mind, however, refused to slow down. A thousand thoughts zinged through it, all the *what ifs*. One caught, and he wondered if it was possible she'd called a friend. Not that she had that many left or, if Jason was to be believed, none left. But he believed at least a few had stood by her as they had through the worst days, and maybe she'd phoned one of them. Maybe she was with them now. Then he thought of Kristy again and knew he was pinning his hopes on a fantasy. If Kristy had bailed on Eloise, she'd burned all her bridges.

Even if her friends did still have her back, the logic was flawed. He was pretty certain they would have let him know she was there. He tossed the doubts aside and decided to make a few calls. His first one, to Kristy, went nowhere. No one was home, and only the voicemail picked up.

His second call was answered on the second ring. "Roberta!" Geez. Didn't he sound cool and collected? Not even a tiny bit.

"Eldon. What's wrong?" The concern in her voice made him feel better, as if he wasn't alone anymore. Jason had to be mistaken. She still had friends. This call proved it. "What's happened?"

He could picture Roberta, who'd been their buddy since they all started a karate class when they were ten years old. The three of them had become tight, given they were the youngest in the class. Roberta lived on the opposite side of town and went to public school, but that didn't make a difference to any of them. They became lifelong friends despite their differences.

"Has Eloise called you?"

"No. I haven't talked to her in a long time. Why? What's she done?"

So maybe Jason wasn't wrong. Roberta knew Eloise as well as anyone. Sometimes she would get frustrated with her, and the two wouldn't talk for months. Then it would pass and they would chat weekly. Apparently that pattern had changed. "She's missing."

"Say that again."

"Yeah, she's missing. We found her car and her purse at the golf course."

"Oh dear, that's awful. Eldon, I'm not that far away and was just headed home. Tell you what. I'm going to swing by the house, and you're going to tell me what the hell is going on. If I can do anything to help, you know I will. I love you guys."

The relief he felt at her words was huge. "You know the way."

"I'll be there in ten."

He thought about calling June and discarded the idea as soon as it occurred to him. He could barely shake her as it was, and if he reached out to her, regardless of how well she was versed on Eloise's routines, he'd never get rid of her. No, he was going pin his hopes on Roberta. She would be able to help.

Divine inspiration was the only thing that could explain how and why the Jaguar was only two blocks away from Eldon Spicer's house. It made it so damn easy to pay a visit. The plan had come together like a child's jigsaw puzzle with those easy-to-fit giant pieces, and not a single one was missing. It was so simple it was amazing it had taken this long to pull it together. Now that it was clear, it was go time, and that was incredibly exciting.

Just the few minutes it took to drive the short distance made her blood roar. It suddenly felt like everything she'd gone through before had been leading up to this major confrontation. Perhaps it was the embarrassment of birthright that she'd needed to wipe clean from the earth, and each of the special ones before was simply the practice she needed to reach the peak. The process resembled the sketches an artist made before he embarked upon his greatest painting.

Yes, that sounded right. This was the masterpiece that would cement a reputation of power and might. No one was as skilled as the Jaguar. No one had eluded detection like the Jaguar. No one had caught even a whiff of connection between those that came before, and they wouldn't now. She was a champion by design, even if birth had tried to rob her of it.

Eldon was sitting on the front steps of his house and looked surprised as she pulled into the driveway. "Hey," he said with little enthusiasm in his voice. Obvious fatigue had made his normally handsome features sad, and his skin had a sickly gray cast to it. This man hadn't slept recently. No biggie. Sleep would be the last thing he'd need to worry about from now on.

It wasn't hard for her to put on a concerned expression. Years of working behind a façade made it easy. It was like changing clothes. Need to be sad. Check. Need to be happy. Check. Need to be a concerned friend. Check.

"Has Eloise called?" Oh yes, just the right note of anxiousness.

"No. Nothing from Jason or the police either."

"Come on. I have a strong hunch I know where to find her. She's done this before."

His head snapped up. "What? You do? What do you mean, she's done this before? She's never disappeared like this that I'm aware of. We've tried everywhere we know to look. Called everyone and came up with nothing. You know where she is? Let's go. What are we waiting for?"

The hope in his voice almost made her laugh. He was in for such a surprise. "Look, it's been a while since I've seen her, and that's my bad. Still, I'm confident I know where she'd go if she didn't want anyone to find her. It's somewhere we used to go when we were kids, and I'll bet you anything that's where she is now."

"Where?" His voice rose, and he stood up from the step. "Where?"

"Just get in the car, and I'll take you there."

He didn't hesitate and began to head to her car, pulling his cell phone out of his pocket as he moved. "I should let everyone know."

"Who's everyone?"

For this to work, he needed to be isolated. "Liz. I'm sure you met her somewhere along the line. She's trying to help track down Eloise too."

The picture lady. Had to be. "Don't think so. Look. You can contact this Liz later. Let's get to Eloise and then make whatever calls you need to."

"Meg and Willow…"

It had to be the rest of the little posse, and they were absolutely not needed right now. "Eldon, do you want to find your sister or not? Put the phone away and let's get on the road. That thing can wait until we've got her safe and sound."

He didn't move to finish punching in the number. He also didn't put the cell back into his pocket. Sometimes he could be such a brat. He had to get into the car, and it would be much easier if he did it of his own free will. His hesitation was frustrating, and anger tried to push the mask of concern off the Jaguar's face. It took effort, but the mask stayed in place. She was that good.

"Absolutely. I want to find her." He finally shoved the cell back into his pocket and went around the car to get into the passenger's seat. Good boy. The easy way was much…well, easier.

Without giving him a second to reconsider, she was backing out of the driveway and zipping down the street. She worked hard not to smile.

"Where is Eloise? Where are we going?"

Hell. But the Jaguar didn't say it out loud. That little surprise could wait until later.

CHAPTER TWENTY-FIVE

The knock on the door surprised Liz until she realized she'd locked the front door when Willow left. Seemed like it was a quick trip, but then again, maybe the restaurant had a pizza ready that someone hadn't picked up. Once before she'd stopped by to grab one and that's what happened. She'd gotten the wonderful pie for half the cost. That was probably what was going on now. Attila would normally go with her to the door, only he was still out back, and she sure didn't need him to protect her from Willow. She paused in the kitchen doorway, staring down the hallway to the front door. She hadn't opened that door without him at her side since the day she'd brought him home. Things really were getting better.

As she walked down the hallway she smiled, thinking she might yet need protection from Willow, only not the physical-violence kind. That was really her own problem and not something Attila could help her with. He was on physical-threat detail, and this was more emotional. He could guard her body, but he couldn't do much for her heart. It had been so long since her heart had been touched that the thought was actually pretty exciting.

She was still smiling when she unlocked the door and swung it wide. The smile faded quickly as she stared into the eyes of a stranger. Suddenly, her nerves buzzed, and the hairs on the back of her neck stood up. Great anticipation morphed into instant warning. Something wasn't right here, and she hit on that fact immediately. She started to push the door shut.

"I don't think so." The force that shoved the door back open was far more than she was expecting.

Liz stumbled backward and tripped on her own feet. She was falling before she had a chance to do anything, including scream. The next thing she knew she was on her back, and the stranger was on top of her. Before her vision went black, she heard, "Sweet dreams, little Lizzy. Buckle up for a little one-way trip."

The next time she opened her eyes, the darkness hadn't abated. She was disoriented, and it took her minute to realize her eyes were, in fact, open, but the room was shrouded in complete darkness. And it smelled old and musty, with something else in the air she couldn't quite put a finger on. Nasty was the word that kept rolling through her mind.

Her hands and feet were bound, too, while a gag prevented her from screaming. She tried, but it didn't work, as the gag cut off any meaningful sound. The restraints on her wrists were uncomfortable, and while she struggled to loosen them it was clear pretty quickly that she was screwed. Then, she realized why. They were thick, plastic, zip ties. Oh hell, no. She'd already been way too close to the bright light. She was not going back there.

This was the first time she'd realized exactly how far she'd come in the last few days. She'd had moments, many moments, when she hadn't wanted to deal with the aftermath of the shooting. Not the pain. Not the recovery. Not the emotion. The depression had been so deep and dark, she hadn't been certain she'd ever find a way out. But she wasn't just a few steps beyond that now. She was about a mile past. Nothing like another traumatic incident to put it all in perspective.

Well, that and a beautiful woman who made her blood pound.

With the pressing darkness and the immobilizing restraints terrifying her, she stifled the scream that still wanted to burst forth. Think. Think. Think. Then a thought occurred to her, and she began to push herself around as best she could, trying to find a doorway, a wall, or anything that she could use to shove the gag from her face. She was scooting pretty well while trying not to think about what she might be moving through, when she bumped into something soft. Instinctively she recoiled and then slowly moved until she touched it again. This time it took only a second to realize that soft something was a body. This time she couldn't stifle the scream, and it came out like a strangled moan. It took every ounce of effort not to hyperventilate.

Please oh please do not let it be a dead body. Her silent plea was answered. The body on the floor not only moaned, but it moved as well. Not dead. Thank God. The thought of being here in the dark with a dead body was more than she could handle. She wasn't that healed yet. Once more she began to move, this time faster. She had to get this damned gag off her face before she lost it completely. She bumped into a wall. A solid wall. Damn it.

She wanted to cry, and then it occurred to her that if there was a wall, there had to be a door, right? If she continued to move along the wall, ultimately she would find a doorway, and praise the gods, she did. After what seemed like hours, she was able to use the edge of the doorway to push the gag away from her mouth. Air filled her lungs, and she gulped, trying to stop the tears that streamed down her face. They were a mixture of relief and pain. The way she had to scrape her face against the doorframe, she was sure her cheeks looked like hamburger, not that she cared. The fact that the awful thing was off made it all worthwhile. Scars be damned.

"Hello?" She said at the same time she began to try to use the same technique to free her hands. She didn't really think it would work. It didn't. "Hello," she said again. "Can you hear me?"

A grunt over to her right made her turn. Finally her eyes had begun to adjust to the darkness, and she could just barely make out a big shape lying on its side. A man. She scooted over. "Are you okay?"

Kind of a stupid question, considering he remained right there. If he was okay, wouldn't he be trying to do the same thing she'd just accomplished? He groaned again, and something in the sound made her squint and move more quickly in his direction.

"Eldon? Is that you?" A sick feeling washed over her.

This time the groan was more of an attempt to speak. Oh, dear God, it *was* Eldon. She was close enough now to be able to make him out. She knew that body, that shirt, those pants. She'd seen them only a few hours ago. Or at least she thought it was just a few hours ago.

"What the hell is going on here?" She got herself turned around so her back was to his head, which put her in a position to feel the knot in the gag tied around his head. It was much quicker this time, even though she couldn't see what she was doing. She untied the knot, and the gag fell away. He coughed and didn't sound all that great. The woman who'd attacked her back at the house had put some kind of rag over her mouth and nose, which had knocked her out completely. Had the same thing happened to Eldon? How she hoped he was going to be okay. But why would some random woman attack either one of them? The world was going crazy.

"Are you all right?" he asked her, once he'd stopped coughing. Leave it to Eldon to dismiss his own problems and focus on someone else.

"I'm a little woozy from whatever that crap was in the rag the bitch put on my face. Beyond that, yeah, I think I'm fine. What about you?"

"I'm pretty sick to my stomach, and my head hurts like the dickens. And I'm not sure my knee isn't broken."

"How?" What had that woman done to him?

"I honestly don't know, but if I had to guess, I was dropped like a bag of hot rocks on my knees. One of them took the fall well, and one of them didn't. It feels like a million hot pokers are going through it."

She flashed back on the face at her door. Not a flicker of recognition. "Who did this? Why?"

His next words chilled her. "Why, I don't have a clue, but I do know who." He coughed again and then threw up.

The pizza Willow had brought back to Liz's house was ice cold and forgotten. Panic so strong she could hardly breathe had filled her when she first got back and found not only an empty house but a barking Attila locked outside. Liz wouldn't have left knowing that she was coming back, and while leaving Attila at the house if she went to run errands wasn't unusual, his behavior was. Something was off, and the dog knew it just as much as she did.

Her hands had been shaking when she'd called Circe and Diana. They were probably getting really tired of hearing from her, but none of that mattered with Liz missing. Her gut feeling was telling her something very bad had happened in the short time she was away. She'd called Meg and was waiting for her and Eldon to get here too. In her mind there was power in numbers. She was pacing in front of the picture window and staring at the street, hoping to see a familiar face, when her cell rang. She hoped it was Liz. It wasn't.

"He's not answering his phone." Meg sounded on the edge of hysteria. She got that.

"He'll call you back." Maybe he was already on his way here. After all, the four of them had become a pack of sorts, and it wouldn't surprise her to see him pull up in the driveway, knowing he was needed even if no one had talked to him.

"No. You don't understand. I've been calling him for hours, and he hasn't picked up once. It goes directly to voicemail. Earlier I convinced myself he was taking my advice and getting some sleep. I told him I'm bringing food over after he'd rested. I've called and called, and I even drove over to his house. He's not picking up, and no one answered the door. I was concerned before you called. Now with Liz missing too, this is scaring the daylights out of me."

The bad feeling in the pit of her stomach ratcheted up. What in the world was going on? "I think you should keep trying, but come on over to Liz's house."

"I'm already in the car."

"Great. Get here as quick as you can."

She was putting the phone back into her pocket as Diana and Circe pulled up in the driveway. The cavalry had arrived, and she'd never been more grateful to see her friends. They would find out where Liz was. After all, that's what Diana did, and she was good at her job.

"Any word?" Circe asked when Willow flung open the door. Diana was a mere step behind her.

"Nothing, and it gets worse." Yes, it was her voice that sounded high and scared.

Diana's eye narrowed. "What do you mean worse? What have you heard?"

"Eldon appears to be missing too." Might as well be blunt.

"Could they be together?" Diana sounded like the professional she was. Calm and focused.

For a couple of seconds she thought about it. It wouldn't be out of the realm of possibility for Eldon to have come over here. Even if that was true, she didn't believe either of them would have left knowing she was on her way back to the house. Not given everything that had happened and not given the drawings. The drawings…why hadn't she looked at them? She spun around without another word and raced to the kitchen. They'd been on the table when she left to go get the pizza.

"What's wrong?" Circe sounded concerned as she followed Willow back to the kitchen.

"The drawings," she said over her shoulder. She stopped in the kitchen doorway and stared. The table was clear except for several pencils and the open pad with a blank page showing. "They were all right there when I left. Right there." She pointed to the table.

"The drawings?" Diana had a hand on her shoulder.

Willow nodded. "Like I told you when I called, she drew two distinct scenes this time. Two women, two scenes."

"Did one of them include a house?"

She had been incredibly frantic when she'd called yet didn't remember telling them what was in any of the drawings, only that Liz had done it again, and she was pretty sure some additional mysterious disappearances were about to be cleared up. "Yes, but how…" She turned to see Circe holding the drawing of the house in her hand. "Where did you find that?"

"On the floor."

"The floor?" Obviously she wasn't firing on all cylinders because it wasn't connecting for her.

Circe must have noticed her frantic confusion. "My best guess, it must have slipped out of the stack, and Liz, or whoever grabbed the other drawings, didn't notice it was dropped."

That hit the mark. Thank God for small favors. It was something, except she didn't really know what that something was. The drawing of the house didn't tell them much. Not like the other drawings that were clear images of faces. With those they would have a much better idea of somewhere to start. Or maybe not. She was assuming the drawings had something to do with Liz's MIA status. Her mind told her they did, or why else would they be gone along with Liz?

What if this drawing had nothing to with anything? She had to stop thinking in terms of *what if.* She'd spent months doing that after the shooting. *What if she'd driven to work that day instead of walking? What if she'd left the house ten minutes earlier or later? What if, what if, what if.* A person could go insane thinking that way.

Like what if she hadn't left to go get pizza?

Stop it. Focus. Right. She was going to make the choice to believe that the drawing was important and that some higher power made sure they had it with them. She might be delusional, yet she didn't care. If she could dream about fire and save her brother, then a drawing of a house could, no, would lead them to Liz. Hopefully, Eldon too.

"Does this mean anything to you?" Diana was holding the picture now and staring at it intently, as if willing it to spill its secrets.

It was a house. A compact rancher that looked worn out and neglected. It was any one of a thousand houses just like it all over the city. "Not a thing." Frustration was beginning to edge out panic.

"Okay. Let's think about this." Diana continued to study the picture. "There's got to be something in here that can help us."

What she wouldn't give to channel that touch of ESP that had graced her during her own recovery. When she needed it, nothing happened. Just her luck.

A knock on the front door drew her attention away from her own lack of skills. Maybe it was Liz…only that was dumb. She wouldn't be knocking on her own front door. She was right. It wasn't Liz or Eldon. Instead, it was a haggard-looking Meg.

Though the answer was clearly written all over her face, she asked anyway. "No word from Eldon?"

Meg shook her head, tears pooling in her eyes. "Nothing. Still going directly to voicemail."

"How do you know there's a problem just because he's not picking up? Maybe he's sleeping?"

She shook her head. "The front door was unlocked. I went in. Nobody home. Car in the garage, keys on the table. No Eldon. What are we going to do? We have to find them."

"Come on," Willow said. "Circe and Diana are here." She led Meg back to the kitchen.

"This look familiar to you?" Diana held out the drawing for Meg to see.

Meg started to shake her head and then stopped. "It doesn't belong to anyone I know."

"I hear a *but* in there." Diana was studying her face intently.

"No, it's not like that. Don't you see it?" She tapped the lower left-hand corner of the drawing.

Now Willow's attention laser-focused on the drawing. She'd missed it before, but as she looked more closely, two things struck her like a stinging slap across the face. The first was a car that, given the look of the house and the neighborhood, was out of place. A sleek, late-model Mercedes. Second was the license plate. A clearly visible license plate.

The big show needed a nice, dark night for maximum effect. The weather gods appeared to be working with the Jaguar, as clouds were moving in quickly and blocking the stars and the moon. It was turning into one of those deep, cloud-cloaked nights where people tended to stay inside. Perfect for the evening's plans.

It was amazing how easy it had been to get them both to the house. Eldon should have been harder. After all, he was a big, strong guy who was smart as hell. Funny how this was the day he chose to be stupid. Or perhaps fitting this should be the day he chose to be dim. His lapse was going to cost him everything. First his sister and now him. Oh, how the mighty fall. It was a joy to be here to see it.

This had been so easy it was laughable. People who lived alone, especially women, should have been more cautious when opening the front door. It was a little disappointing to have it that simple. No telling who could be standing on the other side. She wasn't careful and it was her bad. The Jaguar smiled. Like with Eldon, the cost would be very high indeed.

And like with Eloise, this adventure deviated from the norm. She'd done the planning on the fly instead of carefully, over weeks and months. If this had happened early on, she couldn't have possibly pulled it off. Now, with so many years of experience, she found it relatively effortless and actually very exciting.

With the two of them tucked safely away, it was time to gather the tools she needed to pull off a spectacular show. It would have been a simple matter just to kill them, but hey. Where would the fun be in that? This way, they'd have to sit there and watch each other die slowly. Now that floated the Jaguar's boat.

The drawings that stupid Liz had done lay on the passenger seat of the Mercedes, and they were a big fucking problem. How the hell did she know these things? Not just the precious little blonde she'd been so taken with the first time she laid eyes on her, but she'd sketched Eloise as well. She hadn't been in the ground twenty-four hours, and the bitch was drawing her face. The complications that could cause her were too many to enumerate. She had to be stopped and stopped now. She might have spared Eldon had he not been tied at the hip to Liz. She was the trouble-maker, and Eldon was her sidekick. He'd made a poor choice…just like his sister.

What was about to happen, thanks to the two five-gallon containers of gasoline in the back of her car, was in some ways sad. The house represented everything that had made the Jaguar an exceptional predator and had been the breeding ground for what became a life's incredible work. After tonight, all of it would change. The secret that had been concealed beneath the patio would more than likely be revealed after so many years. The charred bodies that would be discovered inside the burned-out shell might take some time to identify. It just wouldn't take that long. It wouldn't be a problem, for the time it would take to make the identification was all she needed to get away and start act two in a country far away.

All the pieces were in place for the moment it was time to disappear and had been for years. She'd known this day would ultimately come, and to protect herself, she'd have to leave. It had come at last. That didn't mean she'd failed at her life's work, only that it must change. It was the most exciting part of tonight's adventure. Well, besides the flames that would consume the two waiting back at the house. That was going to be seriously enjoyable as well. It was the freedom that waited on the other side of the flames that was most thrilling. A new identity, new hunting grounds, and best of all, no anchors hanging from her feet. True and complete freedom for the first time in her life.

It was dark by the time the Jaguar pulled into the alley. Not directly behind the house. That would never do. Instead, she parked the SUV down the block. She didn't bother to hide the car like she'd always done in the past. Even if someone noticed the beautiful Mercedes and reported it, by the time anyone did that, she'd be long gone.

The gas cans were heavy, but it was a pain that was almost pleasurable, considering what was to happen next. The first chore was to pour a nice trail of gas around the outside of the house to create a beautiful ring of fire. The Jaguar picked up the first can and made a complete wet circle around the building. With no lights on the exterior of the house and the nearest streetlight out, it was easy to move undetected in the darkness. In this neighborhood, few paid attention anyway.

At the back door, the Jaguar paused. What was it? Voices? Putting an ear to the door, she heard the sounds more clearly, and anger surged. It was that damn woman. How in the world did she get the gag off? Her first impulse was to race in and knock her on her ass before putting her hands around her neck and choking the life right out of her. She'd caused her enough problems. It was past time to put her down. Then good sense kicked in, and the Jaguar paused to listen closer to what was being said. What she heard brought a smile. They were making plans about what to do when their captor returned. From the sounds of their conversation, at least the zip ties used to bind their hands and feet were still in place. Good.

The Jaguar moved the second can of gas to the back door and quietly set it down. It would be useful in a couple of minutes. First things first, however. Silently, she opened the back door and slipped inside, careful not to make a sound.

CHAPTER TWENTY-SIX

L iz struggled so much against the zip tie binding her wrists that she could feel the warm blood dripping from the cuts and running down her hands. Despite her best efforts, it was a useless endeavor. She couldn't break the ties and couldn't find anything sharp enough to cut them. All she was doing was breaking through tender skin in a painful, bloody way. Someone had thought this through in minute detail.

"Stop," Eldon said, and he sounded incredibly tired. "You'll just end up hurting yourself." Apparently he was a mind reader. Either that or he could smell the blood running down into her palms.

"We can't just sit here." This wasn't anything like what had happened to her before. She'd been blindsided by that gunshot and had absolutely no control over a single thing that happened from that moment on. She'd been walking across the courtyard minding her own business, and then boom, out like a light with no recollection of what occurred. Right now, she was alert, thinking, and determined. It made a huge fucking difference. She was absolutely not going to be a victim again. No way. No how.

"I don't know what we can do."

The despair in his voice broke her heart. He wasn't the kind of guy who gave up. To hear resignation in his words was crushing.

"We can get out of here before she comes back. You're sure it's your friend?" When he'd explained that his childhood friend, Roberta, an airline pilot with an incredible career and a great family, was the one behind all this, she hadn't believed him. Women like that didn't do things like this, especially a woman who had so much going for her. Did they? After all, here she was tied up and feeling like a lamb awaiting the slaughter. Maybe they did.

"Yeah, it's Roberta all right. Don't you remember her? Eloise and I were in the same dojo with her for years. She was one determined girl, and she seemed to have turned into an incredibly accomplished woman. I always thought it was so cool how she'd raised herself up to become a commercial airline pilot. I mean that's a big deal. She has a husband, some kids, and a beautiful home. On the outside, she has it all. Like I said, a very accomplished woman."

"Who drugs you, drags you to this piece of crap house, and dumps you?"

"Well, except for that part. I guess we all missed the psychopathic aspect of her personality."

"And what did I do to deserve this? Taking me seems about as random as that asshole who shot me. Was I in the wrong place at the wrong time again? I'm way over being scared. I've just crossed the line into pissed off and kicking ass."

As she said it, a brilliant flash of light hit her square in the eyes right before a shoe connected with her face. Pain exploded, and she tipped over backward, her head striking the floor so hard she was seeing stars.

"No, you stupid bitch. You were in the right place at the right time and precisely where I want you to be. You sure as hell won't be kicking my ass." Her laugh was wicked.

"Roberta?"

"Yes, Eldon." Her voice took on a mocking tone. "It's Roberta, you stupid shit."

"Why?"

"Why?" She mimicked. "Why? Now you sound just like your sister before I put an ice pick into her brain."

Liz sat up and nearly vomited both from the pain of the blow and from Roberta's cold admission of murder. She managed to keep it together even as she tried not to picture what this crazy woman said she did to Eloise. "You killed her."

"Duh," she said. "What part of ice pick to the brain are you having trouble with?"

"You're crazy."

"Maybe, but it's really your fault, you know."

Liz wasn't sure if she was directing her accusation at her or Eldon. After all, she didn't know her and vaguely remembered meeting her eons ago, when they were maybe fifteen. That being the case, how could she be responsible for causing Eloise's death? "I don't know what you mean."

"It's pretty obvious, you idiot. You just couldn't leave well enough alone. You had to do these." She threw the drawings that had been on the kitchen table at Liz's feet, or at least she assumed that's what they were since she really couldn't see a thing with the light shining right in her eyes. She heard them as they fluttered to the dirty floor, causing dust to fly up into her face. As it filled her nose and throat, she coughed.

When the coughing passed, she asked, "My drawings?" She wasn't sure if the kick to the head was making it hard to connect the dots.

"God, how stupid are you? Yes, the drawings." The mocking tone was back in her voice. "My life's work, and you were destroying it all. You didn't give me any choice. I had to stop you before you ruined everything."

"I don't..." And then she did. The women's faces that had come to light under her pencil and whose lives had been stolen. Roberta was responsible for taking their futures away from them. All of them. "Why would you kill those women?"

The laughter that filled the room was as dark as the interior and twice as cold. "Why not? It was fun, and they were stupid little cunts."

"You killed Eloise, and she was your friend." Eldon's voice resonated with deep sorrow.

"She was the biggest cunt of them all. She had everything I never did. Money, love, family. She was so stupid, and she threw it all away. I would have ruled the world if I'd started out with the things she had."

"Our family wasn't that great."

Again she laughed. "That might be true, Eldon, but the money makes up for it. Try living in a piece of shit like this and having to deal with a drugged-out, alcoholic mother who liked to wake you up in the middle of the night with a kick to the gut. How about that for a way to start out in the world?"

"I'm sorry," Eldon said. "I didn't know."

"You didn't know. Why not be honest, you asshole? You didn't care enough to find out, now did you? Neither you nor your precious drunk sister. You always said you were a friend, but that was all talk. You didn't care about me or people like me."

"That's not fair. We were your friends, and look at you. You've done well with your life."

"Oh yes, indeed I have. None of it would have been possible without my little side game, and it was going great until you started meddling. It was the only thing that kept me from going insane." She landed another kick in Liz's side.

"You are insane," Liz managed to gasp. "And our friends will find us."

"You think that, do you? Well, truthfully, I'm sure they will, and that's all part of the grand plan. You don't realize how good I am at this or how well I plan things. They will find you. But they'll be identifying your charred corpses, dumbass. I'm going for a new twist on an old game. Now," she said as she moved over to Liz, "I've listened to enough of your crap." She put the gag back into her mouth and then dragged her by her feet to the middle of the room. She did the same to Eldon. "Time to say fare thee well." She laughed heartily and walked out of the room, taking the beam of light with her.

In less than a minute she was back and moving around the room. At first Liz wasn't sure why she was there or what she was doing. Then the acrid smell of gas hit her nose, and behind the gag she began to scream.

Willow felt like someone had just kicked her in the stomach. Her breath whooshed out and her knees buckled. She'd have fallen to the floor, except that Meg caught her. "Oh my God," she muttered. Her whole body shook, and pain like she hadn't experienced since the gunshot assailed her. It was hot and intense.

"I feel it too." Tears were flowing down Meg's face, and her eyes were full of fear.

"It was like someone kicked me." She was recovering her breath, although the pain still lingered. It really did feel as though someone had landed a hard kick to her kidney.

"It's not like that for me. I know something terrible is happening to Liz and Eldon because I feel it right here." Meg patted her heart. "My heart is pounding, and a knot just dropped like a rock in the middle of my stomach."

Willow was steady on her feet again, her mind whirling. She felt much like Meg was describing. "Someone just hurt Liz. I know it, and that means we don't have much time left. We've got to find them right now."

Meg wiped the tears from her eyes. "I know. I know. What are we going to do? I feel so helpless. I don't even know where to start."

Helplessness was exactly the emotion assailing her too, but she refused to say it out loud. If she didn't admit it, it wasn't true. That was her story and she was sticking to it. Pain still radiated through her body, and she had every intention of pushing past it. Oh, hell. It didn't matter whether she said it out loud or not. Liz was in trouble, and she was feeling whatever it was she was going through. It was amazing and as frightening as anything she'd ever experienced. She'd known from the first hello that they had some kind of amazing connection, and it had just been confirmed in no uncertain terms.

"Diana, anything?" Diana had been on the phone since Meg had pointed out the car and the license plate. Diana held up a finger. She said a few more words and then ended her call. She slipped the phone back into the holder at her waist and turned to them.

"All I can say is thank the heavens for the nerds in this world. Without them, the rest of us would be screwed."

"You've got something?" Willow held her side where another sharp pain shot through her. Another blow had landed. *Please let her have something, and quickly.*

"I don't know, but it's all we've got, so I'm going with it."

"Spill it." That was the most forceful Meg had sounded since this whole thing began. The fear in her voice echoed what Willow felt flowing through her entire body. "I don't think we've got much time. Scratch that. I know we don't have much time left."

Circe looked at her closely. "What do you mean?"

She shook her head. "I can't explain it, but it's like I'm connecting with Liz, and some big-ass clock is ticking in the background. It's just about to strike midnight. If we don't track them down soon, it'll be too late. They'll die."

"Is it like with your brother?" Circe knew the story about the visions and the fire.

She started to say no, and then it hit her like a brick to the head. She crumpled to her knees and her vision went black, but only for a moment. Then, just as it had all those years before, the vision in front of her eyes morphed from complete darkness to dancing flames. She could feel the intense heat as it scorched her skin. Willow screamed before she blacked out completely.

She opened her eyes to the concerned faces of Meg, Circe, and Diana. "What happened?" Circe held a damp washcloth to her forehead. Willow pushed it away and sat up with no lingering effects from the crash. Or any that she could feel. Adrenaline had a way of doing that.

"We've got to go, now. Liz and Eldon are together, and they're running out of time. What do you have, Diana? It sure as hell better be something." She pushed to her feet, and everyone followed suit. "Seriously, I'm not kidding. We have to find them like an hour ago."

Nobody was arguing, and she sensed they all felt the same urgency. "Okay," Diana said. They all gathered around her. "Here's what my research guru and favorite nerd uncovered for us."

CHAPTER TWENTY-SEVEN

Eldon didn't pray, and he didn't possess a single psychic bone in his body. Nonetheless, he was praying like a son of a bitch and sending out every vibe he could into the universe, hoping against hope that his entreaty would be answered. If his budding relationship with Meg was worth anything, he hoped to hell it would link them together now. He really, really wanted to see her one more time. And if he did, he was going to plant the biggest kiss he could right smack on her lips.

He wasn't relying solely on prayers and universal energy. No, he was also using good old Boy Scout ingenuity in the form of a piece of broken glass. It was in his hand, and though it was incredibly painful, he had been silently working on the plastic zip tie that bound his wrists together. Blood dripped from the cuts in his fingers, and he was sure they'd require numerous stitches when they got out of here. *If* they got out. Stitches he could deal with. Dying he would prefer not to.

No. He refused to think that way. They would get out, and Roberta would find herself in jail for the rest of her life. That's how it was going to happen. Period. He sped up the pace on the zip ties, ignoring the pain and the warm blood.

His heart was heavy now that he understood why Eloise hadn't picked up on any of the calls he and Jason had made to her cell phone. He'd always hoped she would one day find the strength deep down in her soul to move past her demons and live the life waiting for her. She'd considered herself a weak person. He and Jason, probably, were the minority that recognized she wasn't. In time, perhaps she would have discovered her own inner power. Now that would never happen. He'd let her down. He hadn't protected her.

Protected her from a friend. That part hurt worse than the glass cutting into the fine nerves in his fingers. The cuts on his hands would heal. He doubted the deep slashes in his heart ever would. Roberta had betrayed him and his sister, and he just didn't know how to deal with that kind of treachery. Then again, if he didn't get the plastic zip tie cut off his wrists, he wouldn't have to worry about it. He clearly understood now that Roberta was ruthless and evil. She had coldly killed Eloise and intended to do the same to him and Liz.

He couldn't see her face because she used her flashlight to focus mostly on Liz and to check, it seemed, to make sure the gasoline was distributed all around the room for maximum effectiveness. She most definitely did have a plan, and it involved a great conflagration.

While he might not be able to see her face, he could, however, hear the venom in her voice. She had to be an incredible actress, because the person preparing to take two lives was pure evil. How many others had died at her hand?

"Okay, boys and girls. I'm going to take the gags off, and you know why? Of course you don't. Well, I'll tell you. I want to hear you scream when the flames catch your clothes and your hair. I want to hear how you suffer. You, my dear Eldon, never bothered to listen to my pain, but never fear. I'll listen to yours." She laughed as she yanked the gag first from his mouth and then from Liz's. They both gulped in air as she walked back toward the door, coughing hard as they inhaled the noxious gasoline fumes. If he did survive this, his throat would most likely be scarred.

"What happened to your mother?"

She stopped and turned, the beam of the flashlight making a swath through the darkness. It stopped on his face, blinding him. He shouldn't have said anything, because when she swung the light into his face, he was forced to still his hands. Suddenly he figured out what had happened to the haggard-looking woman who had dropped off and picked up a spunky Roberta every Saturday morning at their dojo. Of course, he'd always thought she was a tired, working, single mother. Looking back and knowing what he did now, he realized it was far more than just that. It wasn't solely weariness that made her face pale and lined. No, now he truly understood that madness, drugs, and alcohol had transformed her into the woman Roberta hated so intensely. The woman she was more like than she would ever admit.

Her laugh was ugly and shook her body, making the flashlight bob. "Why, she's still right here with us. If the sun was shining, I could drag your sorry asses out to the patio, and we could have a little chat with the old bitch."

"You killed her."

"Of course I killed her, you buffoon. She was a horrible person and deserved to die long before I bashed her head in with her favorite frying pan. You should have heard the crunch. God, it was magnificent."

"You're crazy." The light moved swiftly back to Liz's face.

"Shut up, you ugly cunt. I'm not the crazy one. She was. You don't have any idea what went on inside these walls. She made my life pure agony. I simply rewarded her with a one-way ticket to hell, complete with her half-full bottle of vodka. Couldn't put Mommy to bed without her little drinky-poo."

With the light directed to Liz, Eldon once more worked his hands as fast as he could and was rewarded when he began to feel the plastic giving way. A few more slices and he'd have it.

"No one deserves to die." Liz sounded strong and defiant.

"Trust me, sugar. That bitch deserved exactly what she got, and so do you!" Roberta snapped. "I've been working for years without a single person catching on. I had fun and kept my secrets buried where only I knew they were. I could go and visit them anytime I wanted, relive the glorious fun we had together. And then you came along and started to ruin everything. I can't allow you to reveal anything else, and I have to punish you for the damage you've already done."

"I didn't know it was you."

"Doesn't really matter, now does it? These," she kicked the drawings at Liz's feet, "will burn up with you. Easy peasy. No one will ever find them, and that includes Eloise. They're mine for eternity, even if I am leaving this place. You've ruined it for me, and so I must travel on to find greener pastures. New conquests to make."

Eldon almost gasped when the plastic fell away from his hands and the blood began to circulate freely. The tingling in his hands combined with the blood flowing from the numerous cuts made him so light-headed he had to blink to keep the darkness from descending. That and whatever the hell she'd given him before she dumped him here. Drugs were not his cup of tea, and his body was telling him as much. Still, he pushed through the fog and managed to stay alert. They had one chance to get out of this alive, and he was it. Everything smelled of gasoline, and the fumes made his eyes burn and the cuts scream. He didn't care about any of it. He focused solely on Roberta.

Eldon maneuvered around until he was sitting up, his hands still clasped behind his back. If she noticed anything different about the way he was moving, she didn't seem to care. She was in her element, whatever that was. She was making no bones about the fact that she intended to kill him and Liz by burning them alive. Her cruelty nauseated him.

If she was telling them the truth, and he believed she was, she was more than a murderer. She was a serial killer, one he and Eloise had called their friend. His stomach turned, and he had to breathe hard to keep the queasiness at bay, a tall order considering the gas-filled air. When he got out of here, he'd probably need professional help to reconcile a life-long friendship with a serial killer.

He heard the click of a lighter and realized he was out of time. The nausea disappeared as quickly as it came. He didn't have time to be sick. It was now or never. His one chance to save Liz was here. He hadn't been able to save Eloise, and he was damned if he'd fail in his bid to save Liz. He put his hands palm-down on the floor and pushed himself up with every bit of strength he had left. It was enough, even though his ankles were still bound together.

The momentum took him right into Roberta, and they both crashed through the door, but not before he saw the flame of the lighter come to life as she threw it. It flew through the air and into the gas-soaked room.

❖

The Jaguar let out a scream that could have curdled milk. That son of a bitch Eldon had surprised the hell out of her. If anyone had asked, she'd have never believed the bastard had it in him. He was unquestionably the gentle, quiet guy everyone appreciated, yet here he was propelling her out the back door of her own house with a body slam that had far more power behind it than should be possible. It pissed her off. Who the hell did he think he was dealing with? She'd kicked his ass in the dojo when they were kids, and she'd do more than kick his ass now.

She would have the last laugh. The lighter had come to life with a telltale click as she tumbled backward, and she'd enough wherewithal to think quickly enough to put it to great use. She threw the lighter as hard as she could back into the house. The sound of the open flame hitting flammable fluid made her heart swell. That whoosh was such a satisfying sound. Bye-bye, Lizzie.

Now she was on her back with a heavy Eldon on top of her. "Get off me," she screamed in his face. She could hardly breathe with this bear of a man essentially pinning her to the ground. Not only was he a ton of bricks on her chest that she wanted off her body, but she desperately wanted to watch this house of horrors burn for at least a couple of minutes before she was forced to make the necessary retreat. He was preventing her from seeing anything.

Kicking him, she managed to scoot out from beneath him a few inches. With a little more effort she could get free. Since he was all trussed up with the zip ties, all she had to do was roll him off once she got enough space to get her arms free. Then his arms came around, and he pinned her arms. Well, well, well. Crafty little bastard, wasn't he? Except did he really think that would change anything? From his movements it was clear his legs were still held tight together with the zip ties. It was enough to keep him from being a real threat. A nice kick to the balls and he was sure to be putty.

"You're crazy, Roberta." He was still holding her down with his body and his free hands.

"Not even close. I knew exactly what I was doing, and you know what, Eldon. I liked it. I loved it. It was fun killing your out-of-control sister. I enjoyed ending her life, just like I treasure what I'm doing now. Not only that, but I'm going to get away from this place and keep right on doing it. Nobody's good enough to ever stop me."

"Your family, how can you do this to your family?"

He sounded like he really cared about those needy kids who were nothing but big anchors around her feet. And her husband. How great it was going to feel to be free of him at long last. The pretending would stop. The role-playing would end. For the first time in her life she could simply be what she loved the most—the Jaguar. She couldn't care less about her family. They were nothing more than window dressing, and that's all they'd ever been to her.

"You wouldn't understand. You just don't have what it takes to comprehend someone as extraordinary as me. I'm above your boring, everyday existence. I always was. You were just too stuck up in your own hoity-toity world to realize it. Now get the fuck off me." She was missing the fire, and time was becoming an issue. It wouldn't take that long before someone called it in and the fire department appeared. She had to have at least a minute to hear Liz's screams before she made her escape to sunshine, warm waters, and new, exciting hunting grounds.

"Not a chance."

He really was dense, wasn't he? She moved quickly and put a knee firmly in his groin. His intake of breath told her everything she needed to know. The arrow had hit its mark, and this was her chance. With one big shove, she rolled him off her and bounced to her feet. She delivered a sound kick to his stomach and loved the groan that came with it. Oh yes, she was delivering insult to injury, and it felt so incredibly good.

On her feet she stared at the door they'd just crashed through. Flames were licking up the frame, and the wood, dry and neglected for decades, was welcoming the fire's touch. Inside, the faint sounds of muffled screams wafted out. They wouldn't last long. Any minute now the fumes would be more than her little lungs could take, and she'd be fuel for the fire. Fun stuff. She smiled.

She turned and looked at Eldon, wondering what to do now that he'd managed to get himself outside. He was still curled into a ball, his hands cupping his crotch. Mess with the Jaguar, suffer the consequences. Exactly the same lesson his sister had learned at the point of her ice pick. She was going to miss that tool. It was one of her favorites. Eloise's great sin had been that she made one too many drunken, snarky remarks, and payback was a bitch...for her. She wouldn't miss Eloise. Hell. She doubted anyone would miss Eloise.

Her attention returned to Eldon. What to do? She couldn't leave him here. He knew too much. The cops would figure out pretty quickly she was involved. After all, they would find bodies here, and though her skill at going undetected for all these years was brilliant, it wouldn't take a brain surgeon to put all the pieces together once this place went under the microscope.

Then again, what difference did it make if he was still alive when the fire trucks got here? She'd be gone, and no one would be able to find her. Years of hiding in her room in this very house to avoid the kicks and the fists had given her time to learn how to make most excellent plans. Her imagination had grown to immeasurable dimensions during those early years. She'd learned planning, patience, and determination. In the end, those traits had become her defining characteristics. They had made her the Jaguar.

Seconds were ticking by, and she had to make a decision. What to do? In a perfect world, she'd drag him back into the house and let the growing flames do her work. She didn't want to go through the flames licking at the doorframe herself, but really, it was the best solution. What the hell? She wouldn't be in there long enough to sustain any serious injury, and it was the most desirable solution, therefore worth the danger to her own skin. She'd always enjoyed flirting with danger.

Eldon seemed to be on the verge of recovery and was starting to attempt to rise to his feet. That wouldn't do. She hit him with another carefully aimed kick designed to inflict the maximum amount of damage. He collapsed back down to the cracked concrete not far from the spot where her mother's body lay, undoubtedly now a pile of bones. She leaned down and grabbed his feet. She'd dragged him into that house once already, and she'd do it again.

She was laughing so hard as she hauled him struggling and kicking, she barely heard the footsteps that came from around the side of the house.

CHAPTER TWENTY-EIGHT

The tears that flowed from Liz's eyes didn't take any of the sting out of the air. The old saying was true: her whole life was flashing before her eyes in the final minutes she had left. All sorts of regrets made her tears flow harder. This was so different from what had happened to her outside the courthouse.

If she could do it all over again, she would. Not everything, but perhaps what she'd learned during the months since she'd left the hospital. She'd be strong and fearless and not let what someone did to her cripple her life. She'd live every day with gratitude because each new sunrise meant one more day to experience the world. No more PTSD. No more isolating herself. No more pulling away from friends and family. Most of all, no more pulling away from someone who made her heart soar. She would reach out to Willow and let the promise of love take her wherever it would.

The one thing she wouldn't change? Getting Attila. That boy was one of the best parts of her life, even if she did get him for the wrong reasons. She'd believed he would be her protector and her salvation. That wasn't totally wrong. He did protect her, and in some ways he was her salvation, for his unconditional love made her heart grow. He was most precious to her, and she wouldn't change a single thing about Attila.

The fact that Attila seemed to love Willow made her happy even as the smoke continued to fill the small house and the flames grew ever hotter. Willow would take Attila and give him a home.

That gave her a certain amount of comfort in the final minutes left of her life. Her boy would be taken care of.

"Eldon!" It was as loud as she could scream, and the smoke that poured into her throat burned. "Where are you?" She'd heard him crash out the door with that crazy woman, but she'd hoped he'd come back. It was a lot to hope for, as his legs had still been bound by the unyielding zip ties. Though it was dark inside and details hard to make out, she'd swear it looked like he'd managed to get his hands free, though how, exactly, she'd never know. At least one of them would get out of this alive. That was something to be grateful for.

She wished she'd had the chance to tell Willow how much she liked her. The buzz she got every time she touched her and how the feeling in her stomach each time she looked in her eyes was amazing. There was only one way to explain it, even this early on, and that was the beginning of something quite beautiful. Maybe even love. How she wished she'd had the time to find out. It would be really nice after everything she'd gone through to be blessed with someone to love and to share the rest of her life with.

All of a sudden, regrets kicked her ass. Why was she lying here taking this without a fight? She'd survived a damn gunshot, and she was just going to give up here without even trying? That was the dumbest thing she'd ever done. She wasn't that kind of coward.

She just had to figure out how to get out of here. The door, what direction was the door? It was insane in here, and the fumes were making her cough like a smoker on her last leg. Since the flames shot into the air, she'd totally lost her bearings. It didn't matter, though. She had to give it a try. Not trying wasn't an option.

She rolled to her side and began to wriggle like a snake. Her progress was slow, and she didn't have clue if she was moving toward or away from the door. Her lungs burned, and the smell of singed hair filled her nostrils. She didn't even want to think about that.

It was hard work to get anywhere, and her energy began to fail as her movements grew slower. She wasn't going to make it. Damn it all to the hell, she was going to fail. After everything she'd been through already, she was going to burn up inside this decaying monument to one woman's dysfunctional childhood? That was so messed up.

A spark of light caught her eye. Oh, hell no. Her shirt was on fire. All she could think of was to roll, so that's what she did. The smell of burning hair grew stronger, but the flames licking at her clothing faded. It wasn't much. But it was enough. She had a renewed surge of energy and pushed through the intense pain in her chest. She began to try again. Tied up like she was, her movements were awkward and slow. She was never going to make it.

Or was she? All of a sudden, a whisper of fresh air breathed across her face. Her tears flowed stronger. Maybe she was going in the right direction after all. She tried to hurry, yet as she did so, the last of her energy failed her. The flames grew dimmer, the smell of burning hair fainter, until she saw and felt nothing.

Willow didn't even pause. She sized up the situation in a brief glance. Diana did the same and laid out the woman dragging Eldon toward the burning house with one strong and well-placed punch to the head. It dropped her like a bag of bricks. Namaste that bitch.

Her whole body was buzzing, and she knew that Liz was trapped inside that house where flames were licking out around the boarded-up windows and smoke was billowing out from beneath the eves. She ran through the open door without a backward glance. Foolish? Perhaps. Necessary? Absolutely. She was not going to abandon Liz. She'd be damned if she was going to lose the chance to find out how deep the connection between them went. With all her heart, she believed it had the potential to go all the way, and she'd been waiting a lifetime for this. No crazy killer was going to take that away from her.

The smoke and fumes hit her as hard as if someone had smacked her with a baseball bat. She took an involuntary step backward. The air she sucked in burned all the way down her throat, and the smoke stung her eyes so bad she was crying. She ignored it all and pushed forward again. The heat was incredible, and then she stumbled over something, falling painfully to her knees. She touched the obstacles as she went down, and hope surged.

"Oh my God, Liz." Her hope was short-lived. Liz wasn't moving. Willow didn't pause to check whether she was breathing. She got to her feet, grabbed Liz by the shoulders, and backed up as fast as she could. All she had to do was move in the same direction she'd entered in, because she couldn't see anything. It made sense. She'd taken a straight line in, so she'd take a straight line out. It worked, and within seconds she had Liz outside in the fresh air.

"Help her," she wheezed, moments before she collapsed, turning her head to vomit. She'd never felt so horrible, even after the gunshot. She'd never been this scared. She had no idea if Liz was still alive.

After she finished gagging, she pushed to her hands and knees, intent on getting to Liz. Before she could move, strong hands took hold of her shoulders and lifted her to her feet. Two firefighters guided her out to the front of the house, where an EMT truck was parked right behind a ladder truck at the curb. The EMTs took her from the firefighters. "We got her," a big guy in a crisp white shirt said to the man in the bulky yellow jacket and hard hat.

"Liz," she gasped as she tried to wrench away from the EMT. "You need to get to Liz. I don't know if she's alive." The last words came out on a sob. She was fine, and they needed to understand that it was Liz who needed help right now.

The EMT was guiding her gently toward the truck. "Don't you worry. We've got others taking care of her right now."

"Liz," she was still saying as they were putting an oxygen mask on her face. "You have to get to Liz. I think she might be dead."

EPILOGUE

Six months later

Willow sat in one of the padded patio chairs and threw the ball for Attila, who joyfully chased it, picked it up, and brought it back to her so the game could begin again. Liz leaned against the kitchen doorframe smiling as she watched the two of them. How she loved to see them play. How she loved them both.

The doorbell rang, and she turned her head to yell, "It's open." These days she didn't break out in a cold sweat when someone showed up at the door. The alarm pad on the wall in the hallway was still active, although right now the light was blinking a bright green. Locked and loaded wasn't the game plan most of the time these days.

In this instance, she knew it was either Eldon and Meg or Circe and Diana. As it turned out, it was all four of them, and she met them in the kitchen. Six months ago, having all of them together was a somber affair. Today, it was all much different. No one's face was filled with fear or pain. No one's step was heavy.

Willow's face lit up when Liz came back outside with the crew right behind her. "The gang's all here."

"Good morning, musketeers." Willow raised a coffee cup in salute. Everyone laughed and pulled up chairs as well as a bench around the wrought-iron table with the green-striped umbrella.

Liz brought out a tray laden with coffee, tea, and water before turning over the table to Diana. She was the reason they had all come together this beautiful sunny morning. This was her moment for show-and-tell. They'd been waiting half a year for this.

Diana said, "They're going for the death penalty."

"Good," Eldon said. "She deserves it if anyone does."

"Thanks to all the souvenirs they found at her house, including the cross of one of her victims she was wearing around her neck when we arrested her, and Liz's drawings, she doesn't have a chance in hell. One way or the other, whether it's the death penalty or life in prison without parole, she's done."

Willow reached over and took Liz's hand. She thought of the drawings that had poured from her injured fingers during the weeks she spent in the hospital after Willow had pulled her from the burning house. Seven in all. Seven faces with sad eyes and haunted expressions. Each woman was located, their hidden graves discovered in areas ranging from Coeur d'Alene to Newport to Moses Lake. Roberta had chosen her locations well, and they'd remained hidden for many years. Her mother's body was also found beneath the concrete patio slab in the back of the burned-down house.

Roberta had been a diabolical and ruthless killer. Also an incredibly intelligent one. She'd operated under the radar for more years than anyone wanted to think about. At least until Liz woke up in the hospital. It wasn't just Liz's life that had changed on that fateful night in her new house when she'd made the first drawing.

All it took to bring down this particular serial killer was a combination of Liz's drawings and the incredible team of Circe and Zelda. Together their unique skills brought each of the missing home. So many families now had closure, if not a small measure of peace. Roberta, currently incarcerated in a high-security mental facility, went a little more over the edge each time she was confronted with the discovery of one of her murders. She treasured her secrets and resented anyone disturbing her morbid reality. That she'd failed in her bid to kill both Liz and Eldon took away what little bit of sanity she might have been able to hold on to.

It still bothered Liz to know that her work came from a killer's mind. She believed that Willow was right about that. It wasn't the victims she channeled; it was the killer. She'd probably never know the reason. That was okay, even if it was unsettling. The end result was worth the uneasiness. She'd done a lot of good, and that was that. At least she was over it now and wasn't scared of what she'd draw when she picked up a pencil these days.

"Why?" Liz pondered, her mind returning to the conversation at hand. "Why did she do it? I mean, think about it. She had everything. A husband, a family, and a career. She was a commercial pilot, for heaven's sake. How many women would kill to have been in her position? Oops. That might not have been the best turn of phrase to use in connection with her."

"We get it," Diana said with a laugh. "She did have it all, but you know, in my profession we see this all the time. Some people can never find happiness. I sincerely believe some are simply born bad. They never had a chance."

"Eldon," Liz said softly. "What did she say to you?"

Liz noticed Eldon reach over and take Meg's hand. He'd been granted an opportunity two days ago to speak with Roberta. She hadn't seen him since that meeting and was intensely curious to know how it had gone. He looked sad.

"I'd never before seen the fury in her that I did when I looked into her eyes the other day. I think it's been bottled up inside her since childhood, and she managed to camouflage it with a so-called normal life. I thought my mother was painful to live with, but hers made my mom look tame. She was evidently a monster that in turn made another monster. My mother gave us demons to deal with, but she didn't make us monsters."

"Her mother was the first?" That's what the papers had been printing, and it was pretty much what she'd insinuated as she was blowing her own horn before trying to barbeque her and Eldon.

He nodded. "She told me she just snapped one day, and that was how it all started. It felt good so she tried it again. It felt great again, and she just kept going. What kind of person feels good when they kill their own mother?" Anguish whispered through his words.

Diana patted him on the arm. "Don't even try to understand, because you never will. Trust me. What these people do is irrational, and you can't rationalize that."

"Why Eloise?" Liz really wanted to know why she'd targeted Eldon's sister. She might have been a pain, but she didn't deserve to die.

The pain that flowed over his face made her instantly sorry she'd asked. She was about to apologize when he said, "My theory is she was jealous, though she'll never admit it. Despite all Eloise's issues, she still had people who loved her and wouldn't give up on her. Roberta didn't have any of that. She'd killed her mother, she and her husband weren't all that close, and she was totally disconnected from her children. I don't think she had it in her to love anyone except herself. I'm sure any one of those skilled doctors working with her out at the hospital could give us some official diagnosis for why she's the way she is, but frankly I don't care. Fucked up is fucked up, no matter what kind of label you put on it."

Liz thought of all the souvenirs found at Roberta's house when the search warrant was executed. Diana had told them that she'd kept something from each of her victims, ranging from a cross to Eloise's golf glove. The death penalty wasn't a big stretch, considering the hard evidence uncovered so far. It still gave her chills, even though she was confident Roberta would never be free again. It was always frightening when her brand of evil continued to walk the earth.

She banished the ugly thoughts and took Willow's hand, smiling as she did so. "Well, the one thing I know is that I'm glad that asshole, Anthony Washington, shot me."

They all turned and stared at her with identical shocked expressions. She'd expected that. She smiled broadly. "Let me explain. You see, if Washington hadn't shot me, I wouldn't have suffered from PTSD, Willow wouldn't have been here to help me, and Eldon wouldn't have brought me those pads to make the drawings. If I hadn't done those drawings, Circe and Zelda wouldn't have found the murdered women, and if they hadn't found them, they'd still be lost, and Roberta would probably still be killing."

"That's kind of fucked up too," Eldon commented.

"True enough," she said and laughed. "But who are we to argue with the universe. I mean, Meg, would you have thought to introduce me to Willow if I hadn't been such a basket case?"

Meg shrugged. "Yeah. I would have eventually gotten you two together, but it's true. Your PTSD made me think of introducing you when I did. I wanted you to talk with someone who could understand what you were going through. I have only one other friend who's been shot, and is it my fault if she happens to be cute, single, and available?"

"Exactly my point." Liz laughed again.

Willow squeezed her hand. "I think you're right. The universe had a plan for all of us, and look where we are now. Diana has closed another serial-killer case, making her the lead detective at the SPD. Eldon and Meg are getting married in a couple of months, and I have my lovely, lovely Liz. This is a crazy, awful situation that has had a magnificent ending. Really, I see no sense in fighting fate."

Liz looked over at Willow's beautiful face and agreed wholeheartedly. A little over fifteen months ago, her whole life had changed, and for a long time she'd thought it had been changed for the worst. The last six months had been nothing short of magical. She'd recovered well from the smoke inhalation and burns she suffered in the fire. Willow had moved in with her, and their future was looking incredible. Love was an amazing thing. Who would have thought all of this had come to be because one disturbed man started shooting randomly in the courtyard of the federal building. Life was an amazing, intriguing, and wonderful journey.

She leaned over and kissed Willow on the lips. She could hardly wait for what tomorrow would bring.

About the Author

Sheri Lewis Wohl grew up in northeast Washington State, and though she always thought she'd move away, never has. Despite traveling throughout the United States, Sheri always finds her way back home. And so she lives, plays, and writes amidst mountains, evergreens, and abundant wildlife.

When not working the day job in federal finance, she writes stories that typically include a bit of the strange and unusual and always a touch of romance. Her novel *Twisted Whispers* was a 2016 Golden Crown Literary Award winner for Paranormal/Horror, and *Twisted Screams* was a finalist for a 2017 Golden Crown Literary Award.

Sheri and her K9 partner, Zoey, are a nationally certified K9 Search & Rescue team. She also likes to participate in local triathlons and puts her acting chops to use every chance she gets. You can catch her in televisions shows such as *Z Nation* and *Grimm*.

Website: http://www.sherilewiswohl.com/
Blog: https://sherilewiswohl.wordpress.com/

Books Available from Bold Strokes Books

Breakthrough by Kris Bryant. Falling for a sexy ranger is one thing, but is the possibility of love worth giving up the career Kennedy Wells has always dreamed of? (978-1-63555-179-2)

Certain Requirements by Elinor Zimmerman. Phoenix has always kept her love of kinky submission strictly behind the bedroom door and inside the bounds of romantic relationships, until she meets Kris Andersen. (978-1-63555-195-2)

Dark Euphoria by Ronica Black. When a high-profile case drops in Detective Maria Diaz's lap, she forges ahead only to discover this case, and her main suspect, aren't like any other. (978-1-63555-141-9)

Fore Play by Julie Cannon. Executive Leigh Marshall falls hard for Peyton Broader, her golf pro…and an ex-con. Will she risk sabotaging her career for love? (978-1-63555-102-0)

Love Came Calling by CA Popovich. Can a romantic looking for a long-term, committed relationship and a jaded cynic too busy for love conquer life's struggles and find their way to what matters most? (978-1-63555-205-8)

Outside the Law by Carsen Taite. Former sweethearts Tanner Cohen and Sydney Braswell must work together on a federal task force to see justice served, but will they choose to embrace their second chance at love? (978-1-63555-039-9)

The Princess Deception by Nell Stark. When journalist Missy Duke realizes Prince Sebastian is really his twin sister Viola in disguise, she plays along, but when sparks flare between them, will the double deception doom their fairy-tale romance? (978-1-62639-979-2)

The Smell of Rain by Cameron MacElvee. Reyha Arslan, a wise and elegant woman with a tragic past, shows Chrys that there's still beauty to embrace and reason to hope despite the world's cruelty. (978-1-63555-166-2)

The Talebearer by Sheri Lewis Wohl. Liz's visions show her the faces of the lost and the killers who took their lives. As one by one, the murdered are found, a stranger works to stop Liz before the serial killer is brought to justice. (978-1-63555-126-6)

White Wings Weeping by Lesley Davis. The world is full of discord and hatred, but how much of it is just human nature when an evil with sinister intent is invading people's hearts? (978-1-63555-191-4)

A Call Away by KC Richardson. Can a businesswoman from a big city find the answers she's looking for, and possibly love, on a small-town farm? (978-1-63555-025-2)

Berlin Hungers by Justine Saracen. Can the love between an RAF woman and the wife of a Luftwaffe pilot, former enemies, survive in besieged Berlin during the aftermath of World War II? (978-1-63555-116-7)

Blend by Georgia Beers. Lindsay and Piper are like night and day. Working together won't be easy, but not falling in love might prove the hardest job of all. (978-1-63555-189-1)

Hunger for You by Jenny Frame. Principe of an ancient vampire clan Byron Debrek must save her one true love from falling into the hands of her enemies and into the middle of a vampire war. (978-1-63555-168-6)

Mercy by Michelle Larkin. FBI Special Agent Mercy Parker and psychic ex-profiler Piper Vasey learn to love again as they race to stop a man with supernatural gifts who's bent on annihilating humankind. (978-1-63555-202-7)

Pride and Porters by Charlotte Greene. Will pride and prejudice prevent these modern-day lovers from living happily ever after? (978-1-63555-158-7)

Rocks and Stars by Sam Ledel. Kyle's struggle to own who she is and what she really wants may end up landing her on the bench and without the woman of her dreams. (978-1-63555-156-3)

The Boss of Her: Office Romance Novellas by Julie Cannon, Aurora Rey, and M. Ullrich. Going to work never felt so good. Three office romance novellas from talented writers Julie Cannon, Aurora Rey, and M. Ullrich. (978-1-63555-145-7)

The Deep End by Ellie Hart. When family ties become entangled in murder and deception, it's time to find a way out... (978-1-63555-288-1)

A Country Girl's Heart by Dena Blake. When Kat Jackson gets a second chance at love, following her heart will prove the hardest decision of all. (978-1-63555-134-1)

Dangerous Waters by Radclyffe. Life, death, and war on the home front. Two women join forces against a powerful opponent, nature itself. (978-1-63555-233-1)

Fury's Death by Brey Willows. When all we hold sacred fails, who will be there to save us? (978-1-63555-063-4)

It's Not a Date by Heather Blackmore. Kade's desire to keep things with Jen on a professional level is in Jen's best interest. Yet what's in Kade's best interest...is Jen. (978-1-63555-149-5)

Killer Winter by Kay Bigelow. Just when she thought things could get no worse, homicide Lieutenant Leah Samuels learns the woman she loves has betrayed her in devastating ways. (978-1-63555-177-8)

Score by MJ Williamz. Will an addiction to pain pills destroy Ronda's chance with the woman she loves or will she come out on top and score a happily ever after? (978-1-62639-807-8)

Spring's Wake by Aurora Rey. When wanderer Willa Lange falls for Provincetown B&B owner Nora Calhoun, will past hurts and a fifteen-year age gap keep them from finding love? (978-1-63555-035-1)

The Northwoods by Jane Hoppen. When Evelyn Bauer, disguised as her dead husband, George, travels to a Northwoods logging camp to work, she and the camp cook Sarah Bell forge a friendship fraught with both tenderness and turmoil. (978-1-63555-143-3)

Truth or Dare by C. Spencer. For a group of six lesbian friends, life changes course after one long snow-filled weekend. (978-1-63555-148-8)

A Heart to Call Home by Jeannie Levig. When Jessie Weldon returns to her hometown after thirty years, can she and her childhood crush Dakota Scott heal the tragic past that links them? (978-1-63555-059-7)

Children of the Healer by Barbara Ann Wright. Life becomes desperate for ex-soldier Cordelia Ross when the indigenous aliens of her planet are drawn into a civil war and old enemies linger in the shadows. Book Three of the Godfall Series. (978-1-63555-031-3)

Hearts Like Hers by Melissa Brayden. Coffee shop owner Autumn Primm is ready to cut loose and live a little, but is the baggage that comes with out-of-towner Kate Carpenter too heavy for anything long term? (978-1-63555-014-6)

Love at Cooper's Creek by Missouri Vaun. Shaw Daily flees corporate life to find solace in the rural Blue Ridge Mountains, but escapism eludes her when her attentions are captured by small town beauty Kate Elkins. (978-1-62639-960-0)

Somewhere Over Lorain Road by Bud Gundy. Over forty years after murder allegations shattered the Esker family, can Don Esker find the true killer and clear his dying father's name? (978-1-63555-124-2)

Twice in a Lifetime by PJ Trebelhorn. Detective Callie Burke can't deny the growing attraction to her late friend's widow, Taylor Fletcher, who also happens to own the bar where Callie's sister works. (978-1-63555-033-7)

Undiscovered Affinity by Jane Hardee. Will a no strings attached affair be enough to break Olivia's control and convince Cardic that love does exist? (978-1-63555-061-0)

Between Sand and Stardust by Tina Michele. Are the lifelong bonds of love strong enough to conquer time, distance, and heartache when Haven Thorne and Willa Bennette are given another chance at forever? (978-1-62639-940-2)

Charming the Vicar by Jenny Frame. When magician and atheist Finn Kane seeks refuge in an English village after a spiritual crisis, can local vicar Bridget Claremont restore her faith in life and love? (978-1-63555-029-0)

Data Capture by Jesse J. Thoma. Lola Walker is undercover on the hunt for cybercriminals while trying not to notice the woman who might be perfectly wrong for her for all the right reasons. (978-1-62639-985-3)

Epicurean Delights by Renee Roman. Ariana Marks had no idea a leisure swim would lead to being rescued, in more ways than one, by the charismatic Hudson Frost. (978-1-63555-100-6)

Heart of the Devil by Ali Vali. We know most of Cain and Emma Casey's story, but *Heart of the Devil* will take you back to where it began one fateful night with a tray loaded with beer. (978-1-63555-045-0)

Known Threat by Kara A. McLeod. When Special Agent Ryan O'Connor reluctantly questions who protects the Secret Service, she learns courage truly is found in unlikely places. Agent O'Connor Series #3. (978-1-63555-132-7)

Seer and the Shield by D. Jackson Leigh. Time is running out for the Dragon Horse Army while two unlikely heroines struggle to put aside their attraction and find a way to stop a deadly cult. Dragon Horse War, Book 3. (978-1-63555-170-9)

Sinister Justice by Steve Pickens. When a vigilante targets citizens of Jake Finnigan's hometown, Jake and his partner Sam fall under suspicion themselves as they investigate the murders. (978-1-63555-094-8)

The Universe Between Us by Jane C. Esther. Ana Mitchell must make the hardest choice of her life: the promise of new love Jolie Dann on Earth, or a humanity-saving mission to colonize Mars. (978-1-63555-106-8)

Touch by Kris Bryant. Can one touch heal a heart? (978-1-63555-084-9)